# The Orange Blossom Inn

Shae Sikalos

Published by Barefoot Novelist Press

Florida, USA



ISBN: 979-8-218-90191-2

FICTION

For the women who came before me,
and the girl I once was.
May we always find our way home.

# Playlist

**The Night We Met** – Lord Huron
**Slow Burn** – Kacey Musgraves
**Home** – Edith Whiskers
**Cherry Wine** – Hozier
**Lost In My Mind** – The Head And The Heart
**Poison & Wine** – The Civil Wars
**Bloom** – The Paper Kites
**Turning Page** – Sleeping at Last
**Colour My World** – Chicago
**Orange Sky** – Alexi Murdoch
**The Stable Song** – Gregory Alan Isakov
**This Must Be the Place** – Talking Heads

Before the day I came south, before the bruised summer sky and the first sweet shock of citrus on my tongue, there was the old house on Vine Street; the one I grew up in, the one I couldn't bear to call home, not even after my father's heart gave out and left us with silence so loud it pressed against the windows.

I grew up on the kind of street where the only thing that bloomed in summer was police tape, and boots tossed over the telephone wires swung like wind-worn weathervanes, pointing toward trouble. I remember the cracked sidewalk out front, the way the grass grew thin near the porch. I remember sitting on the top step with Goldie on nights when the yelling had finally died down, knees pulled up tight, counting the moths batting themselves against the porch light. Sometimes I'd whisper stories to her in the dark—fairy tales I made up on the spot, spun from scraps of hope and the secret wish that we could ride our bikes out past the edge of town and keep going, never looking back. I used to think I'd run away when I was sixteen. Some girls dreamed of prom or Paris, but I dreamed of a kitchen with quiet corners, a backyard with shadows that didn't threaten, a front porch safe for bare feet. I dreamed of anywhere that wasn't him.

But I stayed. For Goldie, mostly—who was too young to understand why our mother turned the radio up when the shouting started, who never saw the sharp edges of love that turned the world dangerous after sundown. I learned to tuck her beneath the blankets when the voices rose, told her stories about houses that looked after their own. I pretended I was brave so she could sleep. Some nights, when our father's shadow filled the hallway, I'd tug Goldie's hand and lead her out the back door, barefoot and quiet, and we'd lie on the patch of cool grass behind the lilacs. We called it our "nest." The stars would blink on, shy at first, then crowd the sky like children at a window, and I'd imagine what it might be like to live in a house where the walls didn't listen. Where voices never rose, and doors were never slammed, and every room had windows open to the wind.

I learned to recognize the warning signs—the sharp slam of a cupboard, the scrape of a chair, the sound of the television rising to cover the things that went unsaid. My mother would wring her hands in the kitchen; her eyes fixed on the flickering light. When things got bad, she'd send me to check on Goldie. That was her word for it. *Check.* As if it was a small thing. As if I wasn't already doing it, always.

Sometimes I wondered if the house knew what was happening. Houses remember things, I think. They soak up what's left behind and hold onto it in the grain of the wood and the hush between storms. I used to trail my fingers along the banister, feel the warmth there, as if it was holding onto something for me. Maybe that's why it was so hard to leave. Even after the worst, there's a comfort in the familiar. Even when it hurts.

Some nights, I would lay awake, listening to the house breathing around me. I'd imagine what it would be like to leave—not in a rush, not in fear, but deliberately. I'd picture the quiet dignity of folding clothes into neat squares, packing photographs carefully between sweaters, and the gentle click of the door closing behind me. But then, I'd remember Goldie's face—how trusting, how open—and my imagined courage would fade into shadows, leaving me restless and small again. My dreams of escape weren't loud or dramatic; they were as quiet as whispers beneath blankets, soft as moonlight spilling across the floor. But they were always there, waiting patiently for the moment when bravery felt less like betrayal and more like necessity.

People saw us, of course. Neighbors, teachers, the woman at the grocery store who'd slip me an extra cookie at the bakery counter. They saw the bruises they pretended not to see, heard the stories Goldie and I never told. Their faces always held a kind of sadness, or maybe a silent apology— sorry for seeing, sorry for not helping, sorry for looking away.

As I grew older, I promised myself I'd run. I told myself I'd get out, find a place where the air tasted like something other than dread. But when you spend enough years surviving, running starts to look less like freedom and more like a gamble you can't afford to lose.

After my father died, the house changed. I didn't cry. Not really. I felt relief and then the guilt for relief, sharp as a blade. The life insurance payout was modest—just enough to let me look at the map and choose, for the first time, not

based on fear but possibility. Goldie was safe enough by then.
We were both grown, both scarred, both tired of waiting for
rescue. My mother drifted through from room to room as
though she were less flesh than memory, caught between
devotion and relief. She sold the place with barely a word,
dividing up what little was left—dishes, linens. She gave me a
check and said, "Go start your life." As if it was that easy.

I took the money, but I stayed near Goldie at first. I
took a tiny apartment with thin walls and a view of the
laundromat. I learned to love the quiet and almost convinced
myself that solitude was the same as serenity. I tried my hand
at loving men, but mostly I learned what it was like to want
more and expect less. No one ever taught me what kindness
looked like when it lasted.

Sometimes, at night, I'd dream of houses. Not the
one I'd left, but others—old, weathered places on the edge of
towns; wild gardens tangling the porch rails, the light in the
windows warm and wide. I'd wake up with a hunger in my
chest, the ache of longing for a home that was mine and no
one else's.

I think some part of me has always been running. Not
away from something, but toward the hope that somewhere
out there is a place waiting to hold the shape of me. A place
that remembers what it is to be loved, even after all the
storms.

When the listing for Citrus Grove came across my
screen, I felt something flicker inside—a wild, irrational hope.
I stared at the grainy photos until the pixels blurred, as if

looking too long might wear them out. A porch sagged gently under the weight of years; shutters leaned just slightly, like tired eyelids. The listing gave square footage and roof age and the number of bathrooms, but it couldn't measure the way the front steps seemed to be waiting for someone to come home.

I thought of all the houses I'd seen before—bright new builds with their sterile walls and the faint smell of paint; apartments stacked in glass towers where the light never touched anything real. None of them had called to me. But this one… it felt less like an opportunity and more like an invitation.

I imagined the air there—thick with the scent of sun-warmed citrus, heavy enough to taste. I could almost hear the hum of bees in the hedges, the quiet creak of the screen door on a summer night. I didn't need to see it in person to know it was imperfect. That was the point. I wasn't looking for perfection. I was looking for a place that had been through storms and was still standing.

The house looked sad, but hopeful, like me; the paint peeled back to bare wood; the roof sagging just so. There was a softness to it, a promise in the line of the porch and the spill of bougainvillea, that made me believe, if only for a moment, that I could start again.

It wasn't a spontaneous move. It was the slow unraveling of a thousand nights, the quiet planning, the saving and hoping and waiting for the right kind of freedom. Money was always a barrier; courage was the rest. In the end,

I told Goldie I had to try. I promised her I wouldn't go too far, that I'd be close if she ever needed to run, too.

When I packed my car, I tucked my grandmother's afghan into the bottom of my suitcase, slid my journal beside it, and left the rest for another girl to find. I drove south with my heart pounding and my hands shaking, every mile a prayer and a dare.

Houses remember things. I hope this one remembers me kindly. I hope, when I lay my hand against the sun-warmed porch rail, I feel not just the ache of what I left behind, but the quiet thrum of welcome—like a door opening, like a heart unlocking. Even a haunted place might mend given patience and tenderness.

But leaving isn't always as simple as walking out the door. Sometimes, you have to carry the house with you until you find somewhere you can finally put it down.

Chapter One

The house looked smaller than I remembered. Or maybe it wasn't memory I was comparing it to, but imagination—how it had looked in the photos, filtered and softened, framed in late-day light. There, it had looked like a dream. Here, it looked like grief. Grief and gingerbread trim.

The air was warm and damp, soaked with the scent of soil and citrus. A tractor hummed somewhere behind the trees. The gravel crackled beneath my tires as I pulled into the overgrown drive and rolled to a stop beneath a crooked palm tree. From the driver's seat, I could see the porch sagging ever so slightly. The roofline dipped in the middle, like it had exhaled and forgotten how to straighten. One shutter hung loose beside the second-floor window, swinging slowly with the breeze. I half-expected it to whisper something.

Still, beneath the peeling paint and sagging porch, the house's foundation felt sound. It had to be. This house had stood nearly a century already, shaded by trees planted the day it was built— "for luck," the listing said. Or maybe for love.

I stepped out of the car and into the summer heat. A soft wind blew past, thick with honeysuckle and something older, something green and feral. It clung to my skin, sweet and damp, like the air itself was ripened and ready to be gathered. The citrus grove stretched behind the house like a cathedral, leaves glinting, fruit swollen. It was mid-June, late harvest for the Valencias. I'd read that somewhere on the drive down—trying to pretend I knew what I was getting into. The scent was richer here, less perfume and more pulp. The kind that clung to your fingertips long after the rind was gone.

I stood there, letting my eyes follow the neat but unruly rows until they blurred into the shimmer of the heat. The branches arched toward one another overhead, leaves whispering in a language older than the house itself. Sunlight poured through in narrow, angled shafts, striping the ground in gold and black.

The air held the faint metallic tang of rain long past, mingled with the deep, almost wine-rich sweetness of ripened fruit. I breathed it in like it might tell me something—how to stay, how to grow roots without feeling trapped.

I thought of the cramped apartments I'd rented in the city, where the only green I saw was in the wilted basil on my windowsill. This—this was a world you could walk into barefoot and leave carrying something warm and alive. The grove seemed to hum a low, steady note under the rustle of leaves, and I felt welcome.

In the photos, the house had looked Victorian. Romantic. Whimsical. In person, it looked… haunted. Not by ghosts, but by time. Peeling paint, a sun-bleached roof, porch boards that bowed like old piano keys. A Cracker Gothic, I'd learned—a Florida classic.

I stood there for a long moment, my hand resting on the warm metal of the car door, and tried to imagine the first pair of hands that had built this place; the sharp bite of sawdust in the air, the scrape of hammers, white paint, the best money could buy, drying in the sun. It made my chest ache in a way I didn't expect.

I laid my palm against one of the porch posts, paint chalking off against my fingertips. The wood was warm from the sun, and for a moment, I swore I could feel the faintest hum—like the house was alive beneath its wear, holding steady despite everything time had taken from it. Maybe it was only the wind. Or maybe it was the same stubbornness in the bones of the house that had driven me here. I stepped onto the porch and tested my weight on each board. The screen door groaned in protest, hinges rusted, frame swollen with age. Still, I smiled. The door opened.

Inside, the silence didn't feel empty at all, but expectant—as if the house had paused mid-inhale, waiting for something to happen.

The air was thick with heat and memory. Lace curtains wilted in the windows. It smelled faintly of furniture polish and sunbaked wood, the ghost of Sundays long gone lingering in the corners.  Dust danced through a shaft of light on the stairs. I closed my eyes for a moment and imagined laughter echoing down these halls, imagined someone setting a record to spin in the corner of this very room while supper simmered on the stove. I pictured the kind of quiet that wasn't absence but presence—the kind that made space for everything you loved to settle deep into the walls. A vase of dried orange blossoms sat beside the parlor mirror, petals curled inward like secrets. They looked like they'd been placed there for someone long gone, but still loved.

I walked slowly through each room, my footsteps muffled by time-softened rugs. The wallpaper peeled in places. Cracks threaded through the plaster. One of the ceiling fans had lost a blade and hung off kilter.

I trailed my fingers along the banister. It was softer than I expected. The wood had been worn smooth in the center, polished by decades of hands. I could almost feel them—the weight of those who'd climbed these steps before me. The boards creaked in certain spots and not in others, like a house that remembered where it had been walked the most.

I stood in the parlor for a long time. Breathing it in. Imagining it full of light, with rugs and books and wildflowers spilling out of vases. I could see it already. I could see her— the house—in the way you see a woman you know used to be beautiful. Not pretty in the way you notice right away. Beautiful in the way you remember, long after she's gone.

I'd driven twelve hundred miles for this. Left behind my job, my lease, my life. Packed my car with books and tea and too many paint swatches. Told myself I was chasing something new, but really, I was just trying to feel like myself again.

This house had called to me. Not just the porch or the orchard or the promise of quiet. Something deeper. Like it knew something about me that I hadn't admitted yet. Maybe it was foolish. Maybe it was brave. Maybe, like the fruit still clinging to the summer trees, I had one last season in me before the fall.

I backed out slowly, letting the screen door shut behind me with a sigh. The carriage house sat off to the side, half-hidden by a tangle of bougainvillea. Smaller, humbler, than the main house, but sturdy. A place I could make my own.

Its white paint was less peeling than exhausted; it sagged a little like the main house, but it had good bones too. The air inside smelled faintly of cedar and old paper. There was a kitchenette the size of a postage stamp, a small bathroom tucked under the stairs, and a loft bedroom that looked out over the grove. I blew a curl out of my face and stared at the empty space. It wasn't much, but it was a start.

The first thing I did was test the sink. It groaned, sputtered, and spat out a reluctant cough of brown water before dying completely. I stared at it for a beat, then laughed under my breath.

"Okay," I said, setting my hands on my hips. "We'll add plumbing to the list."

I hauled my things inside: a stack of books, my chipped sunflower mug, an air mattress that unrolled with an indignant hiss. I inflated it in the loft beneath the window where I'd eventually wake to the smell of citrus and sun-warmed wood. For now, it was bare. But it would be beautiful. I made it up with sun-bleached sheets, and stood there for a moment, staring out the loft window at the rows of citrus trees glowing in the late light.

By the time I'd finished arranging the essentials—tea kettle, honey, a row of dog-eared novels—the sun had begun to sink, staining the grove gold. I stood in the doorway, barefoot on the cool wood, and breathed deep.

This was it.

The quiet was heavy, but not unfriendly. I'd been running on noise for years—deadlines, rent, the hum of city traffic bleeding through thin apartment walls. Now, all I could hear was the cicadas, the wind through the trees, and my own heart knocking around in my chest like it finally had room.

I walked the grove. Barefoot now, the grass yielded softly under my feet, still warm from the day. Orange blossoms clung to the air like an old hymn—sweet, low, and lingering. Bees moved lazily from bloom to bloom, drunk on nectar, their hum blending with the hush of leaves. The fruit hung heavy, so ripe it seemed to bow the branches in quiet devotion, some fallen to the ground, split and glistening like offerings. I crouched, brushing my fingertips over one—sun-warmed, fragrant—before lifting it, the skin dimpled like the palm of a well-worn hand.

A sudden rustle drew my eyes to the edge of the grove: a small cluster of hens, feathers the color of rust and cream, pecking industriously at the fallen fruit. One looked up at me—sharp-eyed and suspicious—before deciding I was no threat and going back to her feast, while the lowing of a cow rolled across the grove like distant thunder.  I hadn't expected them—any of them—but their presences made something in me ache.

My grandmother used to tell me that animals could sense good hearts. I used to sit in her kitchen, chin on the cool linoleum, while her old tabby wound around my legs and the neighbor's hens pecked at the open back door like they owned the place. Standing there in the grove, the air heavy with oranges and sun-warmed hay, I felt that same quiet belonging. Like the house hadn't just come with animals— like it had come with witnesses.

"Well," I whispered to no one in particular, "guess it's not just me after all."

I split the fruit open with my thumbs, juice bleeding down my wrist. For a moment, I thought of Goldie— barefoot in our mother's kitchen, eating fruit straight over the sink because she hated dirtying a plate. I licked my wrist clean, and the taste hit sharp and sweet.

This wasn't ruin. This was waiting for a heartbeat.

Yet even as the house held its breath, I thought of Goldie, tucked into her tidy apartment back home. She'd promised me she'd be okay—cheerfully telling me she was proud, that I deserved this. But late at night, miles from anywhere familiar, I wondered if she'd known how much I'd held back, how much I'd carried silently to protect her. I wondered if she'd understand that sometimes the only way to truly breathe again was to risk leaving even the things you loved most.

When I came back, the sky was flushed violet and rose. I climbed the porch steps, nearly ready to collapse on my mattress and try to convince myself I hadn't made the worst mistake of my life.

That's when I saw it; a vase.

Not some flimsy grocery-store thing—a tall, heavy crystal vase bursting with pale blush roses and tiger lilies, arranged with impossible care; their scent lush and heady in the damp air. A white card tucked between the stems. I carried it inside and upstairs to the loft, their scent filling the small space until it smelled less like abandonment and more like possibility. I set them on the windowsill where the evening light kissed every petal, and then opened the card.

*Welcome to Citrus Grove, Mina March. Something tells me you're just what this place needed. — Luca Bellante*

I traced the words with my fingertips. Luca.

I'd spoken on the phone with my out-of-state realtor a handful of times—he had the kind of smooth, easy voice that could sell you anything, even a half-ruined house with more termites than square footage. I pressed the card to my chest like proof that I could do this—like maybe I wasn't the only one who believed it—then placed it beside my dog-eared copy of *Pride and Prejudice*. For the first time since I'd signed the papers, I didn't feel like I was standing on the edge of a cliff.

I felt like I'd already jumped.

And maybe—just maybe—the fall would feel a little like flying.

The little electric kettle clicked and sighed from the kitchenette, and I dug out a tin of orange blossom tea I'd been saving for years without knowing what for. Maybe for this. I poured it into my favorite mug—the sunflower one, the one with the chipped rim—and carried it upstairs. The air mattress hissed faintly as I settled onto it cross-legged, tea steaming in my hands. From the loft window, I could see the silhouette of the main house through the branches of the grove, its windows dark and watchful.

It wasn't quiet, not really.

The night had its own language: the low hum of cicadas, the occasional rustle of wings in the trees, the faint hoot of an owl claiming the rafters of the barn. Somewhere distant, I heard a frog croak—lazy and content, like the sound had nowhere else to be. Even the house seemed to listen, its beams settling with soft, contented sighs, like it was glad not to be alone anymore.

I sipped my tea and for the first time in years, I wasn't rushing anywhere.

I wasn't behind on rent or late for work or stuck in a city where everything felt borrowed and nothing was mine. Here, everything was mine.

I set the mug down and reached for the leather-bound journal I'd tossed into the passenger seat during the move. Its pages were soft with use, corners bent from a hundred abandoned starts. I flipped to a blank one, pen poised over the paper. I didn't write much. Just a single line: *This house remembers.*

Because I could feel it. In the way the parlor floorboards sighed. In the gentle tilt of the porch. In the citrus trees, heavy with fruit, offering more than I could possibly take. Outside, the grove murmured with its own secret language. A branch creaked, fruit settling under its own weight. Somewhere close, a chicken gave a soft, drowsy cluck. It was quiet, but not empty. Everything here was alive, breathing in slow rhythm with the night. I glanced back toward the main house and whispered, as if it could hear me, "I'll take care of you."

Maybe it was foolish. Maybe it was sentimental. But as the words left my mouth, a warm breeze drifted through the cracked loft window and brushed over me like an answer. I laughed, soft and startled. "I'll fix you," I said, quieter this time, like a vow.

Downstairs, the sink still didn't work. The floorboards still creaked. The walls were still peeling. But I wasn't afraid. I curled beneath the thin quilt, tea cooling beside me, the flowers perfuming the air, and the sound of the grove wrapping around me like a lullaby. And just before I drifted off, I thought of the note.

*Welcome to Citrus Grove, Mina March. Something tells me you're just what this place needed.*

I smiled in the dark. Maybe I was. I lay back, listening to the steady hum of the grove, and pressed my palm flat against the old floorboards. "We'll do this together," I whispered, to the house, to the land, to myself. The boards beneath my hand felt warm, as if something deep within them had heard me—and agreed.

Chapter Two


The clucking woke me up before the sun. Not a polite sort of clucking, either. No gentle barnyard morning chorus. This was a full-blown feathered uprising—indignant, relentless, like the universe itself had decided I'd slept long enough.

I groaned, pried one eye open, and blinked into the pale ribbon of dawn streaming through the loft window. For a heartbeat, I lay there and listened to the hush beneath the animal riot. The way the walls held the memory of night, the almost imperceptible shifting of the old floorboards as the house exhaled, making room for another morning. Every home I'd ever lived in before had been noisy in its own way: traffic, sirens, voices pressing through drywall. Here, the silence felt deliberate, like a sustained note in a song whose melody I had yet to learn. My air mattress had deflated in the night, cradling me in a sagging vinyl hollow that left every muscle in my back stiff with muted protest. Humidity clung warm and heavy, more like a damp quilt wrapped around me than air.

I sat up slowly. The grove stretched past the window, shadowed and still, except for the faint shimmer of early light sliding over the leaves. I could already smell the earth—sharp, loamy, and awake. The sweet-rot perfume of last season's fruit melting into the soil, the crisp bite of citrus oil lingering from the branches outside. It was the scent of surrender and survival, mingled together. My grandmother used to say you could judge a place by the way it smelled first thing in the morning. I wondered what she would have thought of this: wild, unfiltered, and stubbornly alive. The world felt expectant, like it hadn't decided yet what kind of day it was going to be.

Barefoot, I padded across the creaky loft floor and bounded down the stairs, braving a peak at myself in the bathroom mirror. Dark curls had staged a mutiny, curling wildly in every direction, and there was a faint smudge of mascara beneath one eye like I'd been crying in my sleep. I pressed my palms to my cheeks and leaned closer. Freckles. A dimple that only showed itself when I was tired enough to forget my defenses.

I didn't look like someone who had her life figured out. But I looked like someone who was trying. Maybe that counted. I paused at the window, watching the way the dawn unspooled itself across the grove. Each tree cast long shadows that stretched toward me, as if reaching for an answer only I could give. The chickens gathered in a huddle of feathers below, already fussing over imagined slights and invisible boundaries, their little dramas louder than sunrise.

The clucking came again—louder, demanding. "All right," I muttered, pushing away from the mirror. "I'm coming."

I tugged on a thin cotton dress, tied my curls into something vaguely resembling a bun, and stepped outside. The air hit me like a warm tide. Dew slicked the grass beneath my feet, and the smell of oranges—ripe and heavy—rolled through the grove like incense. Cicadas droned their low, insistent hymn while bees stitched lazy patterns between wildflowers. Somewhere in the distance, a cow lowed—a long, mournful sound that somehow managed to feel like both a complaint and a greeting.

I followed the noise to the barn, wading through grass that brushed my knees. My feet slipped through the dew, soaking the hem of my dress. In the spaces between each step, I could hear the tiny, secret world waking up: a lizard darting from the barn's shadow, a cardinal scolding from the branches above, the faint creak of the windmill at the edge of the property. I breathed it in; let it settle into the hollows of my bones.

And then I stopped.

The trough was full. Brimming with feed. The water bucket—clean and cold, beads of condensation slick on its rim—sat beside a mound of fresh hay. The chickens strutted with self-satisfied clucks, scattering in a flurry of feathers, while the cow—brown-eyed and impossibly soft—watched me with the calm patience of something that already knew how the day would end.

"I didn't… do this," I said aloud, to no one at all.

No footprints. No tire tracks. No note. Just a well-fed barnyard and a silence so deep it felt like the house and grove had been holding their breath, waiting for me to see it.

The cow—God, she had eyelashes too long for this world—ambled forward and nudged my hip with her damp nose. For a moment, I just stared at her—this patient, velvet-eyed creature with lashes like they'd been dipped in ink. There was no apology in her gaze, no doubt, no second-guessing. Just a kind of quiet certainty I'd almost forgotten existed. I envied it—how wholly she belonged to herself. I laughed, startled, the sound cracking like sunlight through a cloud. I scratched behind her ear and felt her lean into it, solid and warm.

"You're not supposed to be here," I whispered. "Any of you."

A hen darted past my ankle like it was offended I'd even questioned it. Another followed, pecking at a button on my dress, bold as brass. I laughed quietly. There was something almost defiant in their movements—a reminder that small things survive by making themselves known, by claiming their ground, by announcing their hunger to the world.

I knelt in the grass, still half-convinced I was dreaming. The earth was warm beneath my knees; the scent of hay and citrus and something faintly sweet—like old honey—hung in the air. It wrapped around me the way a childhood blanket does—not because it's soft, but because it's familiar in some way you can't quite name. I thought of my grandmother's kitchen again, of mornings when the record player hummed Elvis and the whole house smelled of toast and floor polish. How even then, before I knew what I'd be leaving behind, I recognized the rare alchemy of a place that held you without asking you to be anything but yourself.

The wind shifted, brushing the hair at my neck, carrying the breath of the grove. A hen strutted by with the kind of confidence I'd only ever seen in women who'd long stopped asking for permission. One pecked at my shoe, utterly unimpressed by my presence. I couldn't help it—I smiled. These weren't just animals. They were tiny, feathered declarations of survival, too busy living to care whether I deserved to be here.

I pulled my phone from my pocket and snapped a picture of the cow, her face filling the frame like an accidental portrait of serenity. I sent it to Goldie with a quick caption: *The animals were already fed.*

Her reply was immediate: *Um. Like… by who?*

*Unknown. Dairy fairy? Chicken cult? Send help.*

*Creepy or kind?*

*Undecided.*

*Be careful. You're too cute for a true crime podcast.*

I laughed under my breath, leaning back on my hands, letting the morning hum around me, and then turned back toward the grove.

The sun was climbing now, spilling molten light between the trees. I wandered deeper, trailing my fingers along the bark, the texture rough and real beneath my touch. The grove swallowed me whole. Dew clung to the hem of my dress, and bees stitched the air like little golden seamstresses. The chickens murmured in the distance. The cow chewed placidly at her hay.

I closed my eyes, let myself be still, and listened to the slow, certain pulse of this place. The house, the land, the animals—they were all witnesses, silent and unwavering. Maybe I didn't have to prove I belonged here. Maybe it was enough just to be willing to stay.

Eventually, the golden hush of morning gave way to necessity. The chickens had scattered, the cow was content, and my own stomach reminded me I'd brought nothing in the way of breakfast except tea and hope. I trudged back to the carriage house, brushing grass from my calves, heart still thumping with that new, raw kind of gratitude. There was a whole world waiting just down the road—groceries to buy, chores to figure out, faces I hadn't met. I'd need feed, advice, and courage, in that order.

I changed into clean clothes, tied my curls back with a practiced hand, and made a list on the back of an old envelope: peanut butter, bread, coffee, a bucket for water, and maybe—if the universe was feeling generous—answers. The sun was already cresting above the tree line when I slid behind the wheel and rolled toward town; the house and grove receding in the rearview, a promise I wasn't quite ready to leave behind.

------

Citrus Grove wasn't the kind of place that rushed toward the future. It wore its history like summer linen—faded, softened, and utterly unapologetic. Signs above the shopfronts were hand-painted and sun-bleached, edges curling where the rain had found them, but no one seemed in any hurry to scrape them down. The sidewalks cracked and crumbled at the edges, tufted with stubborn little weeds, but the locals simply stepped over them, familiar as kin.

An old man in a straw hat sat outside the barbershop, whittling the same block of wood he'd probably started a decade ago. Children darted through the crosswalk, barefoot and laughing, chased by a stray dog with a limp and a tongue lolling in the heat. Everything and everyone here seemed to know exactly where they belonged. Not just the people, but the buildings, too—stoic under the weight of the sun, painted in shades of memory. Citrus Grove had the sort of patience that could outlast storms, market busts, and whatever progress tried to roll through on four wheels. Not stagnant, not exactly. More like steady. Surefooted.

I found myself slowing down just to match its pace. My car idled past the faded "Welcome to Citrus Grove—Est. 1923" sign, past a row of mailbox flags all painted orange, and into the heart of town.

I was the only thing new for miles, and the town seemed to sense it. Maybe it was only my imagination. Maybe it was hope, stubborn as the fruit clinging to the branches behind my new home.

The scent from the bakery curled around my empty stomach like a warm embrace; a warm, golden haze of yeast and cinnamon and orange zest. I followed it without meaning to, my steps slowing as the bell above the bakery door chimed and I stepped inside.

The light here was soft and forgiving, filtered through old lace curtains and the haze of flour hanging in the air. There was no music; just the hum of quiet conversation, the scrape of a chair, the gentle clink of cups. Even the register rang with a sound that felt old-fashioned, meant for coins, not credit cards.

I ordered a sticky orange roll and coffee at the counter, the girl behind the register greeting me with a smile that was real, if a little shy, like she wasn't used to strangers but didn't mind the occasional one.

As I waited, I watched the town in miniature:

An elderly couple sat near the window; their hands curled around thick white mugs, black coffee steaming between them. They barely spoke, just nodded now and then, turning the pages of their battered newspaper in perfect tandem. It was easy to imagine they'd sat here every morning for the last thirty years, as steady and expected as sunrise.

A trio of young mothers huddled at a corner table; strollers parked beside them like miniature parade floats. Their voices were hushed, eyes darting between their babies—faces slack and peaceful, lost to dreams—and the plates of pastries they traded like secrets. I watched as one woman reached out, gently tucking a blanket around her sleeping daughter, her other hand never leaving her cup.

No one was in a hurry. No one looked at their phone. Even time seemed to lean back and take a long, slow breath. This wasn't a sleepy town, just a contented one. The difference was subtle but important. There was a quiet pride in the way the shop was run, in the way people lingered over their coffee, in the slow parade of neighbors greeting each other by name.

My stomach rumbled, louder than I would've liked, and I bit back a laugh, grateful for the cover of the bakery's gentle noise. I promised myself I'd learn how to linger, too; how to let sweetness—of time, of orange glaze, of belonging—melt on my tongue and stay awhile.

I ducked into the old citrus packing warehouse turned flea market, more out of curiosity than intent. The air inside was cool and scented with orange oil and something sweetly musty—like the memory of a hundred harvests sealed in the cracks of the floorboards.

The place was a maze of stalls and tables, all crowded with the detritus of other people's lives: mason jars filled with marbles, citrus crate labels faded to watercolor, embroidered aprons the color of marigolds. There were old records stacked by the door, their jackets curling at the edges, and a shelf of tarnished picture frames. The black-and-white faces inside smiling at nothing in particular.

I lingered over a bowl of hand-painted teacups—none matching, but all lovely in their imperfection. I wondered who'd last held them, what quiet mornings they'd witnessed.

A woman behind a booth of honey and soaps caught my eye and smiled. "Looking for anything special?" she asked.

"Just getting to know the place," I said, picking up a bar of orange-blossom soap and inhaling deep. It smelled like home might, someday.

She nodded, as though she understood. "Take your time. Nobody's in a rush here."

The grocery store was small, the kind where the produce section doubled as local news headquarters. I picked up peanut butter, bread, coffee, and a carton of eggs so fresh their shells were still smudged with straw. The girl at the register had a high ponytail and an easy smile. She didn't ask for my loyalty card or hurry me along, just chatted about the heat and warned me not to buy milk from the big chain down the road ("It never tastes right").

A handwritten sign taped to the counter read: *Try Joani's Sundrop Lemonade—now with local honey!*

I made a mental note. Another place to discover. Another name to remember.

My hands were full by the time I left; bread tucked under my arm, cold bottle of sweet tea sweating in my palm. I glanced down Main Street—the awnings faded but proud; shop windows displaying everything from hand-thrown pottery to dusty books. Every door was open, or seemed it could be, if you only asked the right way.

I crossed the street, grocery bag swinging at my side, and made my way to Beckett Supply Co.—the hardware store I'd been told was the heart of town, or at least the lungs. The sign above the door was hand-lettered, gold peeling at the corners. The kind of sign that looked as if it had always belonged there.

The bell above the door sang—a sharp, clean note that broke the spell of sunlight and sweet air outside. I stepped into the hush, blinking in the sudden dimness. The place felt cavernous after the brightness of the street; every shelf and shadow steeped in decades of patience. It smelled faintly of hay and mineral oil, a sharper, honest kind of clean than the lemon-scented city shops. Ceiling fans turned overhead, pushing the cool air in languid circles.

For a moment, I was aware of everything: the soft sheen of the concrete floor, the rows of work boots by the door, the tangle of leashes on a peg. There was nothing fancy here, nothing dressed up for company. Just a quiet, built-in confidence, as if sturdiness was in its very foundations, and it had never needed to pretend to be more.

I let the door ease shut behind me, took a breath, and felt the weight of the place settle over me—steady, unmoving, built to last. I hesitated in the doorway, too aware of how out of place I must look: city shoes flecked with barn dust, hair wild from the walk, arms full of groceries instead of grit. Still, there was a comfort here, a promise that if I could just learn the language—of fittings and feed and the quiet dignity of work—I might find a way to belong.

And then I saw him.

He stood at the counter, half-shadowed by the dusty light slanting through the windows, sorting lengths of rope into tidy coils. Broad-shouldered, hands moving with the easy certainty of someone who'd spent his life learning what things needed—not in a rush, not performing for anyone, just *there*.

His shirt was faded; sleeves rolled to the elbows, forearms tanned and strong beneath the thin cotton. A few tousled strands of hair fell across his forehead, damp at the temples. There was a steadiness about him—like the house, like the town itself—that made my heart settle in my chest. He looked up, and for a moment, the anxious static faded. His green eyes were clear, but unreadable. He didn't smile, but he didn't look away either. He just held my gaze, quiet and certain.

The rest of the store faded. I couldn't have told you what music was playing, or if there were any other customers at all. It was just the way he stood, as if the world didn't ask much of him except to be exactly where he was. I felt...present. Steady.

I realized I was clutching the grocery bag to my chest, as if it could guard me from my own awkwardness. My mouth went dry. I tried to remember what I'd rehearsed on the walk over—something about needing chicken feed, or maybe it was garden gloves, or maybe I should just turn around and start over.

"Um—hi," I managed, wincing at the catch in my voice. "I, uh, just moved into the, um, the house at the end of the grove. I think I need… I mean, I know I need…" I trailed off, cheeks burning.

He set the rope aside and regarded me with that same quiet focus, like he had all the time in the world for me to find my words.

"Feed," I blurted. "For chickens. And maybe— something for cows?" I tried to sound like I knew what I was talking about, but the words felt foreign in my mouth, clumsy and uncertain.

He nodded once, unhurried. "Aisle three for feed," he said, voice low and even. "Salt lick is next to the hay. Anything else?"

I shook my head; a wave of embarrassment washed through the relief in my chest, the two feelings tangling tightly together. "I think that's it. For now. Unless you've got a manual for first time farmgirls?"

The barest hint of a smile tugged at the corner of his mouth. Not a laugh, not a tease—just a silent acknowledgment that he'd heard me.

"You'll figure it out," he said simply.

I tried to hold his confidence in my chest as I looked around at the shelves lined with tools I couldn't name and materials I'd never touched. A fleeting thought came to me: how I'd learned early to fix things quietly—broken lamps, squeaking doors, torn curtains—careful not to draw attention, careful not to ask for help. I wondered what it might feel like now, letting someone in, allowing myself to trust, to rely on hands other than my own. My anxiety didn't disappear, but it ebbed, as if I'd slipped out of harsh sunlight into shade. I nodded, gripping my bag tighter. "Thanks."

He just nodded again, already turning to lead me down the aisle, steady as the dawn. He led the way, footsteps echoing on the concrete, and I followed—feeling, for once, smaller in someone's shadow in a way that was not unwelcome. Up close, he was all rough edges smoothed by use: broad shouldered, hands thick fingered and callused, sun-browned at the wrists where the cuffs of his shirt left off. The fabric strained a little at his back when he reached for a bag of feed, muscles moving beneath like he was carved to fit the world exactly as it was.

He didn't ask questions he didn't need answers to. Just loaded the feed into my arms and moved on, wordless but not unkind. The store was hushed around us; the dust and sunlight painting patterns on the old floor. I found myself matching his pace, drawn by the rhythm of it—how certain he was of every step, how the space seemed to part for him and settle in his wake.

He paused at a shelf, lifted a salt lick the size of a cinder block as if it weighed nothing at all, and set it in my cart. "You'll want this," he said, glancing at me sideways— not in the way of someone trying to impress, but someone who'd done this a thousand times for people who needed it.

His eyes caught the light and for a moment, I wondered if this was how women used to feel in the presence of strong men, before the world told them to be wary of strength. Not that he was imposing. Just… present. Like he'd stay until the job was done, no matter what.

I tried to steady my breathing, feeling oddly exposed, as if he might see all the ways I didn't know what I was doing and care anyway.

We made it to the register without incident. He rang up the feed, the salt, the hay, and didn't say a word about my lack of planning or the newness still clinging to my every movement.

"Anything else?" he asked, voice as quiet as the store itself.

I shook my head, suddenly grateful for the lull. "I think that'll do it. For now."

He slid the total across the counter, hands steady. "Welcome to Citrus Grove," he said, and something in his tone made it sound like a promise rather than a greeting. I handed over the cash, fingers brushing his palm for the briefest second—a brush of skin, warm and real and solid. For a moment, I wondered if the world had always been this steady, and I'd just forgotten how to notice.

"Thank you," I said, and meant it more than I expected.

He gave a short nod, like that was all he'd needed to hear, and stepped from behind the counter to carry the feed out to my car.

He hefted the feed into the trunk with practiced ease, barely making a sound. For a moment, we both stood at the back of my little sedan, the heat shimmering off the gravel, the citrus trees watching like a row of old friends. I wanted to say something more—anything to break the hush that felt as solid as the ground beneath us.

"So," I managed, pushing a curl behind my ear. "Any other advice for a city girl suddenly in charge of a barnyard?"

He leaned against the side of my car, arms folded, posture easy as a summer afternoon. "Trust your instincts," he said simply. "And don't let the chickens fool you. They run the place."

A small laugh escaped before I could stop it. "Noted. I'll try to win them over with charm."

He almost smiled. Almost. "Good luck with that."

We both lingered, letting the moment stretch. Finally, I stuck out my hand, a little self-conscious but determined. "I'm Mina. Mina March."

He looked at my hand for a second, then took it—his palm callused, warm, steady. "Westley," he replied. No last name, just the name itself, as if that was enough. It was.

I liked the way he said it. No frills, no need to fill the space with anything more.

He released my hand and started to turn away, but I remembered suddenly—the reason I'd come in, the thing I'd almost forgotten in the hush of the store and the solidity of him.

"Oh—my sink isn't working. Carriage house. It groans, spits, then just… gives up. I've been brushing my teeth with bottled water like I'm on a camping trip gone wrong."

He paused, one eyebrow ticking up. "Probably just a loose fitting. Or a clog." There was that same quiet promise, as if no problem was ever too big. "I'll take a look this afternoon, if you want."

"Really?" I tried not to sound too eager. "I mean—I'd appreciate it. Only if you have time."

He nodded, the hint of a smile at the corners of his mouth. "I'll be there. After I close up."

There was nothing left to say, so I watched him walk back to the store—broad-shouldered, unhurried, the kind of man who kept his word. I found myself hoping he always would.

As I climbed into the car, I glanced in the mirror. My cheeks were flushed, but not with embarrassment—something more like relief, like maybe this town, this house, this beginning, was already offering more than I'd dared to hope.

I took a long breath before turning the key. My errands had taken longer than I had planned—not because the town was confusing, but because everywhere I went, someone stopped to offer a nod or a little wave, as if recognizing a new shape in the town's slow orbit. The engine caught with a friendly shudder as I stole one last look at Beckett Supply through the windshield before easing onto Main Street.

The drive home was short, but I made it last. Citrus Grove's old neighborhoods unspooled behind my windows: porches draped in windchimes, a mother and toddler waving to the mailman, yards gone a little wild but not neglected. There was an intimacy to the way time moved here; the way even the cracked sidewalks seemed to remember every footstep.

When I turned onto my own drive, gravel popping beneath the tires, the carriage house appeared between the trees like a secret kept just for me. I cut the engine, let the hush settle, and listened—for a moment—to the living, breathing quiet.

Inside, arms full of groceries, I stepped over the threshold and let the weight of the afternoon slide off my shoulders. I unpacked with slow purpose; bread, honey, fresh eggs—I realized too late were not necessary—feeling the warm glow of midday sun trace itself across the countertop. It was barely enough for a week, but I knew all too well how to make it feel like a feast.

I caught my reflection in the window—a tired girl, hair wild, arms full of someone else's tomorrow—and thought for a second that maybe, just maybe, I could make something here.

After the groceries, I tackled the tangle of things still waiting in the car. Books first—always. Their spines made a lopsided rainbow on the makeshift shelf by my bed. Then my battered French press, a handful of dishes, a small tin of loose tea that rattled like a charm bracelet when I picked it up. My journal, its leather worn and soft, found a place beside the bed. I stacked the rest haphazardly.

I moved through the little rooms with a slow purpose. I wiped down the counters, found a home for the kettle, hung my sunhat on the peg by the door. Each act was a kind of claiming, a way to tell the house—*I am here to stay.*

Every so often I'd pause, listening. The hush was thick and living, carrying the low, distant rhythm of the grove, the soft ticking of the old wall clock, the whisper of wind through the broken screen. I tried not to think about all the things I didn't know yet: how to feed chickens properly, how to milk a cow, how to belong.

Westley's promise to return sat at the back of my mind—not a flutter, not an ache, but a slow, steady thrum. I could almost feel the shape of it, the way you feel a coming storm before the sky darkens. Not the kind of anticipation that gnaws, but the kind that reminds you to breathe deeper, to make space.

I opened the window over the sink and let in the hot, syrupy air. Somewhere outside, the cow mooed—less a greeting than a reminder that I wasn't the only one finding her footing. I thought about the look in Westley's eyes— steady, unreadable, but kind—and let the image root itself quietly in the back of my mind.

I made myself a mug of tea and sat on the steps outside, legs curled up, watching the afternoon drift by in slow, uneven measures. There was work to do—always—but for a moment, I allowed myself to rest. The house seemed to approve; its boards settling with a soft, approving sigh.

I turned my journal open and tried to write, but the words tangled up in the fullness of the day. So, I just listed what I could see: Sunlight caught in the curve of a glass; wildflowers bending in the wind; a single feather on the threshold; the memory of a voice—*I can fix it*—echoing softly against the hush.

———————————

By the time I heard the engine on the drive, a hush had fallen. Not silence, but expectancy. A space made ready for something—or someone—new.

I hovered by the loft window, the mug of tea cooling in my palms, watching sunlight flicker through the leaves as the sound of gravel crunching grew louder, then stilled. There was something oddly ceremonial about the arrival. I found myself standing straighter, smoothing my dress, suddenly aware of the softness of my own body and the chaos of curls barely contained in a loose knot.

The knock on the door wasn't loud, just a single, measured rap. Still, it startled me—reminded me how little separated me from the world outside. I took a breath, felt it shiver through me, then went to answer.

Westley filled the doorway. Taller than I remembered, broader too, like the doorway had been cut just for him, and still, he barely fit. He held a battered red toolbox in one hand and a spool of plumber's tape in the other. His shirt was the kind of blue that had once been bright and was now faded by years of sun and soap. It clung to his shoulders, the sleeves pushed up to reveal forearms marked by work—scars, sun, freckles, the kind of honest wear you don't see in cities. He was a man built for repair, for holding broken things together.

His eyes found mine. For a moment, I forgot my own name. There was nothing calculating in his gaze, only a quiet alertness—a steadying presence. My heart, which had been fluttering with the thousand little worries of the morning, seemed to land, as if he'd given it permission to rest.

"I said I'd fix it," he said, voice as gentle as the hush that had settled in the grove.

I stepped back, tucking a strand of hair behind my ear. "I appreciate it. I, uh… tried turning the tap. Kicked it. Apologized. Nothing worked."

His mouth quirked, barely a smile. "Plumbing usually needs more than apologies."

He crossed the room in three strides, and for a moment, the smallness of the carriage house felt like a secret, a cocoon. I hovered awkwardly by the doorway as he set down his toolbox and crouched beneath the sink.

"Can you hand me that dish towel?" he asked, not looking up.

I scrambled to oblige, nearly knocking over my mug in the process. Our hands brushed. I felt a spark, not electric—more like the catch of a match, the faint promise of warmth.

He worked in silence for a moment, the only sounds the clink of a wrench and the soft whistle of his breath. I watched the way his hands moved—confident, careful, as if even the pipes deserved respect. I realized how few people I'd known who were gentle with the world around them.

Finally, he glanced up, one eyebrow raised. "You okay?"

"Fine," I managed. "Just… learning the language." My cheeks flushed. "Of, you know, faucets. And… Florida."

He straightened, his presence filling the small room. "You'll pick it up." There was no tease, just steady belief. He positioned himself under the sink; one arm disappeared into the tangle of pipes, the other resting on his chest—utterly relaxed, as if this was the most natural place in the world for him to be. The air felt dense, like it had thickened to hold the shape of this moment.

"Can you pass me the flathead?" His voice was a low rumble drifting up from under the counter.

I scanned the open toolbox, willing myself to pick out the right tool. My fingers hesitated over the choices, and I bit my lip, finally closing on what I hoped was a flathead, knelt down, and stretched my hand toward him.

Our hands met in the shadow of the cabinet—his palm callused and warm, mine small and unsure, but a slip, a misjudged step on the slick edge of the old linoleum, and suddenly I was off balance. The tool clattered to the floor and before I knew it, I was tumbling forward, catching myself on instinct.

My hand landed on the denim stretch of his thigh, his leg a solid anchor beneath me. My other hand braced the floor, so close now I could feel the heat of him—could see, as I ducked to look beneath the counter, the calm way he paused, gazing up at me with faint flecks of gold in his eyes, the kind you don't notice until you're within breathing distance.

He didn't scowl. He didn't even move—just sucked in a quiet breath that felt like a laugh against my collarbone. The room seemed to shrink around us, the air alive with the hum of embarrassment.

"Sorry!" The word tumbled out, barely above a whisper. My cheeks flushed hot, all too aware of the impossibility of the moment—of being a stranger, tangled up on the floor with a man who seemed, impossibly, like a fixture in the house itself.

He didn't move away. Just watched me, something steady and untroubled in his expression. "You okay?" The words were gentle, not just asking, but offering.

I nodded, flustered and suddenly shy, and pushed myself upright, careful not to brush him again. My pulse beat hard and bright, but there was a strange peace in the quiet that settled between us—like the world hadn't broken, only shifted a little.

He shifted slightly, and I remembered I had weight on him. "Flathead?" he prompted softly, and the word broke the tension, grounding me. I found the tool, placed it in his outstretched hand, and he finished the repair in easy, quiet competence; eventually, the faucet giving in to him, groaned, then sputtered to life—a stream of water, clear and bright. He tested it, nodded once in satisfaction, and stood, dusting off his hands.

"All yours," he said, looking at me in that same steady way.

I let out a slow breath I hadn't realized I'd been holding. "Thank you. Seriously—I was about to start brushing my teeth with bottled water and self-pity. But you came. Most people say they'll do something and then never show."

"I don't say things I don't mean."

Something in the way he said it made me want to believe him, even before I'd earned the right. In another life, those words might have been a warning — the kind you learn to read between, the kind you hear right before the follow through never comes. I'd been taught to treat promises like weather: never trust what can change by morning.

But Westley didn't look like weather. He looked like bedrock; like something the storms had already tested and failed to move. The quiet in his tone didn't demand I trust him — it simply offered the possibility and left the choice with me.

I wondered how long it had been since I'd let myself lean into that possibility. Not just believing someone, but believing they could mean what they said without needing to dress it up or make it grand. No oaths. No conditions. Just steady truth, handed over like a tool meant to be used.

And there I was, holding it — clumsy and uncertain, but holding it all the same. Something about that made my chest tighten. A good kind of tight. Like maybe this town wasn't just a restart. Maybe it was a place where people actually *meant* things.

## Chapter Three

Westley stood in the open doorway, toolbox at his side, the weight of late sunlight falling across his shoulders in long, gold strokes. The pipes were fixed, his promise kept, but he lingered—something patient in the angle of his posture, as if waiting for the next line in a conversation I didn't know how to start.

He didn't fidget or fill the silence. He simply stood— steady as the doorframe itself—thumb hooked loosely over the worn handle of his toolbox, boots planted in the dust. The light gilded him—amber pooling at his collarbone,, brushing his jaw. It made the dust motes shimmer.

He glanced out at the deepening sky, then back at me, his eyes darker in the changing light. "Have you eaten?"

The question was simple, but it settled around us with all the quiet gravity of a real invitation. The way he asked—no assumption, just a steady, unhurried kindness—struck something fragile in me. I felt a tremor of nerves—was I imposing? Should I say yes? Did he really mean it, or was it simply what you did for a neighbor, a newcomer, someone not yet woven into the fabric of this place?

The part of me that was always careful wanted to decline, to retreat into the small, familiar comforts I'd carved out in the carriage house. I thought of my mother, her voice always cautioning, "Don't make trouble. Don't overstay." But hunger, curiosity, and something softer—something unnamed, a tender longing not to be alone—urged me forward.

"I haven't," I admitted, my voice too loud in the hush. "Unless you count a slice of bread and two cups of tea."

He gave a slow, approving nod, as if this answer had been expected, maybe even hoped for. "There's a place in town. Joani's place. Good food." He paused, glancing away as if the next words required care. "You'd be welcome."

A thousand small anxieties flickered and faded, melting away with the last rays of sun. I let myself believe him; I let myself want to be welcome. "That sounds… perfect. Thank you."

He offered a small smile, brief and genuine. I stepped back inside to lock up, the old brass key cool against my palm, heart thumping a little faster. The carriage house door clicked shut behind me, sealing in the scent of lavender and lemon balm. I check the windows—one, two, three times— my old rituals of safety, still clinging, even as something new urged me on.

Outside, the world had shifted. The last of the sunlight poured through the trees, gilding over every branch and leaf. Orange blossoms flickered in the breeze, their perfume drifting on the hush that settles before dusk. The gravel path sparkled with mica, stones catching the light like breadcrumbs leading somewhere holy. Each step felt significant, as if the act of walking beside Westley—following rather than fleeting—was its own kind of promise.

Westley's truck waited beneath a canopy of tangled oak and orange, the paint faded and honest, windows smudged with old rain. He moved ahead of me, the heavy door creaking as he pulled it open without a word; I climbed in, the bench seat sighing beneath my weight. The air inside was cool, touched by the day's heat but carrying its own quiet history.

The cab smelled faintly of clean linen and citrus oil. There was an orderliness to the space that surprised me: a folded flannel shirt on the bench, a battered thermos in the cupholder, a field guide to Florida birds tucked into the side pocket. I imagined him here alone, lunch packed by his own hand, the radio low, mornings starting before the world was ready.

He slid behind the wheel, movements unhurried, every gesture considered. He rested his hands on the steering wheel—broad, calloused, the knuckles marked by old work. I thought of how those hands had coaxed his piper back to life, how gentle he'd been with the battered house and with me.

He started the engine, which rumbled to life like an old dog stretching in its sleep. The radio dial glowed soft and orange in the dimness, the music a distant, crackling comfort. For a moment, neither of us spoke. The golden hour had found us both, slipping through the windshield and painting him in that fleeting, holy light. I watched it pool in the hollow of his throat, streak across his cheekbones, turn the brown of his hair to amber.

For one breathless moment, he was transformed—washed clean, radiant, timeless. I wondered if he knew how he looked, how utterly *present* he seemed, not just in the truck but in this life. Did anyone ever tell him? Did he ever believe it, or was he always the one waiting in doorways, steady and silent, carrying his own quiet ache?

The sight of him like that—quiet, unguarded—stirred something. There was a different kind of gravity here, a steadiness that asked for nothing but seemed to offer everything. I thought of the men I'd known who mistook stillness for absence, who filled silences with noise because they feared what might surface if they left space for it. Westley didn't fear the space. He seemed to believe in it, to trust that something good could grow there.

He glanced over, caught me staring, and for a heartbeat I felt seen—exposed, but not unwelcome. His expression didn't change; there was no teasing, just a gentle question in his eyes. A shared understanding, wordless and weighty. I looked away, cheeks warm, pretending to study the town as we pulled onto the main road.

The road unfurled before us, flanked on either side by the ancient groves—row after row of orange trees heavy with fruit, leaves gleaming dark and glossy in the warning light. The scent of citrus drifted through the open window, sharp and sweet, mixing with the loam and sunbaked earth. The air was thick with the perfume of green things settling in for the night; the faint, humming chorus of crickets just beginning to wake.

Wildflowers bent their heads toward the dusk; petals closing around golden hearts. A pair of sandhill cranes lifted off from the roadside; wings gilded by the last, soft light, their cries echoing. I watched as we passed a battered mailbox, painted with faded lemons, a porch swing creaking in the slow wind, shadows growing long and blue across the grass.

We drove mostly in silence, but it wasn't awkward. Westley seemed to believe in the dignity of quiet, letting the engine and the world do the talking. The truck shuttered over potholes, headlights blinking in the gathering dusk, and I let myself be carried along, content to rest in the hush between us. I watched the shape of his hands on the wheel, steady and sure, veins rising beneath the skin. There was something devotional in the way he drove—present, attentive, as if even this small act was worth his whole focus.

I glanced at him again, catching the subtle shift in his jaw, the way his gaze lingered on the road but softened at the sight of a family walking home—two kids, a woman with a basket of mangoes, laughter drifting through the open air. I wondered if he saw the same things I did, if the world glowed for him the way it glowed for me in these in-between hours.

The town looked different in the evening—slower, softer, the gold of daylight lingering in windowpanes and turning the old brick buildings honey warm. I saw faces at doorways, friends pausing to chat on their way home, children tracing sidewalk chalk in the blue shadowed quiet.

The grocery store's neon flickered, casting a pool of color on the pavement; a dog barked somewhere, the sound both lonely and familiar.

We rolled down Main Street, The Sundrop's neon sign blinking to life as we arrived; a lemon in sunglasses leaned against a glass of something tropical with an umbrella. It's yellow light pulsed like a heartbeat against the twilight, promising something sweet inside. Westley pulled to the curb, shifting into park with a motion as fluid as breathing.

I caught my reflection in the window—hair wild, cheeks flushed, something new and eager in my eyes. For a second, I hesitated, caught between the world I'd left and the one I was walking into. All the old doubts crowded in: Did I belong here? Was this a beginning or just a bright detour? But then Westley moved around the truck, footsteps quiet on the pavement, and waited by the door, holding it open as if it was the most natural thing in the world. The golden light behind him made a halo of his silhouette.

I crossed the threshold. In that instant, something shifted: outsider to insider, wandering to welcome. I didn't know what the evening would bring, but I knew this would be a moment I'd want to remember.

The Sundrop's door closed behind us, and the night's hush gave way to a burst of neon and citrus light. For a moment, I simply stood there, letting my senses adjust.

Inside, The Sundrop was a blast of neon warmth and retro kitsch done right—equal parts citrus grove and mid-century bombshell. It was as if someone had taken a Floridian daydream and poured it into a cocktail glass, then garnished it with a twist of the wildest imagination. The walls glowed with colors I didn't know could exist outside a fruit crate label: sherbet orange, turquoise, sunny yellow, all humming in harmony beneath the buzz of fluorescent tubes.

It was atomic pin-up meets roadside fruit stand, but polished, sharp, clean; a curated shrine to all things juicy and joyful. Even the barstools were orange vinyl, bright as peeled clementines, arranged with mathematical precision. It was clearly the work of someone with both vision and a deep appreciation for vintage chaos.

A giant orange jukebox leaned in the corner, crooning something sultry from the '50s, the music threading through the air like spun sugar. My eyes kept drifting to a flossy painting of oranges dripping juice—both promise and peril, lush and a little bit wicked. Every detail in here seemed to shimmer with memory: the citrus-themed pin-up photos lining the walls, the framed snapshots of past Miss Orange Blossoms in big hair and gowns, the orange soda ads for motels long since crumbled into weeds.

It should have felt loud, overwhelming, maybe even artificial; instead, it wrapped around me like warmth after rain. I let myself breathe deep, the scent of oranges and sugar lingering beneath the hum of voices and ice rattling in glasses.

Behind the bar stood a woman who looked like she could bend the universe to her will with one arched brow; a goddess in cat-eye glasses.

She looked like she belonged in a Technicolor dream: blood orange lipstick, black victory rolls, a citrus printed blouse tied neatly at the waist. Her pencil skirt looked sharp enough to cut steel, and her whole presence radiated sassy, witchy authority. I would have trusted her with a secret, or my soul, or both.

She was yelling at someone on the other end of the bar, "Lyle, I swear to God if you bring me one more grapefruit that is clearly a blood orange, I'm going to hex you so hard your exes will feel it!"

A ripple of laughter broke out nearby—customers clearly used to her brand of lightning. I caught Westley's grin, small but real, and suddenly I felt lighter, as if the neon itself was working a spell on me.

Joani—because she had to be Joani, the woman who ran this shrine to Florida weirdness—looked us over as we approached the bar, eyebrows lifting in a silent greeting that dared you to be boring. I slid onto a barstool, Westley settling beside me with a familiar ease, as if he'd done this a hundred times.

Joani gave me a once over that was somehow both surgical and kind. "You new in town, sweetheart, or just lost?"

"I'm Mina," I managed, summoning a half-smile. "New. Just moved into the old house on the edge of town."

"Well, welcome to Citrus Grove. This place is the heart, and I'm the arteries." Her mouth twisted in a sly grin as she wiped her hands on a citrus print towel. "You like grilled cheese and vodka lemonade?" she asked, already reaching for a shaker.

"Those are my love languages." The words came out before I could second guess them. I saw the corners of her mouth turn up, like she approved of the answer, or maybe just the honesty of it.

"See, Westley? She's a keeper." Joani winked at him, then slid a heavy glass across the bar to me, its contents blushing coral pink. She didn't wait for my order; she seemed to know what I needed before I did. The sandwich arrived next, golden and gooey, cut on the diagonal, with a little bowl of something bright orange on the side.

I dipped a corner of grilled cheese into the sauce and took a bite. The taste hit me like sun on my tongue—sweet, tangy, a little bit wild. "This is actual magic," I told Joani, who accepted the praise with the smugness of a benevolent witch.

"Secret's in the oranges and a dash of spite," she said. "Heals what ails you, or at least makes you forget about it for a while."

I let the comfort soak in, the familiar crunch of bread, the citrus bite, the cold snap of vodka lemonade. Each flavor felt like a gentle unspooling, a way to remind my body it was safe here, that maybe I didn't have to keep bracing myself for disappointment. The bar seemed to exhale around me, as if

Joani's words were a spell that loosened something in my chest. I took another bite of the sandwich, let the sweetness of the sauce linger, and listened to the world here. Ice clinked in glasses, someone laughed so hard they wheezed, and a low hum of conversation wove through it all like the constant rustle of leaves in the groves.

I thought of the places I'd left behind—rooms where laughter was just the thinnest skin stretched over something waiting to split. Here, it felt whole. Honest. I caught Westley's profile in the glow of the neon and realized he looked the same way the room felt: solid, unhurried, sure of his place. A part of me wanted to press myself into the seams of this place until I fit, until my edges stopped catching on everything. For the first time in a long time, I could almost believe that was possible.

Westley mostly let Joani and me talk, but I caught him watching our exchange, his expression quietly approving. He didn't interrupt, just listened, his hand wrapped around a chipped mug of beer. There was something restful in his stillness, a steadiness that let the rest of us spin wild and free.

For a little while, we just existed: Joani's laughter in the air, Westley's steady presence at my side, the jukebox spinning out dreams of another decade. The bar filled with other lives—locals drifting in, calling out to Joani, catching up on gossip, the citrus sweet familiarity of a small town. It startled me at first, the warmth of their easy laughter, the open acceptance I hadn't earned yet. It made me ache, made something twist in my chest, remembering nights when laughter had meant danger, loud voices turning sharp without warning. But this was different, laughter without edge, laughter that felt safe. It was a gentle nudge, an invitation, and I found myself leaning closer, wanting desperately to belong, even as old fears whispered caution.

When I paused to catch my breath, Joani leaned in conspiratorially. "So, what brings a girl like you to this little corner of nowhere?"

I hesitated. "The house, mostly. I wanted… I want to make it new again. Turn it into a bed and breakfast, fill it up with people and laughter and light. I want it to be loved. Lived in."

Westley's gaze flicked over, thoughtful. He spoke softly, but his words landed with quiet gravity. "Things break. Doesn't mean you throw them out."

I nodded, understanding more than I could say. "That's my plan. For the house. For me, too, I guess."

Joani gave me a look—one part skepticism, two parts hope. "If anyone can pull it off, it's a woman who eats grilled cheese like it's a sacrament."

I smiled, feeling seen in a way that wasn't uncomfortable, but almost exhilarating. Maybe it was the neon, or the lemonade, or just the safety of being somewhere I didn't have to explain myself.

Around us, the evening pressed closer, the Sundrop's neon pulsing steady against the windows. Joani spun the jukebox to something a little slower, the room softening around its edges. My hands were warm; my heart felt lighter than it had in weeks.

Westley finished his beer, set the mug down with a gentle click. "Ready to head out?"

I nodded, not trusting myself to say goodbye to this pocket of ease. As we rose, Joani called, "You come back soon, Mina. And bring this one with you, or I'll have to hex him into asking you proper."

Westley tipped his head, the ghost of a smile at the corner of his mouth. "Don't think she needs any help, Joani."

I let the night air wrap around me as we stepped outside, the last bright notes of the jukebox fading behind us, and I thought maybe I could belong here. Maybe this was how new lives started: a grilled cheese sandwich, a glass of something bright, a place where laughter echoed off walls painted the color of summer.

The neon glow of The Sundrop spilled onto the pavement and turned every puddle into a swirling, citrus-tinted galaxy. I paused for a moment, watching my reflection blur in the glass; the wildness of my hair, the flush of my cheeks, the echo of laughter still hovering at the corners of my mouth. Inside, Joani's world kept humming—jukebox music slipping through the door as it swung shut, laughter rising in waves, the faint clink of glasses and the perfume of oranges trailing after us into the night.

I glanced back one more time, thinking about all the plans I'd abandoned before they could bloom; all the futures I'd sketched quietly and then erased in fear. But here was something solid beneath my feet—a choice, an investment in myself. Westley was waiting patiently, hands in his pockets, quiet acceptance radiating from him. It struck me how different this was; I wasn't running from something this time—I was finally moving toward something real.

Westley walked quietly beside me, the gold halo of the bar's sign giving way to the cool blue of evening. The air had shifted—lighter, the thick syrup of summer cooling on the breeze; the kind of night that promised sleep would come easy, dreams loose and sweet. For a few steps, neither of us spoke, and it wasn't awkward at all—just a hush that made everything else more vivid: the chirr of cicadas, the distant crackle of a radio from someone's porch, the faint salt tang drifting up from somewhere I hadn't found yet.

Westley unlocked the truck, his keys jingling softly; he waited for me to settle in, then eased into the driver's seat. He didn't start the engine right away. For a moment, we just sat together in the low-lit cab, the residue of the bar clinging to our clothes, the warmth of grilled cheese and citrus vodka still lingering on my tongue.

He reached for the radio, turning the dial until a low, easy song filled the cab; his hand lingered there for a moment, as if anchoring us both to the hush of the moment. "Joani makes it hard to leave, doesn't she?"

"She does." My voice felt softer than before, quieter, but not small. "That's what I want for the house, you know. Somewhere you want to linger, even when you don't have to."

He glanced at me, the lines at the corners of his eyes deepening as he smiled—a private thing, not for show. "I think you might just pull it off."

We started down Main Street, headlights sweeping puddles of colored light across the old brick buildings. The Sundrop's sign flickered in the rearview, growing smaller with every block until it was just another memory.

The truck rumbled over the worn road, suspension creaking in protest, but it felt steady beneath us—a quiet carriage carrying us back to where we began. The night pressed close to the windows; dark velvet streaked with the silver glint of fireflies and the distant blush of porch lamps.

I watched the town recede, replaced by the slow, undulating sprawl of the orange groves, each tree a dark silhouette against the paler sky. Every now and then, a branch reached out, nearly brushing the truck as we passed, the world narrowing to a ribbon of gravel and possibility.

Westley's hands rested easy on the wheel; every so often, his eyes flicked toward me, not quite searching, but curious. I wondered what he saw—if he could read the quiet hope inside me, or if I was just another story passing through his truck.

As we reached the edge of the property, Westley slowed—not at the carriage house turnoff, but farther down, by the old, weathered mailbox leaning at an angle, paint faded from lemon to ivory. He parked beneath a canopy of oaks, letting the engine sigh into silence. For a second, I wondered if something was wrong; then I realized what he was doing—giving us time. Not rushing the end, not cutting the moment short.

He hopped out first, walking around to my side, and opened the door with a quiet, practiced grace. The gravel crunched beneath our feet as we set off toward the house, a good six or seven minutes' stroll up the drive. The darkness was gentle, not threatening; the moon hung low and full above the orange trees, bathing everything in pale gold. The air buzzed with the soft static of crickets, and somewhere far off, a frog sang a note so clear it made me smile.

We walked side by side, not touching, our footsteps falling in and out of sync. There was a comfort in the unspoken rhythm—a sense that we could walk all night, saying nothing, and it would still count as connection. Every so often, I caught Westley's gaze in the moonlight—steady, unreadable, but kind. He seemed content to let me fill the silence, or leave it be.

I talked a little, mostly about the house—my plans for the porch, the wildness of the garden, the hope that laughter might echo off the old floorboards again someday. Westley listened, nodding at all the right moments, offering a small word of encouragement here and there, never rushing me. The longer we walked, the easier it was to let down my guard; the gravel path unwinding beneath our feet felt almost like a promise.

By the time we reached the carriage house, the world had settled into a deeper hush. Westley stopped a few paces back, as if unsure whether to follow further; I turned, feeling the gravity of goodbye tug at me, soft but certain.

"Thank you," I said. "For dinner. For all of it."

He shook his head, one hand drifting to the back of his neck. "Anytime, Mina." His voice was quiet, but there was no doubt in it—no hesitation.

For a breath, I wanted to ask him to stay, or at least not to leave so quickly, but I bit back the urge. This was enough—this walk, this pause, the gift of being known in the smallest ways.

He lingered for a moment, then gave a slight nod and turned to go, boots crunching on the path as he made his way back toward the road. His silhouette, framed for a second by the low, honeyed light from my porch lamp, seemed both impossibly distant and deeply familiar—like something I'd dreamed once and was only now remembering.

I watched until he disappeared around the curve, the hush folding in behind him. The house, waiting, felt warmer for it—brighter, somehow, as if the laughter and light I wanted to invite in were already beginning to settle into the walls.

I closed the door behind me and pressed my back to it, letting the night settle in my chest—a slow, hopeful ache, new but not unwelcome. I didn't know what tomorrow would bring, or what I was growing into, only that this, right here, was the start of something worth holding onto.

Chapter Four

Morning poured through the carriage house in pale gold, spilling across the old tile and waking me before the alarm could try. I lay still for a moment, watching the shifting patterns of sunlight on the wall, letting the quiet fill me. My body ached pleasantly from the day before—real work, the kind that made me feel tired in a way that belonged to living. My mind, though, circled restlessly: last night's laughter at The Sundrop still echoed faintly in my chest, and with it, the sharper ache of hope.

I brewed tea and wandered barefoot onto the porch, setting my mug on the rail because there was nowhere else for it. The morning air was warm and humming with citrus bloom. Orange blossoms drifted in the air; their perfume caught somewhere between dream and memory. The grove shimmered, wet with dew, and I caught myself thinking, if I can make a life here, maybe I can learn to belong to it.

I sat cross-legged on the steps with my tea and a day old hunk of bread, eating breakfast outside because it felt less lonely than standing in the empty kitchen with its single dangling bulb and all that echo. The house was still more shell than shelter, each missing chair or table a small ache I tried to ignore. Somewhere in the grove, a dove called, low and round, as if marking the edges of my morning. I let my gaze drift to the farthest rows; the ones still veiled and thought about how each corner of this place felt like a room in an unlit house—waiting for me to cross the threshold. Maybe belonging could be earned one morning at a time.

I set my cup on the porch rail and opened my phone, scrolling through a string of unread texts. Goldie had sent a blurry photo of her dog tangled in a blanket, the caption a single word: *Survived.*

A knot of affection tightened in my chest. Goldie's presence always lived at the edge of things, a reminder of home and every part of myself I'd left behind. I thumbed out a quick reply—*Come visit me. I have real eggs now*—and set the phone aside, unsure if I meant it.

Inside, I picked at the edges of my new routines. Boxes still crouched in the corners; I opened one and found a weathered copy of *The Garden of Florence: And Other Poems*, the spine cracked and soft from years of re-reading. The house felt larger in the morning, every room holding its breath, waiting to see what I would do with it.

That's when I heard Joani's car long before I saw her—a cherry-red streak, horn blasting out "This Magic Moment" like a battle cry. I grinned despite myself.

Joani swept up the path with a paper sack balanced on one hip and a look of wild purpose in her eyes. "Morning, doll baby!" she called, flinging the screen door wide. "Did you survive your first Citrus Grove hangover?"

"Barely. If you count being up since dawn and arguing with a box of books."

I led her onto the porch, where I'd set down a quilt for us to sit on because there was still no table and not nearly enough chairs.

She deposited the sack between us, releasing a warm cloud of orange and cardamom. "Citrus sticky buns. Fresh. Eat before you faint on my watch. I don't need that on my record."

We sat with our legs tucked under us, sticky buns in hand, sunlight slipping through the screen, making everything seem softer. Joani's energy filled the empty porch, big and easy; for a moment I forgot to feel out of place. I tried to imagine what it would be like to offer her a chair, a real table—a home that wasn't so halfway undone.

She took a sticky bun, tore off a piece, and looked me over as if she could see the shadows I carried. "You know, you're braver than you think," she said. "Most folks would've run screaming after meeting the Grove's oddballs. Or after seeing that busted kitchen of yours."

"Most folks didn't spend half their life wishing for somewhere to run to." My words felt truer than I meant.

Joani grinned. "Well, wish granted. And I come bearing opportunity! I've got orders piling up for screwdrivers and I need oranges—good ones, not that commercial stuff. The Sundrop runs on citrus. I'll pick them myself, if you'll give me a deal."

I blinked, caught off guard by the offer. "You mean… me? My grove?"

She shrugged, reaching for another bun. "You, your trees, your terms. Sell to me at a discount, and I'll make sure you've got a steady paycheck. Festival's coming—Citrus Grove's finest showcase. And…" Her voice slipped sly, "I might've put your name in for the Miss Orange Blossom pageant. Just a little application. You're welcome."

I tried to protest, but Joani steamrolled right over me. "You're doing it, babe. Fresh blood in the pageant, fresh fruit for the market, and a shot at winning a prize—maybe enough to fix up that mausoleum you call a kitchen."

A laugh escaped me before I could stop it—real, surprised. "You don't waste time, do you?"

"Time's a luxury. I take mine with two sugars and a splash of gin." Joani winked. "Besides, you need a win. And the town needs to meet you."

I studied the woman across from me—her cat-eye glasses, her victory rolls, the way she owned every inch of herself. I wondered what it would be like to live like that, without apology.

Even the house seemed to relax a little, as if grateful for Joani's presence filling the emptiness. She noticed things others didn't—a window stuck, a hollow in the porch step, the way I tried not to wince when I shifted my weight on the hard boards. "You know," she mused, "with a little elbow grease and some friends, this place could be magic again."

"I'm working on it," I said, though my voice came out thin. "I've got meetings with contractors this afternoon. If I can afford even one of them."

Joani snorted. "You don't need contractors, you need community. But you do you, honey. Just don't let them talk you out of keeping the bones. The bones are the best part."

She left me with a bag of buns, the smell of cardamom clinging to the air, and the uneasy thrill of being seen—and maybe wanted, for more than what I could pay.

After Joani drove off, I walked back through the quiet house, letting her words sink in. I pictured the festival, the market stalls, the orange trees heavy with promise. For a moment, I pressed my hand to the empty wall where a table should be and whispered, "Soon." Possibility began to fill the space more than dread.

The day stretched ahead, waiting for me to claim it.

The kitchen felt colder with the sun high and Joani gone, every echo a reminder of what the house still lacked. I eyed the empty space where a table should be, then the battered counter, wondering which would collapse first. The room smelled of oranges and old pine and possibility.

The contractors arrived late, both trailing dust and the tired confidence of men who'd seen too many houses like mine fall apart for good. The first looked at the ceiling as if it might come down at any moment; the second ran a hand along the baseboards and tsked, tallying up a list of imagined disasters.

Neither man seemed interested in the bones, only in what they could tear out and replace. "You'd be better off gutting the kitchen," one declared, "Start fresh. It's too far gone." I felt something inside me recoil—a slow, stubborn ache.

"If I wanted to start from scratch, I wouldn't have bought a house with a story," I said.

They didn't hear me. Or maybe they did and simply didn't care. By the time the second one suggested "leveling out the odd corners," I'd already started backing them toward the door.

"I'll be in touch," I promised, though I knew I wouldn't. As they left, I felt a rush of relief and fear all tangled up—the joy of protecting something precious, the dread of being left to figure it out alone.

Outside, the cicadas had begun their mid-morning crescendo. I grabbed my purse and keys, heart pounding, and headed into town. If I couldn't afford someone else's vision, I'd have to find my own.

———————————

The inside of Bennett Supply was a welcome cool and carried the sweet tang of sawdust and metal. Rows of paint cans, boxes of screws, spools of wire—it all looked like another language, one I was determined to learn.

Westley was behind the counter, stacking a shipment of garden hoses. He looked up and smiled, a steady thing that made me feel a little less lost.

"Morning, Mina. Contractors scare you off already?"

I tried for a joke, but it landed with more honesty than I intended. "They wanted to take a sledgehammer to my soul. And my kitchen."

He winced. "You didn't punch them, did you?"

"In my head."

He leaned his elbows on the counter, the sleeves of his shirt rolled up, forearms dusted with flour and wood shavings. "Most folks don't see what's worth saving. But I do."

I felt myself relax, just a little. "I don't know what I'm doing, Westley. But I want to try."

He nodded, then beckoned me down an aisle. "Let's start small. You don't need half of what's on these shelves. Just the basics for now." He handed me a toolbox—sturdy, blue, with space for hope—and a pack of sandpaper, showing me how to test for grit. The handle of the hammer was warm

from his hands before it settled into mine, the weight of it
oddly reassuring. It wasn't just a tool—it was permission to
try, to risk splinters and bent nails in the name of making
something that could last. I noticed a fine smear of sawdust
clinging to his forearm, the pale grains catching in the light
like flecks of gold. He noticed and said nothing, only passed
me a tape measure with the quiet confidence of someone
who believed I could learn the shape of things, if I wanted to.

"Paint?" I asked, eyeing the endless spectrum.

He grinned. "Pick the one that feels like morning.
The house will let you know if it's wrong."

I walked the aisles, collecting a handful of things
under his quiet direction—wood glue, a hammer that fit my
palm, screws and a tape measure, a cheap flashlight, and a roll
of masking tape that Westley said could "hold the universe
together, if you're patient." He didn't hover, just offered a
word here or there, letting me choose.

At the checkout, he rang everything up and tucked a
faded recipe card into my bag—a scribble of his
grandmother's, for orange-blossom cookies. "Little sugar
goes a long way, especially when things get tough," he said,
his voice shy.

He helped me load the trunk, arms brushing as he
handed over the toolbox. "You'll need a way to haul furniture
soon. River's got a line on old trucks if you're looking. Or
you can borrow mine."

I shook my head, smiling. "I'll manage. But if you see a table that won't collapse under a strong breeze, let me know."

Westley's eyes softened, as if he understood exactly what it meant to long for something solid, something lasting. "You'll have more than a table soon. I can help—if you want."

It was the first real offer, not just for labor but for presence. I felt the weight of it, gentle and warm. "I do want," I said, and meant it.

Back home, I carried my new toolbox up the steps, hands shaking from effort and anticipation. The ache of emptiness felt less like loss, and more like a new page.

Chapter Five

The sun was a hot coin pressed to the sky when I pulled into River's lot: Beckett & Rowe Auto — Honest Cars, Honest Folks. Westley parked near the back. The cab was cool compared to the afternoon heat, but I could still taste humidity on my tongue. I smoothed my cotton skirt and followed him through a gate into the lot.

Westley fell into stride with the confidence of someone coming home. I trailed behind, absorbing details: a hand painted price tag on a '99 Jeep—"$5,500 or best offer"—and a stack of old license plates piled like autumn leaves against the fence. Rows of vehicles stretched out before us—some gleaming in the sun, others matte with dust: a cherry red '67 Mustang, a sky blue pickup with heart shaped dents, a pale green sedan whose hood ornament still caught the light. Steam rose from their chrome like lingering promises of the past.

"So, it's *your* lot," I said, glancing at Westley.

"We opened it together. River runs it by himself now."

A sandy-haired man in aviator shades emerged from a small office trailer, chewing a toothpick like a pawn in a high-stakes game. He had ink curling at his wrists and a grin that suggested he'd learned early how to sell dreams.

"Well *damn*, Beckett. If it isn't the prodigal mechanic," he said, clapping Westley on the back. "Didn't know you were bringing me company."

Westley grinned. "Mina, this is River—childhood friend, former partner turned full owner, and certified pain in the ass." Westley said. "Mina's new in town."

I smiled. "Hi."

River tipped his shades and gave me a once-over; not creepy, just amused. "You must be Mina."

"I hear you're the person to see if I want something reliable but not too proud to get dirty."

He grinned. "You want a workhorse, not a show pony. I can respect that. Got some good ones this week. Town trucks, farm trucks, a few older models for charm, if you're into that sort of thing."

"Define 'charm,'" I challenged.

"A stick shift with a personality and a heater that only works if you whisper sweet nothings to it."

Westley snorted. River led us down the rows and I gravitated toward a deep forest green Ford F-150—leather seats, faded chrome. River tapped the side: "This one's solid. Heater works if you whisper. A/C if you curse."

I gripped the door. "Let me test drive."

River handed me the keys. "Chase the horizon."

I slid behind the wheel and let the engine rumble a heartbeat. I eased onto the gravel track. The truck felt right: strong, capable, with stories in its dents. It smelled like citrus air freshener and hay—like home.

Back at the lot, River counted bolts on a workbench; Westley waited by the open door, arms folded. "Well?"

"Think it'll last?"

Westley nodded. "Longer than most men."

River laughed. He gave me a decent price; Westley gave me a nod of approval. I signed the paperwork, handing over a check and the keys to my own sedan and River waved me off with a grin. "Come by anytime."

It felt like the world was giving way, letting me in by inches. With Westley in the passenger seat, I drove to a neighbor's estate sale, the truck rattling and whining, but never complaining. The cab smelled of sawdust, old vinyl, and citrus. Westley pointed out streets, sometimes quiet, sometimes giving the history of this or that old house—"That one's survived three hurricanes, two owners, and a thousand love stories"—his voice low and a little proud.

The table found us before we found it—a battered oak thing, scarred but sturdy, with a pattern of oranges and wildflowers carved into the apron. "It looks like it's survived more than a few meals," I said.

Westley ran his hand along the edge, feeling for weak spots. "Old wood just needs a little patience. Like most things worth keeping."

We found a bed frame, too, paint peeling and sun-bleached, the kind of thing you could picture in a room with open windows and a summer quilt. Romantic in a way I'd almost forgotten that I'd craved. Buying it felt like I had committed a small act of self-love.

---

Westley hoisted the headboard out of the truck bed like it weighed nothing—though I knew solid mahogany like this didn't come feather light. Ornate carvings curled like frozen orange blossoms across the wood. I pictured it in its prime; lacquer unpeeled, edges unshattered.

But in Westley's arms, it looked… small.

I watched the easy strength in his arms as he maneuvered the frame—steady hands, sure steps, the kind of quiet power that made a person feel safe without even trying. He didn't grunt or strain. He just moved with it, as if effort softened in his grip. I'd seen men lift things before, but there was something different in the way he carried this—no flash, no need to perform. Just the steady patience of someone who valued where the thing was going as much as getting it there. It made me wonder if anyone had ever carried me like that—

not literally, but in the way of holding your weight without making you feel like a burden.

"I can get the footboard," I offered, already reaching for it.

Westley glanced back at me and nodded. "You sure?"

"Let me feel useful."

He stepped aside, wiping his palms on his jeans. "Be careful—it bites."

I managed to lift it a few inches before my arms trembled. Westley waited, patient, then caught the weight before it tipped, his shoulder brushing mine as we carried it together. In the narrow stairwell, his presence filled the space—not imposing, just quietly there, a shield against my own uncertainty.

"You okay?" he asked, voice low.

"Totally," I lied, straightening myself out. "Just questioning all of my life choices."

He chuckled, then set the headboard gently against the wall. "Where do you want it?"

I traced the window's frame. "Centered, if it'll fit." I paused, noticing how sunlight spilled across the floorboards, warm and forgiving—revealing their imperfections without judgment, just like Westley's quiet presence. It made me think about how houses, like people, were never meant to be perfect; their charm was often found in their flaws, the worn places that proved they'd been lived in.

It would, but barely. The loft felt cozy—romantic in theory but cramped in practice. Still, it gave the perfect vantage point: golden morning light would pour in, illuminating the bed like a rustic painting.

We began assembling rails and side pieces laying side by side on the unfinished floorboards. This was no click-and-lock nonsense; these were old school fittings that required real tools.

"Here," he murmured, reaching out when I fumbled the wrench. His calloused hand wrapped over mine, guiding my wrist—a heat spreading up my arm, anchoring me in the moment. "That's it," he said. "Steady pressure."

His chest brushed my shoulder as he leaned in. The warmth beneath his shirt was almost dizzying; he was close enough that I could feel the steady rhythm of his breath. "You're good at this."

He paused, then smiled softly. "Done it a few times."

My eyes trailed along the sharp line of his jaw until I met his gaze. "I meant...teaching."

He glanced down, then back at me. "Guess I'm better with tools than words."

"Well," I said, shifting my hand back to the bolt, "you don't need words to be good with your hands." The second the words left my mouth, I froze. Heat flared up my neck, and I prayed the floor would crack open and swallow me whole.

Westley's eyes flicked to mine; amused, almost knowing. "Noted," he said simply.

I groaned and turned away, pretending to tighten the bolt with more focus than necessary.

After a few more quiet minutes, the frame finally came together; it creaked a little but held strong. It had charm, like the rest of the place.

Back downstairs, I struggled with the rolled mattress, but Westley made heavy things look easy—lifting it onto his shoulder as if it were nothing more than a sack of flour. He climbed the stairs, sure-footed, filling the space with a presence that felt not just strong, but reassuring.

"You know, that was going to be my moment of triumph," I said, trailing behind.

"You'll have plenty," he replied, settling the mattress in place. "Just maybe not with fifty-pound memory foam."

I smoothed the pale cream sheets and draped the thrifted quilt—faded coral blossoms against green vines— over the edge. "Think the rest of the house will come together?"

He stood back, arms crossed, surveying the loft. His silhouette in the window light made the room feel protected—like he belonged there, as much a part of the house as any beam or brick. "If you do it like this? Better than you imagined."

I laughed, then reached for my sketchbook. "Want to see?"

He took it with more reverence than I expected and sat on the edge of the mattress, flipping through my charcoal drawings—floor plans, entryway arches, sunlit porches. I watched the way his eyes softened; his brow furrowed in concentration. "These are beautiful," he murmured, tracing a citrus grove sketch with his thumb. "You drew all this?"

I shrugged. "Helps me process. I can't always fix what's in front of me, but I can picture what it could be. That's something, right?"

He met my eyes. "Yeah. It's everything."

Westley set the sketchbook down on one of the nightstands like it was something precious, something that might shatter if handled too roughly.

"You've got real vision," he said, standing and wiping his hands on his jeans. "And talent, too."

"Thanks," I said, heat creeping up the back of my neck. "It's weird to let someone else see it."

His eyes found mine, steady. "I'm glad you did."

He crouched to pack up his tools, sliding the last wrench into the battered canvas bag. The loft felt quiet now, like something had shifted—like the air had taken a breath and was waiting for the next one.

"Look," he said, still kneeling beside his bag, "I know you want to do all this yourself. And I get it. I really do. But there's a lot that needs fixing out there. You're just one person."

"I'm pretty scrappy," I offered, crossing my arms in mock defense.

He gave a soft huff of laughter, shaking his head. "Scrappy doesn't mean invincible," he said. His gaze held mine, steadfast as a grove in winter. "Promise me you'll let me be your backup, not your afterthought."

His tone shifted slightly, not stern, but…weighted, like it cost him something to say.

"What if you fall off a ladder?" he added, quieter now. "What if you cut into old wiring? What if you get hurt and no one knows until—" He stopped. Swallowed.

I sat down on the edge of the bed, suddenly aware of the silence swelling between us.

"It's not just about time or efficiency," he said, finally standing again. "It's about safety."

I wanted to ask who he was thinking about just then. Who he hadn't gotten to in time. But I didn't press. I just nodded and let the moment settle.

Then the rain hit.

Hard.

It was like someone had flipped a switch. Thunder rolled through the rafters; lightning split the sky; sheets of rain hammered the windows—an electric heart pounding over the thrum of my own thoughts.

"What the hell?" I stood and peered through the glass. "It's been beautiful all day."

Westley shrugged, tugging the curtain back to look out beside me. "Welcome to Florida."

The citrus trees bent low under the weight of the storm, and I watched a lawn chair go skidding across the yard like an autumn leaf caught in a gale.

"Want to wait it out?" I asked, glancing over at him.

He hesitated for only a second before nodding. "If you don't mind."

"I don't. Come on, this is perfect tea-and-a-book weather."

I padded down the stairs and into the kitchenette, setting a pot of water to boil and pulling down two mismatched mugs. One had a little cartoon duck wearing glasses and the other bore the faded seal of my alma mater. Westley wandered in behind me, watching with amusement as I added a splash of honey to both.

Together, we crept back up to the loft and sat side by side against the headboard, mugs warm in hand, rain still thundering outside. I noticed his big boots propped—unthinkingly—right on my quilt and raised an eyebrow.

He caught the look immediately. "Shit, sorry," he muttered, swinging them off with one fluid motion. His movements were always gentle, despite his size—always careful with the things that mattered to me.

I curled my legs up under me and reached for the book I'd snagged from the built-ins. It was an old poetry collection, spine cracked and cover worn smooth with age. The shelves were packed—double stacked in places, some books tilted or tucked horizontally on top. Everything from paperbacks with bent corners to ornate hardcovers that looked like they might fall apart if you stared at them too long.

Westley glanced around at the titles. "You read all these?"

"Most of them. I've always loved stories. The way they let you live inside someone else for a while."

"Even the ones with broken spines and water stains?"

"Especially those." I smiled and flipped the book open without looking, letting it fall to a page on its own.

I pressed a hand to my chest. "Like this one." Then I began to read:

> *How do I love thee? Let me count the ways.*
> *I love thee to the depth and breadth and height*
> *My soul can reach, when feeling out of sight*
> *For the ends of being and ideal grace.*
> *I love thee to the level of every day's*
> *Most quiet need, by sun and candle-light.*
> *I love thee freely, as men strive for right;*
> *I love thee purely, as they turn from praise.*
> *I love thee with the passion put to use*
> *In my old griefs, and with my childhood's faith.*
> *I love thee with a love I seemed to lose*
> *With my lost saints. I love thee with the breath,*
> *Smiles, tears, of all my life; and, if God choose,*
> *I shall but love thee better after death.*

The words hung in the air like steam from the tea; soft, heady, lingering.

When I glanced over, Westley's gaze had never wavered, like he was listening with his whole body.

"You just… carry that around in your head?" he asked.

The question lodged somewhere deep. I wanted to tell him it wasn't just in my head—that poems like this sank into the marrow, that they kept you company in the quiet hours when no one called your name. I wanted to ask if he had words he carried like that, too, or if he'd ever had a love that felt like poetry. But the thought of hearing "no" made my throat tight, so I only smiled. "It's stuck there."

"It's beautiful."

I looked down, suddenly shy. "I guess I always wanted to be loved like that. Like someone could see all of me and still say 'yes' without hesitation."

He said nothing, but his fingers brushed mine. The lights flickered once…then went out completely.

The hum of the ceiling fan died, plunging the loft into quiet.

"Oh no," I groaned, setting my mug aside.

Westley stood instantly, his silhouette tall in the dimming light from the windows. "I'll check the breaker."

I followed him down the stairs, the sound of his steps reassuring in the dark. When the lightning flashed, it caught him at the bottom of the stairs—broad and certain, a figure you'd want to have on your side when the world got unpredictable.

He returned a few minutes later, triumphant.

"You're good," I said as the lights flickered back on, warm and humming.

He shrugged, pushing his hair back. "Simple fix."

It was hard not to notice the definition beneath his shirt, the steady rhythm of his breath as he looked back up toward the loft.

I led us up again, and the tea was still warm. Eventually, the rain began to taper off, the thunder receding into the distance. Westley reached for his boots, pulling them back on with slow, practiced movements.

"You didn't drink your tea," I said, nodding to the mug still full beside him.

He glanced at it, sheepish. "I'm more of a strong, bitter kind of guy. But I couldn't say no to you. Not when you were being all sweet."

I narrowed my eyes. "Still could've sipped it."

"I was distracted."

I looked at him then and realized just how much I didn't want him to go. But he stood anyway, slinging the tool bag over his shoulder. "I'll see you tomorrow?" he asked.

"Yeah," I said softly. "I'd like that." And I meant it.

That night, for the first time since leaving the only home I'd known for twenty-seven years, I slept in a real bed; no buzzing air mattress beneath my spine; no faint scent of rubber clinging to my sheets, just soft cotton worn thin with time, a quilt that looked like it belonged to someone's grandmother, and the whispery hush of the ceiling fan sighing overhead.

The air was thick in that Florida way—humid and syrupy, but not in a way I was growing to enjoy. I cracked the window a few inches, letting in a breeze that smelled faintly of rain dampened earth. The cicadas droned a drowsy chorus in the trees. Somewhere in the distance, a frog gave a lazy croak, and I could just barely hear the gentle lowing of my cow from within the barn, like she too was dreaming.

I curled beneath the quilt, pulled it to my chin, and let the stillness settle over me.

This was mine.

The thought came like a quiet revelation. The house, the land, the version of myself brave enough to want something different; it was all mine.

It all felt unreal—this place, this life—as if I might wake to find I had only been dreaming; but the bed beneath me was solid. The silence didn't ache the way it had back in my old apartment. It didn't hum with absence. It was full somehow, like a space waiting to be lived in.

I let go.

I let myself sink.

And somewhere in that in-between place, as the shadows deepened and my breath slowed, he came to me.

Westley.

Not in any big, cinematic way with sweeping declarations or surreal flashes of desire. Just... there. Shadows pooled under the eaves as he stood in the hallway—his fingertips brushing the chair rail as if asking the house for her own blessing. "You stayed," he murmured, and the walls seemed to exhale around us.

It wasn't a question.

He reached for my hand. My heart fluttered. Then I woke.

The light at the window was pale and gold, the kind of quiet dawn that promised heat by noon. The fan still whirred. The quilt was still wrapped tight around me.

But I didn't move.

I reached for my sketchbook, flipped to a clean page, and wrote one word before I forgot the dream: Westley.

Chapter Six


Morning found me before the alarm, sunlight blooming in slats across the carriage house floor, warming the old tiles and the arch of my foot as I slipped quietly from bed. I moved slowly, listening for the hush and creak that told me this house was settling in around me—or maybe, at last, I was settling into it.

I crept barefoot to the little kitchen, trying to preserve the gift of early morning silence. The air was thick with the perfume of citrus and last night's rain, sweet and heavy. I stood for a moment at the window above the sink, mug warming my hands, and watched the world outside: dew still clinging to the grass, the orange trees nodding with fruit, sunlight glinting in every drop. The house, I realized, was less a shell these days and more a body—aching, alive, asking to be filled.

Breakfast was simple: a slice of bread with butter and honey, an egg fried in the smallest pan. I carried my plate to the rickety table Westley had helped me find; the wood scarred and stained with stories I'd never know. It was good, I decided, to eat facing the groves stretched out like open palms waiting. The loneliness seemed softer there, as if the wind could carry it off.

I finished my tea, licked honey from my thumb, and set out into the grove with a basket swinging from my wrist. The air shimmered with the promise of heat. I picked oranges by feel, learning which ones gave under the thumb, which held tight and green.

I lost track of time until a familiar engine rumbled up the drive, slow and easy. Westley's old truck pulled beneath the oak, dust swirling in its wake. He stepped out, toolbox in hand, shoulders squared against the morning sun, and I felt something inside me relax—a muscle unclenched I hadn't noticed I'd been holding.

He raised a hand in greeting, a half-smile softening the lines of his face. "You already start the day without me?" he called, voice warm and easy.

"I don't sleep in much anymore," I said, brushing hair from my eyes and watching him cross the yard. "Too much to do. Or maybe I'm just afraid I'll miss something."

He laughed, that low, easy sound that seemed to fill the air between us. "You're making good progress. Joani says the best oranges are the ones you pick yourself."

"She'd know. She's already put in her order for half the crop." I smiled, pride and exhaustion twining in my chest.

Westley set down his toolbox at the porch steps. "I came to work on the mantle, if you're up for company."

"I'd like that," I said, surprising myself with how much I meant it.

Inside the main house, he laid out his tools with the precision of ritual—measuring tape, chisel, sandpaper, a block of beeswax for finishing. He ran his hands over the wood, humming to himself, and I watched the way he mapped every groove and imperfection, as if reading the house's secret language.

I sat nearby, book in hand, but found myself more interested in the steady movement of his hands, the rhythm of his work. The light from the window fell across his shoulders, catching in the dust and making a halo of him for one fleeting moment.

"Do you want me to read?" I asked, voice soft so as not to break the spell.

He didn't look up, but I saw the smile in his posture. "Only if you want to."

I opened my book—the old poetry collection from the night before—and began to read aloud. My voice, unsure at first, grew steady with the cadence of each line. The words slipped into the space between us, mixing with the scent of orange peel and sawdust, filling the house with something new.

Westley worked as I read, his hands never still but his attention never wandering. Every so often, he'd pause to listen, eyes drifting from the mantle to me, as if he could carve the poem into memory as easily as he shaped the wood.

Outside, the world moved on—cicadas tuning up for midday; a squirrel darting along the porch rail, the sun climbing higher. But inside, the quiet held. It was the kind of silence that felt full, not empty; the kind that belonged to people who had learned, by luck or by longing, how to share space without fear.

When I finished the poem, I looked up to find Westley watching me, sawdust flecked in his hair, a gentle gratitude in his gaze.

"You make it sound easy," he said quietly, "turning words into something you can feel."

I shrugged, embarrassed by the attention but warmed by it, too. "You do the same—with wood, with this place. I'm just learning how."

He smiled, slow and honest. "We're both learning."

For a while, we worked side by side—me with my books, him with his tools. The morning passed in a hush of sunlight and small progress. It wasn't romance, not in the storybook sense, but it felt like the beginning of something that could last: patient, present, and real.

He reached for another piece of sandpaper, his knuckles grazing mine in the exchange. It wasn't deliberate, but the touch held long enough to spark a thread of heat up my arm. I glanced away, letting my gaze rest on the soft curl of sawdust piling on the floor. There was something grounding about the way he worked — no rush, no need to fill the air with talk, as if the quiet itself were part of the craft.

I thought of how, in the city, people measured their worth by how quickly they moved, how much they could cram into a day. Here, Westley measured progress in smooth edges, in the way light slid evenly over the wood. I wanted to learn that kind of patience — to make something beautiful without worrying who would see it first.

Outside, a breeze stirred the scent of orange blossoms through the open window. Westley's eyes flicked up, catching mine, and for a beat it felt like he could see every place I'd been splintered and didn't flinch from any of it. I looked away first, pretending to read, but the words blurred until all I could hear was the steady rhythm of sand on wood, like a heartbeat you could build a life around.

Joani's arrival announced itself the way a summer storm did—loud, cheerful, impossible to ignore. Her Bel Air rattled up the drive, its chrome flashing in the sun, engine purring like a half-wild cat. The paint had dulled, the hood ornament slightly askew, but it wore its age the way Joani wore her victory rolls: proud and unbothered by the passing years. I could almost imagine the car had been in her family forever—passed down, patched up, never replaced, just loved and kept running.

She rolled down the window and hollered, "Rise and shine, farmer girl!"

She swept onto the porch with a grocery bag balanced on her hip and a stack of glossy flyers in the other hand. "Don't shoot, I come bearing gifts," she declared, grinning behind her sunglasses. "And urgent festival business. I can't let you embarrass me by showing up unprepared."

I held open the screen door, laughing. "You're a vision, Joani. You know that?"

She dropped the bag on the floor and flung herself into a chair, fanning herself with the festival flyer. "Flattery'll get you nowhere. Actually, that's a lie—flattery gets you everywhere, especially in this town."

She unloaded her offerings: a tangle of citrus shaped hairpins ("For the pageant—think Doris Day meets Florida roadside"), a jar of homemade lemon balm, and a dress wrapped in crinkly pink paper. "Consider this a starter kit for blending in. And standing out. Both are required."

"Joani, you're ridiculous," I said, but my heart softened at the sight of her gifts.

She leaned in, sharp eyes softening. "You're still on the fence about this, aren't you?"

I shrugged. "I don't want to make a fool of myself. Or you. Or Citrus Grove."

She snorted. "Babe, this place was founded on the backs of fools and dreamers. You'll fit right in." She slid the flyer across the table. "Orange Blossom Festival, main street.

Booth assignment's in the corner. You and me—right across from the kettle corn."

She ticked off festival advice with the confidence of a woman who'd survived every small-town tradition twice over. "Sell what you've got—eggs, honey, oranges. Smile, but don't let the old timers haggle you down to pennies. Oh, and whatever you do, avoid Mrs. Hathaway's pickled okra. That's not food, it's a dare."

I snorted into my tea. "Duly noted."

Joani studied me for a moment, then gave a satisfied nod. For a split second, Joani's eyes softened into something deeper—recognition or understanding, maybe. It was the kind of look that made me think she knew exactly how far I'd traveled, and just how much of myself I'd left behind to get here. "You're getting color in your cheeks. That's how you know you're doing something right." She eyed the mantle where Westley's tools were lined up. "And look at you— already got yourself a handyman. My work here is done."

I shook my head, grinning. "It's not like that."

She raised an eyebrow. "Sure, and I only come for the sticky buns."

Before I could answer, my phone vibrated—Goldie's name lighting up the screen. I thumbed open her latest volley: *Send me a photo of the sunrise and your ugly new boots. Also, do NOT name the chicken after me. Miss you, weirdo. I'll come soon. Swear.*

My heart tightened and loosened at once. I snapped a quick shot of the porch view and my bare feet, replying: *Only if you promise not to elope with a surfer before you visit. No boots yet. Miss you more.*

Joani craned her neck. "That the famous little sister?"

Goldie's name on my screen felt like a thread tied to home, tugging me just enough to remind me I hadn't drifted too far. I clung to it the way you hold warm hands in winter—not out of fear, but because it felt good to be held. I nodded. "She's threatening to visit. You'll like her. She's impossible not to."

Joani reached for a sticky bun, breaking it in two. "Good. You need more trouble in your life. But in the meantime, we'll get you ready for this festival. Citrus Grove is about to meet the new March girl, whether she likes it or not."

We spent the next hour planning our booths—how to string orange blossoms along the table, which jars of honey would catch the morning sun, what dress might make me look less like an escapee from a Jane Austen adaptation and more like someone who belonged. Joani, part drill sergeant, part fairy godmother, peppered her instructions with stories about past festivals: the year the pie eating contest ended in disaster, the time the mayor's goat got loose on main street.

The morning passed in a happy mess of laughter, honey, and lemon balm, the house brighter for it. Joani's energy was infectious, and for the first time, the festival didn't seem so terrifying—just another story waiting to be told.

When she finally gathered her things, she kissed my cheek and gave the porch one last approving nod. The smell of summer and sugar tangled in the air until I couldn't tell where Joani ended and the house began. "Don't let the nerves eat you up, babe. You've got grit. This house picked the right person. And remember—nobody ever made history by blending in."

She sauntered to her Bel Air, running her hand over the faded hood with the kind of affection that belongs only to those who understand the beauty of holding on. Before she climbed in, she called back, "Runs better than any of those plastic things they sell now. Built to last, like good women and stubborn houses."

I watched her rattle off down the drive, leaving the sound of her laughter, the scent of lemon balm, and a promise of belonging in her wake.

It was late afternoon, the kind of sultry Florida day that made even the orange trees sigh, when the call came—an unknown New York number, too familiar in its area code to be mistaken for spam. I hesitated, thumb hovering, but the sense of unfinished business pulled me in.

"Hello?"

"Hi, Mina? This is Luca Bellante—we spoke briefly during the closing on the Grove Street property." His voice was polished, professional, but with a cadence that suggested he was used to getting past people's defenses.

I straightened instinctively, as if he could see me through the phone. "Yes, that's me. Everything's fine with the house, if that's what you're wondering."

He laughed, low and practiced. "I'm sure it is. I just wanted to check in, see how you're settling. I'll admit, I was surprised your offer went through. That place had quite a few interested parties."

His words made me bristle, though I tried not to show it. "Sometimes the right letter at the right time can change a mind," I said, surprised at my own candor.

He paused, then: "Ah, yes—the famous letter. You made quite an impression, apparently. I suppose I could have written one myself, but I'm more of a numbers guy. Results, not sentiment."

There was a subtle barb tucked in there, something that made me feel childish for having dared to believe a letter could matter more than a check. Still, I stayed polite. "It worked out for me."

He softened, almost purring. "I'm not bitter, Mina. Sometimes the best deals are the ones you lose. Teaches you to play smarter next time. So—how are you finding Citrus Grove? Small town living treating you all right?"

I could picture him leaning back in a glossy office chair, confident, a little bored, trying to turn a loss into an opportunity. "It's quieter than I'm used to. But I think I needed that."

"That house has potential," he said, circling back. "A smart investment, but also a real fixer-upper. I hope you're not trying to do it all yourself?"

There it was: the familiar script. Flattery as warning. "I've got help. Local, mostly."

He hummed. "Smart. You'll want someone who knows what they're doing, or you'll spend twice as much fixing mistakes. Maybe I can offer some advice—if you ever want a second opinion. I'll be in town this weekend, working on a property. If you have time for a drink, I'd love to meet in person."

His tone made it sound casual, but there was an expectation hanging in the pause, a kind of challenge. I felt old habits stirring—the desire to say yes, to make things easy, to avoid disappointing anyone. And beneath it, something else: curiosity. What did he really want?

"Sure," I said, already regretting it and trying to convince myself it was just good manners. "Friday works."

"Perfect. I'll text you the place. Dress casual—this isn't New York." He paused, then, "But you could pull off Fifth Avenue if you wanted. See you soon, Mina."

He hung up before I could reply, leaving me with the echo of my own uncertainty.

I set the phone down, pulse tapping at my wrists. It wasn't just the invitation that unsettled me—it was how easily I'd slipped into old patterns, making room for someone else's expectations before I'd even had a chance to define my own.

I tried to shake the call off by going outside, letting the heat and the steady hum of the grove anchor me. I collected eggs, gathered fallen branches, rinsed a handful of lemons for an infused honey. I set out a jar on the fence rail, watching the sunlight swim in the golden depths. It struck me that, for all my longing to belong here, it was still too easy for one stranger's voice to shake my sense of self.

Goldie's texts came in quick succession—two photos of her dog in sunglasses, a string of emojis, and finally: *Don't say yes to any man in loafers. Love you. Call me after.*

Her voice, even in pixels, grounded me. I replied with a picture of the grove at sunset, the sky bruised and lovely. *No loafers. Just bare feet. Miss you.*

---

Friday came sticky and bright, the kind of evening that promised storms. I chose a dress I already owned—a cotton print with a pattern of wildflowers and the soft memory of home. I tied my hair up, left my makeup in the drawer, and tucked my anxiety away with the rest of my city habits. The mirror didn't fight me. It didn't demand transformation or apology; it only gave me back a girl who looked like herself, sun touched and unpolished, as if Citrus Grove was already softening her edges.

Luca's text arrived just before seven. *I'm at Magnolia's. Booth by the window.*

Magnolia's was the new place in town, glass and reclaimed wood, all open beams and Edison bulbs. When I stepped inside, Luca was waiting, half-smile already in place, tapping at his phone.

He looked up, assessed me—head to toe, not entirely unfriendly, but cataloging all the same. He rose, greeted me with a kiss on the cheek, and gestured for me to sit. "You made it. Good. I was beginning to think you'd changed your mind."

I shrugged, finding my voice. "I said I'd come."

We ordered drinks—he, something imported; me, sweet tea with lemon. He told stories about Manhattan, about closing deals, about a penthouse with a river view. Each sentence was smooth, shaped for an audience, and though he asked about the house, the questions felt more like an appraisal than real interest.

"You know," he said, "not everyone could take this on. A woman alone, all this land. It's…brave. Or maybe a little crazy."

I sipped my tea, forcing a smile. "Sometimes you have to risk a little crazy for something you want."

He leaned in, lowering his voice, eyes glinting. "And what is it you want, Mina?"

The question was so direct it startled me. I faltered, the answer tangled somewhere between honesty and self-preservation.

"I want a home. Something I can build myself."

He considered this, then offered the faintest, condescending smile. "Ambitious. But I hope you'll let someone help you, or at least talk you out of any disasters. Some lessons cost more than they're worth, trust me."

We talked around each other for the rest of the meal, his charm circling like a hawk, never quite landing. He paid the bill with a flourish and led me out, his hand at the small of my back—guiding. Outside, the storm finally broke. He offered a ride home; I declined. He pressed but relented when I agreed to see him again the following weekend, a flash of annoyance buried beneath a parting compliment.

Back in the carriage house, I pulled off my shoes and let the thunder shake loose the last of my nerves. I wiped off my makeup, braided my hair, sat at the window and let myself feel the distance that remained between the life I wanted and the one I was trying to leave behind.

In the hush after, I realized the air inside felt lighter, the table solid beneath my hands, the sound of rain on the roof more honest than any promise.

Chapter Seven

By midsummer, mornings didn't feel borrowed anymore—
they belonged to me, as much as this patch of earth or the
house itself. I moved through the small rooms with purpose,
steps finding their own worn path: tea steeping, sunlight
spilling sideways across the floor, the hum of bees drifting
through the open windows. The place was half-unpacked,
half-reborn. I didn't mind the mess; it felt like evidence of a
life finally in motion.

The air shimmered with the smell of orange blossoms
and wet grass. Out back, the chickens announced themselves
at daybreak, demanding and alive. Some mornings, I lingered
there longer than the work required, leaning on the fence
with the eggs still warm in my palm, letting the grove's breath
wash over me. It was alive, changing from moment to
moment, carrying traces of wild mint, damp bark, and the
faint mineral tang of the well water I'd hauled for the garden.
Sunlight slipped through the leaves in broken coins, catching
on spider silk, on the glossy backs of beetles, on the
trembling curve of a blade of grass.

I thought about how, months ago, I'd woken to car
alarms and the groan of garbage trucks; how every day had
been claimed before I'd even risen. Here, I could take the
world in small sips, deciding for myself what to swallow and
what to leave untouched. Even the animals seemed to
understand the rhythm.

I gathered eggs, tucked them in the crook of my arm, and left a jar of honey out front beside the "Fresh—Pay What You Can" sign. These small offerings—eggs, honey, fruit—felt like tokens of faith, both in the land and in myself.

Goldie texted early: *Still wild? Still barefoot? You better be eating real food. If not, I'll drive down there and force feed you oranges like a goose.*

I grinned, shot back: *You wouldn't dare. I'd win. Also, come visit. The bed is finally real.*

It was a day threaded with gentle expectation—the kind that feels heavy with something about to tip. I was half in the rhythm of work, half waiting for the break in it.

The sound of a truck rolling slow up the drive cut through the hush. Westley's arrival was always quiet, but I felt it—a soft jolt, as if the house recognized him even before I did. I wiped my hands, feeling the sticky imprint of citrus on my skin, and stepped out to meet him.

He stood at the edge of the porch, box of tools in one hand, gloves in the other, shirt dark with old paint stains and new sweat. He looked like he'd been up for hours, the sun catching the edge of his hair and turning it almost gold. Not beautiful in any delicate way, but sturdy, like something that wouldn't break no matter how much the world tried to wear it down.

"Hey," I called, leaning against the doorframe. The screen rattled with the breeze.

"Hey yourself." He gave a half smile—hesitant, almost bashful. "Didn't mean to interrupt."

"You never do," I said, and meant it.

He gestured with the box. "Thought you could use a moisture meter, couple of pry bars. Got a shop light in there too, for when the sun quits early."

I laughed. "You know me too well."

He set the tools just inside, hands moving with the ease of someone who trusts himself. There was a pause, a kind of gravity between us, where everything felt possible and a little dangerous.

He cleared his throat, glancing at the ground. "You got plans tonight?" The question was casual, but I could hear something careful in it—like he was bracing for an answer.

"Actually, yeah. Dinner. With Luca...my realtor."

Something flickered in his eyes—not anger, just a silent calculation, a storm held behind good manners. "That so?" Westley nodded once, slow. "No judgment. Just—don't let him talk you into anything you don't want." He didn't say more, but I heard the rest.

He lingered another moment, then offered, "I'll swing by after. If you're not too tired. Could look at the parlor. Save us time tomorrow."

I smiled, grateful for the way he asked, not assumed. "I'd like that. Ten?"

He met my gaze, steady and unafraid. "Ten."

He turned to go, boots thumping down the steps, the house and I both watching him leave. His presence settled in after he'd gone—the good kind of ache, the kind that promises something real.

Inside, I set the new tools by the door, feeling the choice between worlds humming under my skin. Tonight, I'd put on a dress and be what someone else wanted. But for now, I was exactly myself—barefoot, unhurried, and a little more whole than I'd been yesterday.

I changed clothes three times before settling on a sundress that felt neither too eager nor too apologetic. When Luca's message chimed—a photo of the restaurant's neon sign, captioned *Your table's waiting*—I swallowed my nerves and stepped into the dusk.

His car was already waiting at the curb, glossy black and humming with newness. He leaned out, sunglasses perched on his head even though the sun had already dipped behind the oaks. "You clean up well, March," he called, and I tried to laugh, though it felt more like performance than pleasure.

We drove with the radio low, and the windows open to the humid breath of summer. I watched the landscape rush by—the wild tangle of green, the tangled dreams of someone trying to outrun the ache of belonging.

Luca asked questions about the house—its bones, its history, how much I'd paid and whether I planned to "flip it" or hold on. He spoke with the brisk certainty of someone who saw properties as lines on a balance sheet, every word quietly negotiating for control.

At the restaurant, he pressed a hand to the small of my back, guiding me past the host stand. We were seated near the window, string lights catching in his hair. There was something dreamlike about the way he praised me—lavish, bright, and a little too sweet, like flower juice pressed to my eyelids. I tried to see myself as he described: dazzling, rare, meant for more. But with every compliment, I felt myself slipping further from the girl I'd been, and closer to someone I might not recognize if I looked too long in the mirror.

He ordered for us both without asking, reciting the chef's specials with the authority of someone used to being obeyed. I let it happen, telling myself it was easier, that it was a kindness, even as my own voice shrank to a shadow at the table. I watched his hands—well-manicured, all movement and show—and wondered what they would feel like if they ever reached for something without first weighing its worth.

The conversation drifted from architecture to ambition to travel—cities he'd conquered, deals he'd made, people who'd disappointed him. "You're not like most," he said, the words dropping between us like petals, but I couldn't tell if it was a compliment or a warning.

I smiled in all the right places. I drank the wine he chose, let him brush a stray curl behind my ear as if claiming some small, tender territory, and the whole time, a strange duality unfolded inside me: part of me floating high above the scene, watching a woman who could be anyone—pleasing, pretty, not quite present; the other part rooted firmly in the seat, feeling the scrape of the chair against my bare knee, the cool ghost of loneliness clinging to my skin.

The night blurred at the edges. Dessert was delivered with a flourish—something citrus and rich, almost overwhelming in its sweetness. "A taste of home," Luca said, his eyes locked on mine. I took a bite, let the sugar and tartness explode on my tongue, and wondered if this was what it meant to be wanted, or simply acquired.

On the ride home, he talked about renovations, investments, and hinted at new possibilities. "I could help you, you know. Set you up, get you out of that shoebox." His tone was warm, persuasive, but I felt a tightening inside—as if the air itself was a contract I hadn't agreed to sign.

He parked at the end of my drive, engine idling. "You're different, Mina. I like that." He leaned in, his kiss a practiced thing—soft, then insistent, tasting of citrus and confidence. I let it happen, more out of politeness than passion, and pulled away gently when the moment stretched too long.

"Thank you for dinner," I said. My voice sounded steady, even as my heart galloped.

He smiled, all teeth. "Anytime. I like a challenge." He
touched my wrist, thumb circling as if trying to memorize the
shape of my pulse, and then he was gone, the car's red
taillights flaring and fading down the lane.

I stood in the quiet for a moment, letting the night
cool my skin. There was something about the way his absence
left the air—a relief, a small ache, a sudden clarity. I crossed
the yard barefoot, stepping carefully over dew-wet grass, and
unlocked the door to my quiet house.

Inside, the familiar hush settled around me, steady
and good. I put the leftovers in the fridge, slipped out of my
dress, and stood for a long time at the window, watching for
headlights that never turned back.

Tomorrow, I'd sand old wood and scrape paint, let
the world shrink to the size of a single room, a single beam of
light. But tonight, I let myself feel the strange blessing of
emptiness—the space where something real might finally take
root.

I had just changed—tank top, no bra, old pajama
shorts—when his knock landed, soft as rain against the
screen door. I froze for half a breath, suddenly aware of bare
skin, the cling of cotton, the way cool night air pressed
through the cracks and found the warmest parts of me. For a
flicker, I felt both exposed and inexplicably sure—like I could
trust the moment to hold me, or at least trust him to.

I padded over and let Westley in. He stood on the
stoop, toolbox in one hand, lantern in the other, his eyes

lingering on me just long enough for something electric to pass between us. The faintest pulse of interest flickered in his gaze—honest, respectful, and just a little hungry—but it faded into warmth as he met my eyes and I didn't shrink from it.

"Didn't mean to catch you off guard," he said, voice low, almost apologetic. He tipped his head toward the main house. "Parlor's calling."

I grabbed a cardigan, but left it unbuttoned, and together we crossed the yard beneath the moon, the grass cool and damp against my feet. The air bit at my skin, raising goosebumps and drawing tight little peaks beneath the thin cotton of my tank top. I felt every inch of it, awake and aware, as if my body was a question the night was daring me to ask.

He noticed—of course he did. His eyes flicked, lingered, then respectfully retreated. But there was a softness there, and a kind of gratitude too, as if he knew I was giving him something rare and unforced.

Inside the main house, the air was warmer, thick with the scent of orange oil and old wood. He set down his tools and started laying out supplies, but neither of us spoke at first. The only sounds were the hush of our breathing, the creak of the floorboards, and the slow beating of my own heart.

He gestured for me to sit by the hearth as he worked on the trim, and I curled up, knees hugged to my chest, cardigan slipping off one shoulder. It was easier to talk with his back turned, both of us half-busy with something else.

"Why Citrus Grove?" he asked, gentle, with no demand in it.

I stared at the bare wall for a long moment, the words surfacing and breaking like slow bubbles. "I needed… to leave. Where I was, it hurt to stay. There were too many things I couldn't make right, too many stories that weren't mine to fix." I bit my lip. "My family fell apart. Some things happened when I was young—things nobody talks about. I spent a long time running, trying to outpace the echo." I looked up, finding his eyes in the lamplight. "I guess I wanted to find a place where I could breathe again. Where I could remember who I was before."

He was silent, letting the truth fill the space. Then he nodded, quiet but certain, as if he'd known some version of that pain himself. "That makes sense," he said simply. "Some places… they're poison if you stay too long."

We worked like that—side by side, trading tools and small directions. Every so often our hands touched, sparks that weren't shocking, just warm. I told him about the house, about Goldie, about the way Florida sunlight felt different than any I'd known. He listened.

At one point, the silence stretched between us, long and full. I realized I was still in my pajamas, feet bare, cardigan sliding down my arm, and I didn't care. He glanced over, eyes lingering with quiet reverence, and for a moment, I felt as beautiful and alive as the house itself.

He sanded the trim with careful strokes, then spoke again—so soft I almost missed it. "You're not the only one starting over, you know."

I looked up, surprised. He met my gaze, a small half-smile there. "Most people only see what's broken. Not the work it takes to mend it. Or the patience." He set the sander aside and knelt by the firebox, hands rough with old calluses and new splinters. "You're good for this place. You'll see."

Something inside me loosened, then settled. "Thank you," I whispered, and meant it.

He packed up quietly, but lingered in the doorway, the lamplight catching the line of his jaw, the breadth of his shoulders. "If you need anything, you know where to find me."

I nodded, letting my cardigan slip fully off the other shoulder, not out of seduction but simple comfort. "I do."

He hesitated—just for a heartbeat, as if considering whether to say more. In that brief hesitation, I saw a flash of vulnerability cross his face—an unguarded moment where his eyes seemed to say what his words couldn't. It felt like catching sight of something rare, a glimpse behind a door he'd always kept carefully shut. But then he simply smiled, soft and real, and let himself out into the night.

I stayed there in the warmth, my body humming from the cold, the work, and the truth of being seen. The old house creaked around me, settling, and for the first time in a long while, I didn't flinch from the echo of my own heart.

Chapter Eight

The days leading up to the Orange Blossom Festival unfurled like silk—soft, unhurried, golden at the edges. Each morning brought a rhythm that felt less like surviving and more like inhabiting: tea brewed before sunrise, the porch cool beneath my feet, the house humming with possibility. I woke with the sun and found myself looking forward—sometimes even hopeful, which still surprised me.

Joani's visits became a ritual, her laughter echoing down the drive long before I saw the flash of her Bel Air. She swept in with her arms always full—homebrewed concoctions, occasional odds and ends she said made her think of me, and gossip; a chaos of good intentions. "Get up, babe, there's work to do!" she'd call through the screen, and the house would seem to breathe in her wake, swelling just a little at the seams.

Westley fell into step as naturally as breath. He'd show up with a toolbox or a fresh loaf of bread, sleeves rolled, hair a little wild from the drive. He belonged to the morning, shoulders wide as the doorway, bringing quiet with him like an offering. Together, we mended: sanded the mantle, painted trim, scrubbed old tile until it glowed beneath our knees. I read poetry as he worked, sometimes pausing to watch the play of light across his hands—strong, careful, shaping more than wood.

Even Joani seemed to recognize the peace that came from this arrangement. "Look at you two," she teased, arms crossed, lips quirking. "Who knew labor could look so romantic?" I flushed, but inside I felt anchored—seen without being demanded, held without being claimed.

We made festival plans around the kitchen table, spreading out flyers, lists, jars of honey, fabric scraps. Joani mapped out booth arrangements in looping script, her bracelets jangling with every gesture. She quizzed me on festival etiquette ("Never trust a judge who won't eat a sample. Never sit your oranges beside Mrs. Carmichael's marmalade, she's ruthless with a spoon.")

We picked fruit in the afternoons, sun-warm and fragrant, our hands sticky with juice. Westley's easy laughter carried across the rows, and sometimes he'd pass me an orange, split in two, just for the taste. I learned which branches bent with promise and which clung too tightly, refusing to let go. The grove had its own vocabulary—rustles and sighs, the sharp scent of torn leaves, the thud of fruit hitting the basket. Westley moved through it as if he'd been born to its language, hands sure, steps easy, pausing now and then to test the weight of an orange before setting it gently in my palm.

I caught myself memorizing these moments without meaning to: the low sound of his voice when he asked me to hold the ladder steady, the quick half-smile when he caught me watching him, the way his shadow sometimes fell over mine and stayed there a beat too long. None of it felt like a

performance; it was just him, as constant as the sun passing
overhead.

Once, I glanced toward the road and imagined Luca's
sleek car pulling into the drive, his gaze sweeping over the
same scene. I wondered if he'd see the quiet joy here, or only
the labor—if he'd understand that some work nourishes
more than it drains. The thought slipped away as Westley
tossed me another orange, grinning like he knew I'd catch it.

At night, I found myself less restless, more at ease in
my own skin. The carriage house felt different—fuller, as if it
had been waiting for this kind of living; this blend of labor
and laughter and quiet. I caught my reflection in the window
sometimes, hair wild, cheeks sun-touched and barely
recognized the girl I'd been in the city—hungry, brittle,
always bracing for loss.

It was Joani who handed me the package, wrapped in
tissue and the faintest trace of cologne. "Special delivery, doll
baby," she announced, dropping it in my lap as if she'd been
waiting for the moment. "From your mysterious admirer."

Inside: a dress. Soft, expensive, a blue so pale it was
nearly silver. A slip of card tucked beneath the folds—Luca's
name, a message in handwriting too precise to be loving: *For
your next big night. –L.* The fabric pooled across my knees,
beautiful but strangely cold. I tried to imagine myself in it—
belonging, dazzling, adored. Instead, I just felt suddenly,
deeply tired.

Joani watched, sharp eyed. "Pretty thing," she said, not quite smiling. "But is it you?" I shrugged, folding the dress back into its box, unsure whether to be grateful, flattered, or wary.

That evening, I set the box at the foot of my bed, a small, elegant challenge waiting to be answered. Outside, the crickets sang their late summer hymn. Inside, I breathed in, steady and quiet, letting the day settle in my bones. Tomorrow would bring its own kind of weather.

Morning broke warm and gold, light flooding across the patchwork quilt and into the spaces between my fingers as I reached for the day. I woke with the sensation of having slept deeply, as if the house itself had exhaled all night—an easy, living thing. For a moment I lay still, listening: birds in the grove, the click of cicadas, the faint thump of someone's car radio on the far side of the property. Then, closer—a footstep on the porch.

I sat up, the box with its cold blue dress catching the light at the foot of my bed. I barely glanced at it; all I felt was the living warmth of sunlight at my back, the kind that asked you to get up and open the door. I did.

Westley was there, backlit by morning; sleeves pushed up and hands full—fresh coffee with steam waving a morning greeting, a broad shouldered steadiness that seemed to belong to another century. "Thought you might be running low," he said, offering the coffee as if it were some ancient, sacred gesture.

I smiled and accepted his offering, feeling a heat in his hand still lingering. "Your timing's perfect. Come in—unless you want to stand here and watch me make a mess of the coffee."

He ducked inside, filling the small kitchen with the scent of clean laundry and something sharp—citrus, wood, sun. The space always felt bigger when he was in it, as if the walls remembered how to breathe.

I moved through my morning with a sense of ease that was almost unfamiliar: cracking eggs, slicing into the bread, spreading butter that softened instantly in the humid air. Westley found my mismatched plates and set the table by the window. He worked quietly, but there was nothing awkward in it; the silence between us was the soft kind, a space where nothing urgent needed to be said.

We ate in companionable quiet, facing the sun-drenched yard. His knee brushed mine under the table—a small, accidental contact that sent a warm thrill through my skin and straight to my heart. I wondered if he noticed, or if it was just the natural consequence of two people who'd started to move in time with each other.

After breakfast, he lingered, thumb tracing the rim of his mug. "You free this afternoon? I thought I'd tackle the window trim in the main house."

"I'm always free for that," I said, a smile slipping into my voice. "You're the only person I know who can make home repair sound like a date."

He grinned, warm and inviting, and for a moment I felt what it might mean to belong to a place, to a person, to a day unfolding.

The first drops began to fall as our work began. Thunder cracked somewhere distant; the house shuddered. I moved to the window, watching as the wind pressed the orange trees flat, leaves flashing silver in the gust. "These Florida storms could wake the dead," I said, voice quiet.

Westley joined me, his presence a steady counterpoint to the rising wind. "Ghosts aren't so bad. It's the living you have to watch out for."

We worked together, a silent choreography: propping up the porch rail, wrestling the stubborn kitchen window shut, stacking towels by the door just in case. Each small effort felt like an act of faith—a belief that this old house would hold, that we would too.

When the power flickered out, Westley lit the candles I kept for hurricanes, their soft glow gilding the woodwork and the curve of his jaw. I made tea on the gas stove, the ritual soothing in its smallness. We sat on the floor, backs against the cool plaster, knees drawn up, steam curling between us.

Outside, rain battered the world to silence; inside, it was warm, golden, and quiet. Our laughter was muffled but true. There was no sense of the everyday routine—just this: two people alone with the storm, sharing breath and heat, making a haven in the chaos.

At some point, I realized I was leaning closer, that my bare shoulder brushed his arm, that I didn't mind at all. Westley's hand, rough and gentle, found mine, and neither of us pulled away. My skin tingled from the contrast: the cool air at my back, the impossible heat where he touched me.

"I should go," he said softly, after a long moment. But he didn't move.

"You could stay," I said. "The couch pulls out. It's not much, but—"

He looked at me, gaze searching. "You sure?"

"I want you to." The admission felt big, bigger than the storm, bigger than the house itself.

He nodded once, the corners of his mouth curving upward, but there was a seriousness to the way he watched me—a respect, a patience, as if he understood what it meant for me to ask. A hush passed between us—then, as if on cue, the storm eased. The steady roar gave way to a softer, splintering quiet. Westley glanced out the window at the silvery wet world.

"If we're gonna make it to the carriage house before the next round, it's now or never," he said, mouth twitching into a challenge.

"Then let's run," I said, heart already leaping ahead.

We gathered up shoes, flashlights, and leftover mugs, and when we pushed open the door, the air was thick and electric, the world gleaming with rain. Halfway to the carriage house, thunder cracked again, and we broke into a sprint, laughing so hard I could barely breathe. I slipped on the grass and nearly fell, but Westley caught my arm, steadying me. His other hand reached up, gentle, tucking a sodden strand of hair behind my ear. In the wet hush, with water streaming down my cheeks and his palm warm against my temple, I felt a heat that had nothing to do with weather—like he was carrying the Florida sunshine itself, lit from within, and I could bask in it forever if I just stood close enough.

We tumbled into the carriage house just as the next downpour roared to life, shaking rainwater onto the tile. For a moment we just stood there, breathless, laughter nearly drowning out the thunder. The world outside vanished, and I was suddenly aware of how close we were, how the house smelled of orange blossoms and storm.

By now it was after two in the morning. "My grandma always said nothing good ever happens after 2 a.m.," I managed, voice unsteady from adrenaline—or something else.

Westley grinned, a rare flash of teeth. "Guess we'll have to prove her wrong."

He took the couch with a grateful sigh as I fetched him a pillow and a blanket, the space between us alive with all the things we didn't say.

I climbed the stairs to the loft, peeling off my damp jeans and trading my soaked t-shirt for one warm and dry. The fabric clung softly to my skin, all comfort and relief, nothing like the cold, unfamiliar dress still boxed at the foot of my bed. As I let my hair tumble free from its ponytail, I turned toward the railing and saw him below, lying on his back, arms folded behind his head.

He looked up just as I caught him, the candlelight throwing shadows across his face, his eyes catching on the bare length of my legs, the outline of my chest beneath the shirt. For a second, he didn't look away—just drew a careful, shuddering breath, as if he had to will himself into stillness.

I felt bold and exposed, all at once. Confident, and a little afraid. The night air cooled my skin, raising goosebumps along my arms—but I didn't flinch or cover myself. Not with him.

He offered the faintest of nods, a silent promise of respect, then forced his gaze to the ceiling. "Goodnight, Mina."

I turned out the light and climbed beneath the quilt, feeling the echo of his warmth settle into my bones.

Chapter Nine

I woke to a hush that felt almost holy—the kind of silence
that follows a summer storm, when every leaf glistens,
unburdened. The rain had stopped in the night, leaving the air
washed clean and cool. My body ached with the sweet fatigue
of work and laughter and longing; my mind was still tangled
with fragments of a dream I couldn't quite recall, except that
it ended with a gentle hand reaching for mine.

Westley was gone.

At first, the emptiness of the house startled me, but
there was no sting to it—no aftertaste of abandonment. Only
the soft imprint of his presence, the memory of warmth
where he'd sat on the worn couch, the faintest scent of soap
and sawdust lingering in the air. On the kitchen counter,
beside the chipped mug I favored, sat a note in his careful
handwriting: *Didn't want to wake you, store opens early. Tea's
steeping. I'll see you at the festival.*

I smiled, tracing the edge of the note. He had a way
of slipping out without leaving, of making space without
making distance. I poured the tea he'd left for me, the water
still warm in the pot, and drank it slowly at the window,
watching the morning sun ignite the dew on the grass. Every
blade shimmered, every orange on the trees seemed rounder,
brighter, as if the storm had polished the world just for me.

The grove looked almost shy beneath its own beauty, each branch bending under the weight of its new washed leaves. Drops clung to the fruit like small suns, catching the light and scattering it into a thousand fleeting prisms. I wanted to step outside barefoot, to let the damp earth press its cool truth into my skin, to feel the world in a way the city had never allowed.

I thought about storms—not just the kind that rattle windowpanes, but the kind that strip you bare, peeling away every certainty until you're left with nothing but yourself. This one had left no damage, only clarity. Maybe that was the mercy of it: to remind me that not every force that shakes you is out to ruin you. The air itself seemed to hum, low and patient, as if promising more good things just beyond the horizon.

My skin felt different—lighter, somehow. I moved through the small rooms with a sense of ease that was still new, finding myself humming as I packed eggs into cartons and polished honey jars for the festival. The table we'd scavenged, the shelves we'd built, even the battered kettle on the stove: all of it felt like evidence of a life I was actively shaping.

I avoided the blue dress at first—the box was still at the foot of my bed, folded with a precision that felt clinical, a little cold. I trailed my hand across the lid but left it closed. Today, I needed comfort, not performance. Joani would laugh at the idea of me swanning around in borrowed silk before noon, and I found myself grinning at the thought.

My phone buzzed. Goldie, as ever, right on time:
*Sunrise check-in. Show me your farmer tan. I want proof of life before I brave these Florida highways. Miss you, weird girl.*

I snapped a picture of the sun-warmed space, sent with a one-word reply—*Home*—and set the phone aside, heart easing at the connection.

A second message arrived, this one from Joani: *Festival game plan tomorrow at ten. Come ready to hustle, doll baby.*

I pressed my palm to the windowpane, watching the way the breeze moved through the grove, stirring shadows and light. There was a wildness in me that felt mirrored by the world outside—a sense of being on the edge of something important, a threshold waiting to be crossed.

I finished my tea, then spent the next hour moving through the house in small, deliberate rituals: setting out jars of honey, checking my inventory of eggs, winding fresh string through the baskets for oranges. Each task was grounding, almost sacred—a way of declaring to myself that I belonged here, that I had chosen this place, this work, this version of myself.

The carriage house was quiet, but the hush felt earned, like a song winding down after its last bright note. I breathed in, slow and sure. Whatever else the day brought—festival, flattery, closure or ache—I was ready. The storm had passed, but something else was just beginning.

———————————

I dressed for dinner with the same sense of ritual I used to pack my apartment not that long ago: methodical, detached, going through the motions. The pale blue dress waited for me, pressed and lovely, but when I slipped it over my shoulders, it felt unfamiliar—foreign, like a memory of someone else's longing. The fabric was cold against my skin, elegant but not mine.

Joani's voice echoed in my head—*"Pretty thing. But is it you?"*—and I shrugged into a cardigan, needing a buffer between myself and the dress's too smooth perfection. I braided my hair, applied a careful sweep of mascara, and stared at my reflection in the carriage house window. I looked polished, composed; if I squinted, I almost looked like the kind of woman Luca might have wanted.

The evening was warm and heavy with the aftertaste of rain. Luca arrived in a black sedan—impeccably detailed, of course—stepping out in a crisp linen shirt, a bouquet of expensive white lilies in hand. "For the new queen of Citrus Grove," he said with a half-smile, offering the flowers as if closing a deal.

We drove in practiced silence, the car cool and quiet as a mausoleum. He played music low—something smooth and unthreatening, the kind you barely notice until you realize you haven't heard your own thoughts for miles. His compliments were plentiful but oddly hollow; each one carefully measured, bright and superficial. There was something dreamlike about the way he praised me—lavish, bright, and a little too sweet, like flower juice pressed to my eyelids.

The restaurant, a swanky new bistro on the edge of town, was all gold fixtures and dim lights, meant to evoke intimacy but somehow feeling staged. Luca ordered for both of us without asking—wine, appetizers, steak rare for himself, salmon for me. "You seem lighter," he observed, eyes sliding over my bare shoulders, his smile thin and knowing. "Citrus Grove must suit you."

I tried to answer lightly, but the conversation kept turning toward the house—his missed opportunity, my "unexpected" win, the way things "always work out for the right people." Every word was a veiled negotiation. The meal became a dance of subtle criticisms and small boasts: the city, my accent, the "charm" of an old house compared to the stability of a new build. He admired my boldness, but only as long as it didn't cost him anything.

Halfway through dessert, he leaned in, voice pitched low for significance. "You know, you could do better than this little town. I've got friends in Miami—connections. I could make things happen for you." His hand brushed mine, the contact deliberate, possessive. "You deserve more, Mina."

His words landed like an offer, not a compliment. I looked at him and saw the edge beneath the polish, the hunger for control masquerading as care. I remembered every time I'd mistaken attention for affection, every time I'd tried to mold myself into someone else's vision.

A hush grew between us. I tried to pull my hand away, but his fingers tightened—a small, iron warning hidden in the gentleness of his grip. I glanced around, suddenly aware of how exposed I was, how careful I'd have to be. His eyes met mine, flat and expectant, his smile barely touching his lips.

"I think I'm where I need to be," I said, my voice steadier than I felt. He didn't let go. Luca's mouth tightened. "You're making a mistake," he said, the words barely louder than the flicker of candlelight between us. "Don't embarrass me. Not here."

His thumb pressed a warning into my palm. For a heartbeat, I froze—my mind racing, pulse thudding loud in my ears. But something in me refused to yield. I gently twisted free, forcing my hand back to my lap. For a heartbeat, I wavered. The urge to say yes—to step back into comfort, let someone else take the lead—flickered through me. But it passed, as quickly as it came. I thought of the storm, of Westley's quiet presence, of Joani's laughter and the steady ritual of my mornings. I thought of the house, its bones and stories, the wildness of the groves. I remembered what it felt like to breathe.

I squared my shoulders, found my reflection in the window beyond Luca's face—a ghost of the girl I'd been, vanishing by degrees. "Thank you for dinner," I said, this time with no softness left to offer. "But I don't need saving. Not anymore."

His eyes flashed—a promise, or maybe a threat—but he said nothing else. I rose quickly, gathering my bag with unsteady fingers, my heels clicking too loud on the tile as I left. He watched me go but didn't follow. As I pushed through the door into the warm night air, my heartbeat slowed. I felt the evening's gentle breeze like a reassurance—reminding me that some steps, even the hardest ones, lead you closer to yourself.

Outside, the air was thick and sweet and rel. I drew it into my lungs and kept walking, every step away from the restaurant a step back into myself.

Chapter Ten

The house loomed up out of the darkness as I climbed from the car, heels dangling from my fingers, their straps already forgotten. Not welcoming, not cold—just waiting. A silent thing with its own breath and memory, as if it watched and measured each night I returned, deciding what kind of person I would be by morning.

Tonight, its windows glimmered faintly under a low ceiling of clouds, their light softened by the heavy, humid air. Somewhere in the grove, a bird called once, then fell silent.

I thanked the driver and stepped onto the gravel drive. The stones pressed cool and sharp against the soles of my feet, each step a reminder that I was here. I moved slowly, as though hurrying might shatter the delicate quiet the world had draped over itself.

At the porch, I paused. The light above the carriage house door buzzed faintly; its glow bending and blurring in the damp air. Moths spiraled toward it, their wings flashing in the yellow light before vanishing into night again. The smell of wet grass and salt thickened the night; the kind of scent that found its way under your skin and stayed there.

Inside, the door clicked softly behind me and, in that hush, I finally exhaled.

The blue dress shimmered under the kitchen light—delicate straps, a hush of silk, a lie. It had looked beautiful out of the box, expensive, the sort of thing someone like Luca might picture me in. The right size, and yet it didn't fit. I could still fill the way it had rested against my skin at dinner; an elegant noose, perfect for the role he'd written in his head.

I reached for the zipper and pulled it down in one smooth motion. The fabric slithered away, whispering as it fell, puddling at my feet in a sigh of surrender. Even the silk beneath seemed to slip from me of its own accord. I left it there, each layer falling away until nothing remained but the truth of skin and bone.

I stood for a breath, the air meeting me without flinching. Then I bent, gathered the dress in one hand, the rest in the other, and carried it outside. The night opened for me as I stepped onto the porch, and the breeze was cool enough to raise goosebumps along my arms.

The trash bin sat beneath the far corner of the porch light, waiting. I lifted the lid, breathing in the faint rot of coffee grounds and eggshells within. I dropped the dress in, and it landed with a soft sigh against the heap—one more thing gone soft in the Florida heat.

For a moment, I gripped the bin's edge, letting my fingertips bite into the plastic. My pulse felt steady in a way it hadn't all night. A strange sense of liberation rushed over me, not just from the silk dress but from the invisible binds I'd let others place upon me. I thought about how many things I'd worn for someone else's sake—how many rooms I'd walked into costumed in their idea of me, speaking lines they would never admit they had written. The rustle of leaves whispered secrets, a gentle reminder that my story wasn't theirs to write.

The lid fell shut.

Let it wrinkle and rot.

Let the night go with it.

I stayed there, naked beneath the porch light, chest rising and falling. The smell of orange blossoms carried on the air, mingled with the damp earth and the faint mineral scent of the well pump; I drank the night in: frogs and cicadas, the distant sound of a truck rumbling past on the highway, its sound fading into the distance until only the night remained.

The breeze moved over me as though it had been waiting. I closed my eyes and drank it in, feeling my hair shift against my shoulders, my skin prickled by the cool.

It felt like coming up for air.

And for a long moment, I just… stood. Felt how exposed I was, and how safe. No one's gaze but my own; not watched, not measured, not stripped down for someone else's pleasure or approval. Just… seen. By the moon, by the trees, by the self I'd been avoiding.

*Not everyone who unlocks a door deserves to be let inside,* I thought, glancing over my shoulder at the closed door behind me. For once, the only one with the key was me.

A breeze lifted a curl of hair from my shoulder as I stepped off the porch and walked into the darkened grove, the grass still wet from last night's storm. Cool blades kissed my ankles; damp earth gave a little under my weight. The world smelled rinsed—orange blossoms, clay, and the faint green bite of torn stems. Above me, the trees arched into a quiet cathedral, leaves black against a cloudless sky. I slipped farther in until the porch light thinned to a pale memory.

The first branch I reached brushed my shoulder like a greeting. I trailed my fingers along the low branches, letting my palm ride the glossy leaves, feeling their waxy smoothness and the tiny seams along each edge. I cupped a low hanging orange, feeling the cool, living weight of it in my hand. The stem held fast. It would let go when it was ready; I understood that and moved on.

Crickets thrummed, the frogs sang their nighttime hymn, my heartbeat slowed, and I belonged to the world again. I smiled at the knowledge that I'd joined the shift that belonged to animals and people not afraid of the dark. Everything here breathed without asking permission. I felt wild and private and holy.

Maybe I'd played the fool, letting myself be courted by a man who wore his ambition like a mask. Wasn't that the way of midsummer? To wake in a strange place and find you've given your heart to someone with the head of an ass.

136

I had said yes too often because yes was easier. It smoothed the way, quieted the room, earned me a kind of safety that wasn't safety at all—just a clean, curated surface for other people to walk on. Somewhere between the blue dress and the candlelight and Luca's small, pinning hand, I'd remembered the girl I used to be: bright for other people, quiet for survival, a chameleon who mistook disappearing for peace. Standing here bare as a peeled fruit, I felt the opposite of small.

A lone orange thumped softly into the grass. I laughed, startled by the simple luck of it. I picked it up and pressed the cool sphere to my sternum, the rind giving slightly under my thumb. The world had been loud for days—Luca's polished voice, Joani's gossip-fueled prods, Goldie's distant laughter on the phone. Here, though, only the wind moved, shaking loose petals that drifted at my feet like parchment blessings. The breeze exhaled for me as I peeled the orange: the strands of pith clung like tiny white hands. Then I pressed a segment to my lips and sank teeth into the sweet flesh. Juice spilled down my chin, down to my chest, and left a line down to my navel, sticky and sweet. I let it stain me.

I ate the segments one by one, savoring their brightness, each bite a reclamation. *This is mine*, I thought, swallowing the sun-bright taste. This skin, this night, this hunger.

I sat in the grass, dampness cooling the backs of my thighs, and pressed my hand to my heart. I let the wildness move through me—the ache of wanting, the sweetness of finally, quietly, choosing myself.

For a long time, I just sat. The world kept spinning; the stars didn't care if I was clothed or clever or claimed. The only approval I needed was my own. I lay back, leaves scribbled against the sky, a narrow clearing opened to a seam of stars where the clouds had pulled apart and let the Florida night air settle on my damp skin like a second breath. If someone had walked into the grove just then, they would have found a woman bare, striped faintly with dirt, marked with her own fruit—nothing tidy enough for a picture, everything true enough to live in.

When I stood, grass stuck to the back of my calves. I brushed it off, then gathered the discarded orange peels and scattered them at the base of the tree; a bright offering around the roots, Ants swarmed the new bounty with a discipline I envied. Waste became sweetness; mess became work; work became home.

And in that small, fierce conviction, I found my way home.

I told myself one last truth before I climbed the steps: wanting is allowed. So is changing your mind. So is walking out of a restaurant under your own steam, so is dropping a dress in a bin and never fishing it back out, so is eating an orange under a sky that doesn't care what you wear to dinner. My chest felt light enough to float. My legs felt strong. I had the key.

On the porch, the bulb buzzed, and a moth the size of my palm settled for a breath against the screen; its wings patterned like a pair of eyes. It lifted away without sound. I opened the door and let the house breathe me in.

Inside, the night would meet water and soap and a clean sheet. The last of the grove clung to me—petal, dirt, a ribbon of juice dried to sugar at my sternum. I carried it upstairs like proof.

Inside, the air was cooler, the scent of wood and faint citrus still lingering from the afternoon. I shut the door behind me with a quiet click and leaned against it for a moment, palms flat to the grain. The house always seemed to listen; tonight it felt like it understood.

In the kitchen, I turned the tap until the water ran cold, cupping my hands to drink. The shock of it chased the heat from my tongue, sent a small shiver along my spine. I let it drip down my wrists before twisting the tap shut, droplets falling to the floor like beads of glass.

The shower came next—its bite bracing, almost medicinal. I didn't rush. I let the water find every place that still carried the day: the silk's phantom weight along my shoulders, the faint scent of lilies in my hair, the ghost of Luca's hand against my palm. Each rivulet carved a clean path, taking pieces of the evening with it. The drain swallowed them without ceremony.

When I shut the water off, the silence felt wider, as if the house was holding space for me to decide what came next. I toweled off slowly and climbed to the bedroom.

Naked, damp, I crawled into bed, sheet drawn up to my chin. The ceiling fan turned lazily above me, its hum syncing with the steady beat of my heart.

Tomorrow there would be the festival—the bustle, the noise, the pleasant exhaustion of smiling at strangers and speaking about honey jars as if they were treasures. There would be Joani, irreverent and certain, already mapping out her plans for my future. There might be Westley, steady in the crowd, his presence quieter than all the noise around us.

But tonight belonged to no one else.

I closed my eyes and let the grove follow me into sleep: the wet grass against my calves, the cool press of an orange in my hand, the sweet sting of its juice against my lips. The night hummed, not with threat, but with possibility.

Chapter Eleven

I woke to a house made new—sunlight threading the curtains, the scent of citrus and bread and cool linen in the air. My limbs ached in the way that feels earned, not punishing. My skin, washed clean of last night's sorrow and silk, was bare beneath the sheets. For the first time since I'd crossed the state line, there was no ache to fill, only a slow and certain fullness spreading from my chest to my fingertips.

I moved through the rooms, pausing to press my palm against the doorframe, the countertop, the old glass of the window. Each touch a quiet claiming. My life. My place. My body. I did not flinch from my own reflection; I looked, and I lingered. There was nothing here to hide.

It felt almost as if the house and my body were in conversation; that it was acknowledging my touch. The cool glass of the window didn't recoil; the worn countertop did not bristle. Every surface seemed to say, "You're here now. You've stayed." In the reflection, I saw not just my face but the soft lines of my shoulders, the slope of my collarbone, the constellation of freckles I used to hide beneath makeup. My body was a room I could enter without knocking, without apologizing.

In the kitchen, I made breakfast just for myself—a ritual that felt more like celebration than necessity. I warmed milk from the morning's first pail, swirling honey into it until the scent rose like a blessing. The bread was yesterday's, a little stale at the edges, but thickly sliced and toasted golden in the pan. I halved an orange, letting its juice run over my fingers. I ate slowly, savoring each bite, letting myself be both hungry and satisfied. The bread gave way beneath my teeth with a satisfying crackle; the honey sinking into its pores like sunlight into soil. I thought about all the mornings I'd rushed through meals in another life—eating only after others were fed, swallowing without tasting. Here, I could linger. I could let the juice run over my fingers and not wipe it away right away, as if some part of me needed proof that sweetness could be messy and still be mine.

It struck me then how much I had changed. Not in loud ways, but quietly—cell by cell, word by word, meal by meal. This was not a girl fleeing an old life; this was a woman staying. Rooting. Taking up space at her own table, setting her own pace.

I carried my mug outside, feeling the grass damp and alive beneath my feet. The sun was up now, burning mist off the orchard. The hens greeted me with lazy clucks. Moo-donna, sleepy and content, raised her great head as I crossed the pasture, and I pressed my cheek to her side, grounding myself in the steady rhythm of her breath. The world did not need me to be spectacular; it only needed me to be present.

There was work to do, but no hurry. I swept the porch, watered the potted plants, gathered eggs from beneath warm straw, and sang to myself—just for the pleasure of it, no audience required. I was not preparing for anyone's arrival, not making a show of thriving. I was simply living, and that was enough.

I let the screen door swing shut behind me and stepped barefoot into the backyard, the hem of my cotton shirt brushing my thighs. The grass was still damp, and my toes squelched into the earth. I didn't mind. I wanted to feel something real. Something solid. Something alive that didn't expect anything back.

The pasture was humming with late summer life; green and gold and sun-warmed. The hens scratched lazy circles in the dirt, and the bees moved with that single minded hum of purpose, all rhythm and bloom. Moo-donna raised her head when she saw me and let out a soft, approving grunt.

She blinked her big, sleepy eyes at me like she knew. Like she understood. When I spread a blanket near the pasture's edge and sank down beside her in the grass, she didn't shift or fidget, just exhaled a long, slow breath and let her warmth settle around me.

We sat like that for a while, the two of us. I leaned my back against her side. Let the sun kiss my bare legs. Let the sound of bees and the breeze in the orange trees fill the sacred silence I hadn't known I needed. Moo-donna's hide was warm beneath my palm, a living quilt stitched with the patience of seasons. She chewed slowly, unconcerned with the passing of time, her great eyes soft with the wisdom of someone who has nothing to prove. Milk and bees and eggs and fruit — all of it beginning in the quiet work of female bodies, each one producing without apology, without permission slips signed by the world. It was a sisterhood of cycles and yield, and in their company, I felt inducted into something older than language.

It was a woman's world here. Female lives, complete in themselves. The bees didn't wait for permission to build. The hens didn't look over their shoulders when they laid an egg. Moo-donna didn't apologize for the space she took up or the softness of her body or the slow, steady way she moved through the world.

It made me wonder: how much of my life had been shaped by the hope of being chosen? But this—this soft, sunny moment in the field—I hadn't been chosen by anyone but myself.

And that was enough.

I closed my eyes and let Moo-donna's steady breath anchor me. Her side rose and fell like a tide. The hens pecked nearby. The breeze caught a curl of my hair and lifted it, gentle as fingers through pages.

This was the real world. This pasture, this sun, these creatures who needed nothing but quiet consistency and care.

I didn't need saving. I didn't need champagne or grand gestures or a man with ocean eyes promising things he didn't mean. Instead, I craved the slow rhythm of a life quietly chosen. The mornings spent tending to small tasks; afternoons lost in sunlight, evenings curled beneath familiar blankets. It was a different kind of romance—not built from whispered promises or stolen glances—but from steady, quiet days strung together like beads, each one worn smooth by touch and time.

I just needed this. A full breath. The press of warm fur at my back. The low cluck of hens who understood more about resilience than most people ever would. I opened the little book I'd left in the barn weeks ago and turned to the ribboned page.

> *You do not have to be good.*
> *You do not have to walk on your knees*
> *for a hundred miles through the desert, repenting.*
> *You only have to let the soft animal of your body*
> *love what it loves.*

Moo-donna snorted.

"Same," I murmured, turning the page, my cheek pressed to Moo-donna's warm side. Her breathing was slow and steady, like she understood every word. The hens clucked softly nearby, pecking in the grass without concern for yesterday or tomorrow. Bees danced in lazy loops above the wildflowers, drawn by sweetness, never shame.

My body softened. My throat unknotted. No penance. No hunger to be perfect. Just the permission to want what I want. To love what I love. My fingers curled in the grass, damp and sweet smelling. My spine settled into the earth like it belonged there. I read a little more, then just lay back and let the sunlight dapple across my closed lids. I might have dozed. I know I dreamed.

In my dream, I was walking barefoot through the grove at night, each tree bowing as I passed. The fruit glowed faintly, as if lit from within, and I knew without tasting that each one held a memory I'd made here — the first orange picked, the first jar of honey sold, the first time I'd chosen myself over someone else's wanting. I filled my skirt with them until the fabric sagged, heavy and fragrant, and carried them home. When I woke, my arms still felt the weight.

When I finally stood and rolled up the blanket, I felt better. Not fixed. Not magically whole. But better. Like maybe I could keep going. Like maybe I didn't have to be perfect to be loved.

And then I went inside and showered, brushed my hair, washed the sheets, lit a candle with notes of sage and tangerine and honey. I opened the windows and let the light in. The house didn't just wait. It welcomed me.

Chapter Twelve

Joani was pure, distilled sunshine—orange peel and bourbon, summer dresses and laughter, and the sort of history you could wear like perfume. When she arrived, the house brightened by degrees, as if it, too, had been waiting for her to come fill its quiet with something alive.

She breezed through the door with a bakery bag and a mason jar of something golden fizzing in her grip, already calling, "Rise and shine, festival queen! You look like a woman on the cusp of trouble."

I snorted, tucking my knees beneath me on the couch, hair damp, skin still warm from the shower. "Good morning to you too."

Joani's bracelets jingled as she set the scones on the table and popped open the jar, pouring two generous glasses. The kitchen air was thick with the perfume of fresh pastry— citrus zest and sugar still warm from the bag. Joani opened the window just enough to let in the hum of bees and the green scent of mown grass, sun pouring over the weathered countertop and glinting off her hairpins. I watched her move with easy purpose, unwrapping her treasures: glass jars of wild honey, a worn tin of rouge, a little atomizer of orange blossom water. Every gesture was a blessing; every scent a benediction. I couldn't remember this house ever feeling so alive. "Breakfast of champions," she said, sliding one of the glasses across to me. The drink smelled of citrus and whiskey—a recipe she'd probably invented in a moment of inspiration and a touch of mischief.

I lifted the glass. "What is it?"

She winked. "Secret weapon. Ellie used to say, 'Never let them see you wilt before noon.'"

Joani's energy was contagious; I let myself bask in it, the two of us encircled by the subtle kind of sisterhood that needs no explanation. She pulled out her makeup kit—"Time to work my magic, babe. God, I haven't done makeup on skin this smooth in years"—and I sat while she dabbed foundation, dusted blush, coaxed a little color onto my lips. "Enjoy it. I'd give up my favorite push-up bra to go back to your collagen levels."

I laughed. "Noted. I'll savor it for the both of us."

As she worked, Joani hummed an old tune, and I caught myself relaxing, even looking forward to the strange newness of the pageant. She laid out a dress on the bed: lemon yellow swing, delicate orange blossom embroidery trailing across the bust—vintage, soft, and undeniably hopeful. Joani beamed, "Ellie gave me a few pieces when I was a teenager trying to figure myself out. Said, 'Style is just a story you wear on the outside.' I never forgot that."

Joani parted my hair with gentle fingers, her touch confident and familiar as she twisted each strand around a curling iron, coaxing it into soft, tumbling waves. "Every pageant girl needs a bit of Old Hollywood," she declared,

misting my hair with orange blossom spray. The scent clung
sweetly, reminding me of dusk in the grove—gold and green
and utterly new. In the mirror, my reflection sharpened, the
familiar planes of my face softening into something almost
glamorous. For a moment, I looked at myself and saw not the
outsider, but a woman on the cusp of her own story,
belonging at last.

"You look radiant," she declared. "And I'm judging
this year, so I can't enter. But that doesn't mean I can't live
vicariously through you."

"That seems ethically questionable," I teased.

She shrugged, unbothered. "The mayor owes me a
favor and the other judge is my cousin. It's Florida, babe.
Nobody's clean."

We both laughed, and then Joani reached into her bag
and pulled out a battered photograph in a frame, the glass a
little cracked at one corner. She handed it to me with a
gentleness I hadn't expected.

The woman in the picture was stunning. Poised,
crowned in curls, a sash crisp across her halter dress. But it
was her smile—a closed-lipped kind of sparkle, as if she knew
something about the world no one else did. The brass
nameplate read: Eloise Beckett. Miss Orange Blossom 1954.

"Who's this?" I asked, tracing the edge of the frame.

Joani glanced over her shoulder, her voice low with memory. "Ellie? Oh honey, she was it. That's Eloise Beckett. The matriarch of Citrus Grove. She didn't just win crowns; she built the stage they handed them out on—parades, bake sales, the first library drive, the women's guild, Sunday school, theater costumes. Grace and lipstick, but the kind of woman who wasn't afraid to shovel compost in a silk scarf. Rosie the Riveter in pearls."

I studied the photo, feeling both admiration and something like longing. "She's…beautiful."

Joani smiled softly. "Half my closet's inspired by her. Some of it was hers. She took in every stray—me included. Fixed up this carriage house when it was just raccoons and old paint. Let me live here for pennies when I was twenty and lost as a goose."

I traced the name again. "Beckett. Any relation to Westley?"

Joani blinked, then barked a laugh. "That's his grandma, honey. Wait—don't tell me you didn't know this was her house you bought?"

I stared at her, heart thumping, memory flickering with every conversation and look I'd shared with Westley. "He never said."

Joani shook her head, muttering, "Lord, that boy. I'll wring his neck later."

A thump at the porch—River's voice booming, "Load's ready!"—and Westley's quiet reply. Joani popped her head out the bathroom, "Don't you boys dare peek, we're in full transformation mode in here!" Westley's voice drifted through the door, gentle: "See you there, Mina."

I watched Joani study me in the mirror, her hands gentle as she finished the final touches. I caught my reflection—smiling, luminous, haloed in those perfectly set waves. It struck me, quietly, that this wasn't just about the pageant or the dress or even the town. It was an introduction, yes, but also an invitation: "Hi, I'm Mina. This is my story." I felt it in my bones—the rooted certainty that I could be new here, and known. Not just by them, but by myself. As though my face had given away those private thoughts, Joani paused, voice suddenly soft. "I know. It's okay to be seen, Mina. You deserve that."

I looked down at the dress again. It was beautiful— vintage, citrus colored, the kind of thing you'd wear on a porch swing with a glass of sweet tea and the sun on your skin. I didn't know if I was ready, but I knew I'd never be alone on that stage.

———————————

Main Street simmered with festival heat, the kind that made everything shimmer at the edges. It felt like stepping into a memory not yet made, something I knew I would carry with me long after the banners were packed away. Even now, in the swirl of voices and laughter, I sensed the roots I'd begun planting—tentative but deepening, stretching into the

151

soil of this town until leaving would feel like tearing away a part of myself—bright tents flapping in a lazy breeze, children darting between tables, the scent of kettle corn and sun-warmed citrus swirling together in the air. Somewhere, a band played something upbeat and familiar, but the notes drifted like pollen, nearly lost beneath the drone of the crowd. Fairy lights were strung from lamppost to lamppost, twinkling even though the sun hadn't set yet, casting the whole town in a dreamy sort of glow.

Joani led me to the makeshift dressing area behind the stage, clutching her clipboard like a lifeline. The dress fit so seamlessly it might as well have been part of me; the lemon yellow fabric swishing softly as I walked. My hair, glossy and perfectly waved, tickled my shoulders; every time I touched it, the orange blossom scent caught in my throat. Backstage, nerves tangled with laughter and last-minute instructions; Joani hovered near me like a benevolent storm. I paced back and forth behind the curtain, pulse skipping in time with the distant music.

Joani had dabbed powder over my nose three times already. "You look like springtime kissed by a storm cloud," she murmured, adjusting the orange blossom pin in my hair.

I laughed nervously. "That's very poetic for a woman holding a flask in her cleavage."

She winked. "It's got electrolytes."

I barely noticed the contest announcements, the thrum of applause as contestants took the stage. My mind buzzed with the story Joani had told me—Ellie Beckett, Miss Orange Blossom 1954, the matriarch in pearls and silk scarves, the same house, the same family. Westley's house. His story tangled with mine before I'd ever set foot in Citrus Grove.

I hovered near the edge of the stage, nerves flaring in my chest. Joani squeezed my hand, steady and bright. "You're not here to perform, doll baby. You're here to belong. Let them see you." She tucked a stray curl behind my ear, her voice low. "Ellie would be proud."

Joani squeezed my hand once and stepped off toward the judges' table, fluffing her hair and applying one more layer of lip gloss before taking her seat. She gave me a thumbs up as she sat.

The MC, a grinning middle-aged man in suspenders and a straw hat, took the microphone and began introducing the panel of judges, including Joani, "local business owner, event chair, and unofficial mayor of the fun around here."

I stepped out onto the stage in a blur of heat and nerves and applause. The pageant wasn't about perfection. It was about charm. Community. Citrus Grove.

The lights above the stage were hot, the air prickly with anticipation. I took my place, listening as the emcee's voice boomed through the speakers: "Mina March, newcomer to Citrus Grove!" My name echoed off storefronts, met by a scattering of applause—familiar faces, strangers, and a few surprised gasps.

I looked out at the sea of people and saw Joani's grin from the front row, a lighthouse in the blur. I caught a glimpse of River near the trucks—off to the side—Westley, half-shadowed beneath the canopy, hands jammed in his pockets, watching with a look I couldn't name.

I answered the questions—about what brought me to Citrus Grove, what I loved most about the town, what it meant to build something new; the answers came haltingly at first. But then it grew steadier, each word a stone in the foundation I'd been quietly laying for weeks. I smiled. I waved. I made it through without tripping. I only swore once, quietly, when the microphone snagged my hair.

Somewhere in the crowd, someone cheered my name. I laughed, the sound bright and real.

When the winner was announced, I barely heard it. "And the crown goes to… Mina March!" The sash slid across my shoulder, the weight of the crown soft and surprisingly warm in Joani's hands as she pinned it in place. Someone snapped a photo, confetti fluttered overhead, and for a moment, I felt as golden as the light pouring down from the late afternoon sky.

Joani hugged me tight, her voice fierce in my ear. "See? You belong. Welcome home, Miss Orange Blossom."

I stood in the center of the stage, the dress bright against my skin, the crowd's faces softened by sunlight and shadow. All I could think was: I am here. I chose this. I am not a visitor. I am not the in-between anymore.

After the photos, the speeches, the swirl of congratulations, I slipped away—out of the glare and into the quiet shade behind the stage, crown in hand, heart full and aching. I needed to find Westley. There were questions that only he could answer now, and I was finally ready to hear the truth.

The crowd blurred at the edges—faces washed in sunlight, laughter bubbling through the warm near-July air, everyone a little sticky with anticipation. Main Street shimmered beneath the weight of citrus banners and bunting, the scent of sweet tea and fried dough blending with orange blossom and sunscreen. It should have felt overwhelming, but after this morning's quiet transformation, I drifted through the festival as if wrapped in silk, buffered from the noise by a kind of interior brightness I'd never known before.

Joani moved through the crowd like she owned the town—one hand waving, the other holding her clipboard aloft like a queen's scepter. Her laughter cut through the din, and everywhere she went, people stopped her for hugs, gossip, old memories. I stayed in her wake, half-shadow, half-celebrant, still not quite used to being noticed—let alone seen.

I'd always imagined the festival as a pageant of small-town clichés: pie eating contests, sticky toddlers, sunburned fathers, gossipy women in floppy hats. And there was all of that, of course—but now it felt different. I was not a tourist passing through, nor a ghost of my own making. People greeted me by name—Mina March, the new Miss Orange

Blossom—smiling as if I belonged to them now, and they to me.

Joani made introductions, but her voice was distant, my attention snagged by flashes of memory: Ellie's photograph, the echo of Westley's name on Joani's lips, the realization that the house I loved was tangled, root and branch, with the lives around me. Every gesture, every warm "congratulations!" held the weight of generations—of women who had come before me and chosen to build a life here, each one carving out a place with callused hands and stubborn hope.

I was passed from neighbor to neighbor, their congratulations as sweet and cloying as orange blossom honey. Mrs. Carmichael pressed a sticky bun into my palm, her hands sunspotted and sure. "You belong here, sugar. You're one of us now." Her words landed soft but sure, and I couldn't help but believe her.

Children ran wild between the booths, their laughter threading through the sticky air. Someone had set up a dunk tank, and River's booming voice called out for volunteers— his hat already askew, cheeks pink with mischief. I watched as Westley, sleeves rolled and hair mussed from the sun, handed out lemonade at Joani's booth, his smile quiet and steady. He caught my eye once across the crowd and raised his cup in a silent toast, sunlight catching in the fine dusting of sawdust that always seemed to cling to him.

I touched the crown on my head, still surprised by its gentle weight. The dress clung to my body, warm from the sun and fragrant with orange blossom spray. Every step felt lighter than the one before, as if the earth itself had risen to meet me.

But even in all this celebration, there was a part of me that drifted—untethered, searching. I wondered how many other women had stood here, blinking in the festival sun, their hearts wild with questions no one could see. I wondered what it would mean to go home tonight, wearing this crown, knowing the story of the house was bigger than me. I wondered what Westley would say when I asked about Ellie.

A marching band played, the high school's majorettes tossing orange batons to the sky; their routines met with applause and laughter. I stood at the edge of it all, new and still unfinished, hungry for the answer only he could give.

The speeches blurred—mayor, judges, the MC's easy jokes. The pageant contestants gathered around one last time for a group photo, their dresses a bright collage of color and hope. Joani winked from the judges' table, her lips quirked in secret encouragement. I took my place in line, feeling both seen and unseen, carried along by a river of tradition I was only beginning to understand.

When the parade of winners ended, I slipped away— barefoot, crown in hand, the dress trailing behind me like a golden echo. The festival hummed on without me. My heart was already elsewhere, moving toward the one place, the one person, where the next piece of my story waited to be spoken aloud.

The festival had faded to a dream when I found
Westley on the porch of the old house—leaning against the
railing, half in shadow, half in the mellow spill of the porch
light. He straightened when he saw me, the set of his
shoulders both proud and uncertain.

"Congratulations," he said softly. "Miss Orange
Blossom."

His words made me smile, though my heart was
beating so hard it almost hurt. I set the crown on the step,
then joined him, folding my hands in my lap.

"Joani told me," I said, my voice quiet but steady.
"About your grandmother. That this was her house before it
was mine. That you…" I trailed off, searching his face for any
flicker of confirmation, or regret.

He was silent for a moment, the breeze playing at the
curls on his forehead. "Yeah," he finally said, staring out
toward the dark grove. "This was Ellie's place."

"Why didn't you tell me?" The question came out
gentler than I expected. "Not just about her. About you."

He shrugged, jaw flexing, eyes averted. "I don't know.
Maybe I wanted to see what you'd make of it, without the
story weighing you down. Or maybe it just—hurts, more than

I thought it would, to talk about her." His voice was quiet, not quite apologetic, not quite defensive.

I sat with that for a moment. The hum of distant music, the scent of orange blossoms rising as the air cooled.

"You know," I said, "it would have mattered to me. Knowing. But I'm here now. I chose this place."

He looked at me then, his gaze uncertain and searching. "I know you did."

The silence between us was full, but not final. There was so much I wanted to ask—about the house, about his family, about why it felt like the walls remembered things he couldn't say. But I could feel how far he was willing to go tonight, and I didn't want to press further than he could bear.

I reached for his hand, laying my palm lightly atop his on the porch rail. He let it rest there, didn't move away, but didn't close the distance either.

"Maybe you'll tell me the rest someday," I said. "When you're ready."

He nodded, a slow, grateful movement.

A breeze lifted the hem of my dress, the citrus sweet air wrapping around us like a gentle embrace. We sat together for a while, not speaking, letting the night be enough.

When I rose to go, I picked up the crown and met his eyes. "Thank you—for everything you've done. Even the things you don't talk about."

He half-smiled, tired but genuine. "You make it easy, Mina."

I left him there on the porch, feeling the ache of questions left unanswered. But it was an ache I could live with, for now. I crossed the yard to the carriage house, crown clutched in one hand, and stepped inside, the sense of belonging both heavier and sweeter than before.

I wasn't sure how long before the rest of his story would surface; before the words would come, and the wounds would open. For tonight, the space between us was not a wound, but a door—unlocked, waiting, patient as the slow turning of a key.

Chapter Thirteen

Morning spilled in slow and gentle, slipping through the kitchen window and stripping the floor with honeyed light. I was halfway through my coffee when I heard the crunch of gravel—the old, comforting sound of Westley's truck in the drive. Something in me braced and relaxed at the same time, like the click of a lock tumbling open.

I pulled on jeans, slipped into sandals, and stepped out to meet him, feeling the grass cool and damp beneath my feet. Westley was already rounding the porch; arms burdened with a stack of battered leather photo albums and a paper sack heavy with glass bottles. He looked as if he'd slept hard and badly, hair mussed, a faint smudge of grease or soil on his jaw. There was something in the way he moved—quiet but purposeful—that made me feel seen, as though I'd been waited for, not merely expected.

He met my gaze, eyes tired but gentle. "Hey," he said.

"Hey," I managed, my throat thickening unexpectedly. He hefted the bag.

"Brought you Joani's sparkling lemonade. The kind with all the bubbles, none of the hangover. Figured you could use it."

It was such a small, considerate thing—but the kind of thing that unties knots in your chest before you realize they were there. I smiled, blinked too fast.

He shifted, awkward in a way that felt honest. "Got some old photo albums. Thought you might want to see what the house looked like…before. When it was home. When it was hers."

I reached for them carefully, almost reverently. Each album felt like holding someone else's heart—its pages fragile, its weight more emotional than physical. I wondered how many quiet evenings Ellie had spent turning these pages, tracing faces with a fingertip, holding onto memories that slipped like sand through her grasp. I knew what it meant to search for something solid amid shifting tides of time. The leather was soft and worn, the corners battered by decades of hands. Each album was heavy—not just with photos, but with years. I wondered if memory always weighed this much.

He led me to the porch swing, where the wood still smelled faintly of paint and pine sap, the chain creaking in a way that made me think of rocking chairs and long, drowsy afternoons. We sat close, knees barely brushing, the albums a small mountain between us.

I opened the first cover. A black-and-white snapshot greeted me—raw beams of a half-built house, sky open overhead; a single orange sapling staked in the yard. Time pressed in on every page: children with toothy grins and grass-stained knees, women in Easter dresses laughing on the porch, sunlight slanting through magnolia leaves.

Westley pointed at one photo. "That's Ellie. My grandma. Just a kid there. Her daddy built this house for her mama—said every home needs roots. They planted those citrus trees the same day they hammered the first nail."

His voice was thick with pride and something softer, sadder. I traced the photo's edge, feeling the pulse of history beneath my fingertip. "It's beautiful."

"She was beautiful," he echoed, voice barely above a whisper. "Smart, too. Tough as nails, sweeter than tea. She had a way of making everyone feel like they belonged here— even when they didn't."

I flipped the page: Westley as a boy, gap-toothed and wild, standing with a hen tucked beneath his arm, beaming in front of the very porch where we now sat. I laughed, and he did too, the tension easing between us.

"I think she'd have liked you," he said. "Ellie always rooted for the ones who showed up with dirt under their nails and dreams bigger than their doubts."

He thumbed through more photos: parades, pageants, and summer picnics. Then, the parlor—once pristine, now a little faded in memory but alive in the photo; the wallpaper patterned with orange blossoms, velvet armchairs waiting to be sat in.

"I want to bring this back," I said quietly, running a finger along the image of the wallpaper. "If you don't mind. I could make it look like this again."

He looked at me, eyes shadowed with something like awe. "You'd really do that?"

I nodded, feeling the truth settle somewhere deep. "Of course I would. It deserves to be remembered. She does."

For a long moment, we just sat in the hush, the morning alive with the song of mockingbirds and the distant rumble of trucks on the highway. I felt the urge to reach for his hand—almost did—but settled instead for letting my leg rest against his, a quiet connection.

"She's still here, you know," he said after a while. "Not here in the house. She's…she's alive. In a nursing home a few towns over. It's not fancy, but the garden's nice. She loves the hibiscus."

I turned, startled. "I didn't realize…"

His mouth twisted. "She started slipping a few years back. I didn't notice soon enough. Not until it was too late. I thought I was doing the right thing; running the supply store my grandpa left behind, then the car lot when River didn't step up right away. I thought if I just worked harder, I could be everything. Do everything. Be like her. Keep everything running."

He swallowed. "Friday dinners turned into phone calls. Then phone calls into nothing. I got busy. I thought she was fine. She always *seemed* fine. Until one day, I showed up and the place was falling apart. The goats were gone. The animals hadn't been fed in days. She hadn't bathed. And when I walked in…"

He stopped. "She called me by my grandfather's name."

He went silent, the confession hanging in the air between us, fragile as spun glass. I saw the way his fingers gripped the edge of the photo album, how hard it was for him to let this out.

"I had to sell the house," he continued, voice rough. "To pay for her care. I hated it. I hated myself for it. I felt like I'd let her down. Like I'd let everything she built fall apart."

I found his hand and set mine over it gently. "You didn't. Not really. It was always going to come back to life. Maybe just…needed the right time. The right people."

He let out a shaky breath. "Your letter—it was the first good thing I'd heard in a long time. The way you talked about wanting to make this place a home again. It felt like…maybe there was a second chance. Not just for the house. For me, too."

I squeezed his hand, feeling my own eyes sting. "You were never alone in this."

He blinked, looked at me. "Would you want to meet her? Ellie?"

"More than anything."

He smiled—a real, tremulous thing—and nodded.

The porch fell quiet again, but the silence was full and golden and good. Around us, the trees shifted in the breeze, and I realized the house was still listening—soaking up the new stories as hungrily as it remembered the old.

Somewhere in the distance, a mockingbird sang. The scent of honeysuckle and orange blossom twined through the air, and I knew, without question, that this was what coming home felt like—not just for me, but for Westley, too.

He watched me trace the edge of the photo with my thumb, the leather cover warm from the sun. There was a look on his face—guarded hope, or maybe just relief at finally letting some of the weight slip from his shoulders.

"You'd really want to meet her?" he asked, voice quiet.

I nodded, heart tight. "Of course I would."

Westley let out a breath that sounded like it had been trapped for years. "She gets tired easily. Some days she doesn't remember. But I think she'll know you. Or at least— she'll know what you're doing here. And that matters."

I reached for his hand this time, our fingers brushing—not quite tangled, but closer than we'd ever been. "Let's go," I said. "Today."

He blinked, surprised, then nodded, as if he'd needed someone else to grant permission to move forward. "Alright. Let me grab my keys."

---

The drive out to the nursing home was a long ribbon of sunstruck pavement, citrus groves and telephone wires spinning past in a blur of green and gold. Westley was quiet, his knuckles white on the steering wheel, but not distant; it was the hush of someone bracing for old ghosts, not turning away from them.

I held the photo albums in my lap, flipping through pages as the landscape changed from rural sprawl to the tidy hedges and hibiscus that marked the edge of town. My heart beat fast—part nerves, part something softer, the kind of hope you can't quite say out loud.

The nursing home was a low brick building rimmed with bougainvillea, pink and wild against the walls. The place felt both gentle and sad, like a home you leave only when you've lived too many stories to hold inside.

Westley signed us in, shoulders broad and steady. I followed him down sunlit halls lined with framed photos and quilt squares, the scent of lemon cleaner and peonies thick in the air. He stopped outside a door with a painted ceramic sign: Ellie.

He knocked softly. "Grandma? It's Westley. I brought a friend."

She turned in her chair, lap covered by a patchwork quilt, a book open and forgotten in her hands. Her eyes—clear, green, the same as Westley's—fixed on us, sharp as new leaves. I felt her gaze move through me, measuring.

"Well, well," she said, voice sandpaper and honey. "You're prettier than I imagined."

I laughed, nervous, but she waved me closer. "Sit. Don't hover. You're not a nurse, are you?"

Westley grinned, some of his tension melting away. "No, Grandma. Mina's fixing up the house."

"The house?" Ellie looked past me, toward the window as if she could see the porch from here. "She's a stubborn one. Gets it from my father. And you're the girl who sent the letter."

I nodded, surprised. "How did you know?"

Ellie's smile flickered. "Houses remember. Even when we forget."

She took my hand, fingers dry and soft, skin mapped with time. "Thank you for not tearing her down. Some folks just want new things. But you—you see her for who she is."

I blinked hard, pressing her hand between both of mine. "I'm trying to make her whole again."

She patted my wrist. "A woman after my own heart."

Westley hovered nearby, eyes rimmed red. Ellie beckoned him close. "And you, mister. Have you finally learned to ask for help, or is this girl just magic?"

He managed a crooked smile. "Bit of both, I think."

Ellie squeezed my hand. "Let the house teach you, dear. She knows all the secrets—where to patch, where to let the light in. Don't be afraid to put your own name on her, too. A place belongs to whoever loves it best."

The visit was quiet, golden sun slanting through the curtains, the tick of a wall clock. Ellie drifted in and out, sometimes mistaking Westley for his grandfather, sometimes lucid enough to ask about the porch swing, the color of the kitchen walls, the way the bees sounded at dusk.

When it was time to leave, she held my hand and said, "Don't let him run off. He's got a good heart. But he's stubborn as a mule."

I smiled, promise curling warm in my chest. "I'll try."

Westley leaned in to kiss her cheek. "Love you, Grandma."

She looked up, softer now. "I love you, too, West. Take care of her. And yourself."

The walk back to the truck was silent, as we both held the moment as long as we could.

We drove back in the waning gold of late afternoon. The car windows down, orange-scented air swirling around us, both of us lost in thought. I pressed my forehead to the glass, watching the grove slide past, feeling changed and unmoored, but more myself than I'd been in a long time.

Back at the house, the world felt quieter. Not empty—just waiting. Westley carried in the albums, set them gently on the table, and without a word, started pulling out the paint cans and brushes for the kitchen cabinets.

"Want to keep me company?" he asked, not quite looking at me.

I smiled, the answer already written in my bones. "Always."

We worked side by side as dusk poured into the house. My hands found the rhythm of sanding, brushing, wiping down the trim. Westley hummed under his breath, voice soft as the first crickets outside. Now and then, our eyes met—not shy, but searching, as if memorizing each other in this new light.

There was no need to fill the quiet. The house creaked; the bees droned; the last light pressed gold along the floorboards. It was enough. It was everything.

As night came, I poured lemonade into old mason jars and handed one to Westley, our fingers brushing—longer this time. We sat on the porch steps, drinking in the cool, letting the hush of a good day settle between us. I thought of

Ellie, of what it means to carry a legacy, to choose a home and let it choose you back.

Westley looked at me, something hopeful and raw in his eyes. "Thank you for today. For seeing her. For… everything."

I rested my head on his shoulder for a heartbeat; the world shrinking to just this—sunset, paint on our skin, the memory of kindness. "Thank you for letting me."

And in the fading light, with the house breathing around us, I felt it: the promise of healing, not just for a place, but for the people who choose to call it home.

Chapter Fourteen

River had warned me about Poker Night, but nothing could have prepared me for the sheer, saturated Florida-ness of it. It was like stepping into a sun-warmed honey jar, the way The Sundrop was strung with orange paper lanterns and thick with laughter, the walls humming with jukebox twang and the low shuffle of card decks. Joani stood at the center of it all; her loud tank top warned, "Bless Your Heart and Mind Your Business," and her bracelets jangled as she shouted, "Somebody put out that dang cigarette! This ain't the Elk Lodge and I just got my hair done!"

I spotted River at the bar with his boots propped up on a milk crate, cradling a beer. He hollered as soon as we spotted me, "Look alive, people! Mina's here—nobody bet the house."

"You didn't think I'd show, did you?" I teased, sliding onto the next stool.

He shrugged, all mock solemnity. "I doubt everybody. It's a public service." He nudged a glass my way—iced tea, strong enough to crack a tooth. "You're sitting in on a legendary night, March. Try to keep up."

Behind us, Joani called out, "You in, doll baby? Or just here to look pretty and make Westley sweat?"

My cheeks flushed, but before I could answer, Westley appeared at my side, sleeves rolled and forearms still streaked with white paint from the afternoon. He smelled of citrus, sawdust, and the faintest hint of woodsmoke. His hand brushed my lower back as he guided me toward a table, a whisper of touch that sent warmth chasing up my spine.

Joani shuffled the cards with one hand, shot me a look. "Well, somebody's gotta keep Westley humble. Sit down before I sic the town florist on you."

Said florist—a woman named Cherry, dressed in fuchsia from jumpsuit to garden gloves—flashed me a wide, lipstick-matching grin. "It's true, honey. I play for blood and for begonias."

Laughter rolled like summer thunder. I took my seat next to Westley, close enough that the brush of his arm made every nerve light up. "You ready to learn the real reason people come to Poker Night?" he murmured, voice low and secret, just for me.

"I thought it was the bar tab credit," I deadpanned, but my heart hammered under the soft fabric of my sundress.

"Watch out for Joani," he warned. "She's been known to hustle her own family."

Joani arched an eyebrow. "That's not hustling, it's called skill. Deal her in!"

The cards hit the table in a rapid fire rhythm, and I caught myself falling into the music of the moment—the jostle of bodies, the twang of the jukebox, the thrum of something electric under my skin. Joani's perfume—orange blossom and bourbon—curled through the air, and River kept a running commentary, needling everyone in a way that somehow felt like affection.

At a nearby table, someone slapped a pair of fives down and declared, "Cowboys," before scooping a modest pile of bottle caps and gum wrappers into her lap.

"This isn't even real money," I whispered to Westley.

"Bar tab credit," he said. "Don't underestimate it."

I watched two rounds before he nudged my knee with his under the table. "You're up."

"I don't know how to play."

He leaned in, his voice a hush against the shell of my ear. "Don't worry. I'll go easy on you." His breath was warm, a secret against my skin. "For now."

The first two hands, I folded fast. "She's sandbagging," River whispered. "Watch out, Joani."

Joani didn't look up from her cards. "Sandbagging? Last time someone accused me of that, I won his truck." She winked at me. "He still bikes to work."

Someone whistled. Mr. Humphrey, the retired science teacher, squinted at his hand. "Do threes beat queens?" he asked.

"No, Darwin," Joani fired back without missing a beat. "Not even in an alternate universe." The table broke up.

We played through three hands—Joani narrating, River heckling, and the townsfolk coming and going in a current of laughter and spilled drinks. A candle burned at the center of the table, its little flame flickering each time someone leaned in too close, the scent of melted wax and wood smoke curling through the bar.

By the final hand, the air was sticky and full of secrets. Westley dealt, slow and deliberate, and I couldn't help but notice the way his fingers brushed mine as he passed the cards. The little candle at the table flickered, making the shadows dance across his face.

As the game went on, the bar's energy softened, condensed. Someone had propped open the side door, and humid night air drifted in, smelling of honeysuckle and fresh-cut grass. The sweat cooled on the back of my neck, and I felt the ghost of Westley's gaze like the brush of fingers.

When the last card hit the table, Westley leaned over, his lips so close to my ear that I could feel the tingle of every word. His hand—warm, a little rough—rested gently on my bare thigh. My skin prickled, heat radiating from his palm. For a heartbeat, everything hushed.

Joani, from across the room, cupped her chest dramatically. "Someone's bluffing. I can feel it in my boobs."

River lost it, laughter like a barn door slamming open.

Westley didn't even flinch. He watched me, eyes gentle but unyielding. "You're bluffing," he whispered, thumb brushing just above my knee, slow and deliberate.

I shivered. "And if I am?"

His fingertips traced the soft curve above my ear, brushing back a stray piece of hair and lingering at the nape of my neck. The sensation was dizzying—a promise, a question, a slow accumulation of sun on stone.

"If you're bluffing," he said, his voice pitched so only I could hear, "then I hope you never stop."

I swallowed, my pulse a wild drumbeat in my throat. "Call me, then."

He laid down his cards—two low hearts and a pair of tens. Barely a breath better than mine. I won.

Joani threw her hands up like she'd won herself. "Mina March, slayer of egos! That's what I like to see. River, pass me that flask!"

The dog under River's chair stretched, tail thumping. Someone started up "American Pie" on the jukebox, and the whole bar seemed to vibrate with joy.

But my focus was Westley—his hand resting just above my knee under the table, thumb making small, grounding circles. The heat of him. The promise.

"You're dangerous," I murmured as I raked in the fake winnings.

Joani clapped twice. "Somebody get me a fresh pitcher and June Kravitz, keep your paws off the centerpieces. That woman left last week's garden club with more than just a trophy."

Mr. Humphrey, face earnest, said, "You're a natural, Mina. Next week we're playing for pie. Fair warning, Joani cheats."

Joani gasped, hand to heart. "Only when it counts, darlin'."

The game wound down, and Westley's eyes found mine—steady, sure, saying all the things he wasn't quite ready to say out loud. In this town of oddballs and loud hearts, I realized I'd been adopted without even noticing.

As we gathered our things, Joani hugged me tight, pressing orange blossom and bourbon into my shoulder. "Poker's like venereal disease in Citrus Grove—sticky and hard to shake. Welcome to the family, babe." I laughed, but beneath the humor, there was a warmth that felt like belonging. I'd spent years trying to stay invisible, only to realize that being seen—even in all my messiness and uncertainty—was the kind of gift I hadn't known to ask for.

Each smile, each teasing remark, tied me more firmly to these people and this place, knitting me into the tapestry of Citrus Grove. And for the first time in a long time, I felt the truth of it all the way to my bones.

When we spilled out into the gentle darkness of Citrus Grove, the night clung to us, heavy with crickets and the scent of orange blossoms. Westley's hand found mine, fingers threading through, gentle and sure. He didn't pull me close, didn't rush. He just held my hand as if it was the most natural thing in the world.

Westley offered to drive me home, the way he always did when the night pressed thick and velvet against the small-town streetlights. I didn't protest, even though my car sat parked by the curb. The truth was, I wanted more time—the excuse to linger, to draw out the warmth of the night a little longer. Logistics could wait until morning.

He parked at the end of my long, shadowy drive, the headlights catching the dew-silvered grass. Neither of us moved at first, letting the engine tick cool and the hush settle in. Somewhere far off, a bullfrog sang from the pasture.

The walk up the drive was slow, fireflies blinking low in the grass. Our hands brushed, fingers grazing, and I let mine linger, unsure who reached for whom first. By the time we reached the porch, I felt lighter than I had in years.

Westley paused at the bottom step, the glow from the porch light dusting his hair with gold. I turned, suddenly aware of how close we stood, his hands slipped to each side of my waist, steady and gentle. I could feel the warmth of his palms through the thin cotton of my dress, the quiet surety in the way he held me—not pulling, not pushing, just waiting. My heart stuttered, wild and willing.

"Did you see Cherry try to pay her tab with a bouquet?" I asked, the memory bubbling up suddenly, too good not to share. "She actually bartered three dahlias for a round of shots and a bag of pork rinds."

Westley grinned. "And Joani threatened to make her wear the garden gloves all week if she tried that again."

I laughed—a true, irrepressible thing, rolling up from my belly until my whole body shook with it. Westley stepped closer, drawn by the sound like a moth to a porch light. For a second, we stood in the dark, my laughter spilling out and my chest pressed to his, every inhale bumping against the solid warmth of him.

He didn't say anything—just drank in the sight of me, eyes crinkling, lips parted like he might try to memorize the taste of my happiness.

I wiped a tear from my cheek, still catching my breath. "Sorry. I don't know what's gotten into me tonight."

"I do," he murmured, voice low and sure. "You're finally letting yourself have a good time."

He reached up, tucking a wild curl behind my ear, his fingertips trailing the nape of my neck. His thumb grazed the edge of my jaw, and my breath caught—half expectation, half invitation.

I swallowed, heart hammering. "You're bluffing," I whispered, borrowing back his words from earlier.

He smiled, slow and a little sad, folding his hand just like at the poker table. "Not tonight," he said. "Not unless you call me."

The air between us snapped tight—electric, humming with possibility. I stood there, breathless, wanting to bridge the small distance, knowing it was my move to make. For a split second, I thought about closing that last bit of distance—the final lean, the first kiss—but I held still, savoring the weight of possibility.

And for a heartbeat, neither of us moved. Just two people on a porch, soaking in the last bit of night, the slow build of wanting that felt like the promise of a storm.

Chapter Fifteen

The morning after Poker Night felt like waking in a world spun from gold. Light filtered through the thin cotton curtains, spilling over my tangled sheets in slow, syrupy lines. It took me a few moments to remember where I was—not just in Citrus Grove, not just in the carriage house, but *here*—wrapped in the quiet aftermath of laughter that hadn't belonged to someone else.

I rolled to my back, sheets cool and twisted around my legs, and stared at the whorled plaster ceiling. The ghost of last night's laughter lingered, warm in my ribs. I pressed my palm over my heart and just… breathed. There was no rush, no demand, no list waiting to be checked. Only the soft ache in my shoulders from too much joy, the lingering tingle of Westley's palm on my knee, the memory of Joani's perfume—a mix of orange blossom and bourbon—dancing through the air.

Outside, Florida did what it always did in July: sang. Cicadas thrummed in the live oaks. The breeze smelled faintly of citrus leaves and gardenia, sun-heated and dense. In the next room, Moo-donna's bell clanged against the pasture gate, insistent and familiar, as if she'd come to expect me not just as caretaker, but as kin.

I stretched, every muscle uncoiling, and padded barefoot to the kitchen, collecting my scattered dress from where I'd flung it over the arm of the sofa. The tile was cool beneath my soles, and the old farmhouse sink gleamed, full of last night's dishes soaking in citrus-scented water. I could hear the slow creak of the back porch swing, the faint thud of something—someone—moving just beyond the screen.

It took only a heartbeat to know it was Westley.

He didn't knock. He never did, not anymore. He just showed up—boots planted in the earth, every movement careful, like he was learning the steps of the new rhythm we'd found together. I leaned against the doorframe and watched him through the screen: sleeves pushed up, jeans soft from years of wear, hands already stained with soil. He was digging in the garden bed, coaxing a new line of squash up a trellis, humming quietly, the sound low and soothing as thunder before rain.

I let myself linger in the doorway, soaking up the sight of him—the way the sun painted his skin gold, the gentle set of his shoulders, the way he existed here, in this place, as if the house itself had dreamed him up.

He looked up when he heard the squeak of the hinge. "Morning," he called, soft and warm as the sun rising over his shoulders.

"Morning," I echoed, tucking a wild curl behind my ear. My voice felt different in the morning light—less hesitant, less unsure. Like I'd been speaking someone else's lines all my life, and now I'd finally found my way back to the script that belonged to me.

He straightened, dusted his palms on the thighs of his jeans, and crossed the small patch of grass between us. "You sleep alright?"

I considered lying, the old reflex to say "fine" without thinking, but the truth came out instead. "Best I have in years." The smile that bloomed on his face was quiet, private—something meant just for me.

He glanced at the sky, where clouds gathered in fat, white pillows. "Looks like we'll get rain later. Think you'll melt if you come help me check the irrigation lines?"

"I'm tougher than I look," I said, holding out my hands for the gloves he always kept tucked in his back pocket just for me.

We worked side by side in the garden, sleeves rolled, hands in the dirt, the air between us as easy as breath. The morning felt alive. Sunlight slipped through the citrus branches in scattered gold, catching on Westley's forearms as he knelt beside the irrigation lines. I stole glances when I thought he wouldn't notice, memorizing the quiet steadiness in the set of his shoulders. This wasn't the kind of work that asked for words; it was the kind that stitched you to a place, thread by thread, until it began to feel like it belonged to you—and maybe you belonged to it, too. Westley showed me how to check for leaks, how to wiggle the tubing just so until the water ran clean. "See?" he said, grinning, "You've got the touch. Citrus Grove's finest farmhand."

Moo-donna wandered over to the fence, nose twitching, and Westley greeted her like an old friend. "Morning, Queen." He slipped her a piece of sweetgrass and she licked his palm with a dignified grunt.

"She approves," I said, watching the way her soft brown eyes blinked at us, heavy-lidded and wise.

"Only because you're here," he teased. "She's got taste."

The sun rose higher, dappling the yard in shifting, golden light. Birds darted through the low branches, their song braiding through the hush of morning. I could feel the day gathering itself around me, every moment settling like a blessing.

After we finished, Westley reached into his truck and produced a small, faded American flag—its stripes a little worn, the blue still brave and bright. "Joani says you need this for the Independence Day Festival tonight," he said, pressing it into my hand. "Tradition."

I turned the flag over, thumb catching on a loose thread. "You always go to the festival?"

He shook his head, gaze thoughtful. "Usually not. It's… loud. Crowded. Easier to stay home. But that message Joani sent out to all of us made it sound like more of a command than a request."

My heart thudded, a slow, hopeful ache. "Guess we'd better not disobey her."

His smile was slow and warm. "I'll pick you up later, then?"

I nodded, tucking the flag into the pocket of my overalls. "I'd like that."

Something passed between us then—a quiet understanding, maybe, or shared relief in knowing we were both choosing this.

Before he left to go help River haul tables into town, he paused at the back step, looking up at me with that same quiet wonder. "You look happy," he said, voice low.

I wanted to tell him that I *was*—that for the first time, happiness felt like something I could hold in my own hands. Instead, I just smiled, and he smiled back, and the whole day shimmered with the bright, impossible joy of belonging.

When the truck rumbled away, I stood on the porch for a long while, flag clutched in one hand, the scent of fresh earth and mown grass filling my lungs. The world felt open, abundant, sweet as honey. Tonight would come with its chaos and color and fireworks. But for now, I let myself simply *be*. Rooted, soft, a little sun-warmed and wild.

———————————————

The knock came just after noon, followed by the unmistakable creak of the screen door easing open. It had that slow, musical groan only old wood can make—half invitation, half warning.

"Don't shoot, it's just your neighborhood citrus witch!" Joani's voice rang out, bright and irreverent, full of the day already.

I laughed from the bathroom, mascara wand in hand, trying not to poke my own eye. "Back here! Come on in before Moo-donna gets ideas about guarding the door."

She materialized in the doorway a beat later, arms full—bakery box dangling from one hand, an armful of silky fabric, and a giant canvas tote bursting with makeup and jewelry. Her sunglasses were perched like a crown on her curls, and she wore a sundress printed with giant lemons and tiny bees, the skirt swishing around her knees like sunshine itself. Everything about her, from her stride to her grin, felt like festival season in human form.

"Peach turnovers, waterproof eyeliner, and backup earrings," she declared, placing the bakery box on the dresser with exaggerated care, like she was unveiling a rare gem. "Because I know you, and I know you didn't pack proper accessories when you moved in. Bless your heart, but your jewelry game is tragic."

I grinned, stepping out to meet her. "You're a menace, Joani."

"And yet, beloved." She winked, already rifling through my dresser drawers for a brush. "Some of us are just born to rescue the under-accessorized."

She paused, taking in the space. The carriage house glowed with soft, filtered midday light. My stack of old books leaned precariously on the window seat. Fresh paint brightened the walls. One of Ellie's crocheted afghans had found a permanent home on the reading chair, and the whole place smelled faintly of orange blossom and sun-warmed linen. Even Moo-donna's bell could be heard faintly through the open windows—steady, grounding.

"Well, I'll be damned," Joani said, hands on her hips, sunglasses sliding down her nose. "You've turned this little shed into a whole damn apartment. It's downright cozy."

"You like it?" I asked, unable to keep the hope from my voice.

"I love it. It's you. All of it." She stepped closer, running her fingers along the edge of the vanity I'd sanded last week, her rings catching the morning sun. "Soft. Thoughtful. Stubborn in all the right places. Like a lemonade pie with a ginger crust."

A blush rose to my cheeks. "I'm still settling in."

"You look settled," she said gently, then turned toward the mirror with a conspiratorial grin. "Now scoot. We've got a small town to impress."

We got ready together, shoulder to shoulder like teenage girls before a dance—there was a giddy, almost illicit joy to it. Joani plucked a dainty pair of cherry earrings from her stash and handed them to me. "These are lucky," she whispered. "Trust me." I borrowed her lipstick, a daring red she called "Firecracker," and she fussed with my hair until it fell in soft, lazy waves around my shoulders.

She spread her makeup kit across the dresser like a general planning a campaign—primers, powders, setting spray, and enough color to paint a sunset. "Tilt your chin," she commanded, dusting a shimmer onto my cheeks. "Good. You ever worn real eyeliner before?"

I laughed. "Not without ending up like a raccoon."

She cackled, delight crackling through the room. "That's what I'm here for. There's no crying in citrus beauty."

We swapped stories as we worked—her gossip about the town council ("The Mayor's toupee is held together by nothing but pride and Gorilla Glue, swear to God"), my memories of the first night in the house, the little wins and missteps I'd had since. The room filled with a sense of occasion, of something about to happen. I realized, somewhere between blush and mascara, that I wasn't nervous. Not really. Just open—ready.

"Westley's picking me up," I said, trying for casual, though my reflection gave me away; cheeks a little pink, smile just a little too wide. Joani only hummed in response, dabbing concealer beneath her eyes. She didn't ask about him. Not directly. And for some reason, I was grateful.

"Wear the white dress," she said, rifling through my closet before I could protest. "With the red flowers. It screams 'summertime heroine.' Shows off your legs, too. You need to show off your legs."

I did as she said, slipping the dress over my head. The fabric was light, cinched at the waist, and it swirled around my knees like a dream. In the mirror, I saw someone new— still me, but sharper at the edges, sunlit and a little wild.

Joani stood back, hands on her hips, inspecting me like a masterpiece. "You look like trouble," she said, grinning.

"So do you," I shot back, and we both laughed, high and bright.

A knock at the door, sharp and punctual, ended our reverie. I glanced at the clock—right on time. Joani slipped her sunglasses back on like armor, smoothing her skirt. "I'll get it. But only so I can give you a dramatic send-off."

I trailed after her, nerves prickling under my skin.

I opened the door to find Westley on the porch, freshly showered—or at least not covered in sawdust for once—wearing a pale button-down and his good jeans. His eyes flicked over me in a quiet sweep, landing somewhere between admiration and restraint, like he wanted to say more but was holding back.

"You look…" he started, but the sentence faded. "Ready for a parade."

Joani slid past me, pecking my cheek on the way. "Y'all behave yourselves," she said breezily, already descending the steps. "I'll see you there. Gotta swing by the community center to help set up the popcorn machine."

Westley, ever the gentleman, called after her, "You sure you don't want a ride?"

She turned, one eyebrow raised. "What, and play third wheel all afternoon? Not a chance, sugar. Besides, I've got a reputation to maintain."

He laughed, shaking his head. I watched Joani stride down the path, fearless as ever, the sunlight catching on her lemon-bright dress and bouncing her shadow along the grass.

Then she was gone, and I was alone with him again.

He opened the truck door for me without a word. Our hands brushed as I climbed in, the contact sparking something that had been flickering all week. My skin tingled where his fingers had grazed mine. As he rounded the front of the truck, I glanced down at my lap, smoothed my dress, and tried not to smile too hard.

By the time we reached the square, Citrus Grove was in full bloom—streamers fluttering, sun high, the whole town awake with possibility.

Citrus Grove's Fourth of July festival was less an event than a living, breathing thing—an annual exhale of joy that threaded through every street, porch, and patch of open field. By the time we rolled up in Westley's truck, the square was already pulsing with life, the air thick with the sticky promise of sunburn and sweetness.

Westley parked beneath a sprawling live oak, its branches thick with Spanish moss that glimmered silver in the late morning light. From here, the whole town looked like a carnival painting come to life. Red, white, and blue bunting draped every fence post and storefront; flags fluttered from mailbox to mailbox. Somewhere, a child's shriek of delight rose above the din, trailing behind a cluster of helium balloons bobbing in the heat.

I took Westley's offered hand as I stepped down from the cab, the cool leather of his palm a small anchor. For a moment, we just stood there—me in my white dress and cherry earrings, him in his pressed shirt and jeans, both pretending not to notice how the town seemed to tilt its head in our direction.

The square was a sea of folding chairs, lawn blankets, and hand-painted signs: PIE CONTEST, DUNK TANK, BEE KEEPING DEMO. The scent of kettle corn and funnel cake drifted above it all, chased by the sharper tang of grilling sausages and freshly cut grass. Somewhere near the bandstand, a bluegrass group tuned their instruments, the twang of a banjo curling through the air.

Westley and I wandered side by side, moving slow enough to take everything in. My dress swished around my knees; I felt the warmth of his presence at my side—a constant, steady thing, like a porch lamp left on all night. People called out greetings; some waved, some just nodded with the subtle pride of neighbors watching one of their own come into her own.

"Miss March!" Mrs. Kinney, the mayor's wife, bustled up in a hat festooned with miniature flags. "Are you competing in the pie contest this year? Because if not, I'm putting all my money on Joani. That woman can bake circles around the rest of us."

Westley leaned in. "You ever tried Joani's bourbon peach pie?"

I grinned. "Last week. I think it re-wired my brain."

Mrs. Kinney beamed, patting my arm. "Welcome to Citrus Grove, sweetheart. It's about time someone pretty shook things up around here." She bustled off before I could reply, trailing the scent of gardenias.

Children darted between tables, faces streaked with face paint and sticky with snow cone syrup. A local dog, wearing a stars-and-stripes bandana, lopped past with a hot dog bun in his mouth, trailed by a pair of laughing teenagers.

I could feel the weight of eyes on us—not cold, not critical, just curious. In the months since I'd arrived, I'd been the woman with the old house, the newcomer. Today, I was something different: Westley's date, maybe. Or at least, his chosen companion. The realization sent a little thrill down my spine.

We found Joani at the lemonade stand, arguing with the volunteer about the proper sugar-to-water ratio ("I swear, you use any less than two cups and it's just sour rainwater, darling"). She spotted us and waved a lemon-shaped fan in our direction.

"Well, look at y'all!" she called, voice carrying. "Don't you two look like a Norman Rockwell painting with just a dash of Florida scandal?"

River materialized from the crowd, a cold soda in each hand and a band-aid on his forehead. "I tried to dunk the mayor," he stage-whispered, handing me a soda. "Turns out, that's only funny until you actually do it."

Westley raised an eyebrow. "You banned yet?"

"Two strikes left," River said cheerfully. "Plenty of time."

Joani swept in, looping her arm through mine and giving Westley an approving once-over. "You look good, Beckett. But I'm not letting you two sneak off just yet. We've got a three-legged race to lose and a pie to defend." She winked at me. "Besides, you promised to help judge the watermelon carving contest."

I let myself be tugged along, laughter bubbling up, carried on the current of Joani's relentless energy. The group moved as a unit: Westley with his easy stride, River telling bad jokes ("Did you hear about the chicken who won the parade? He was egg-cellent!"), Joani with her clipboard and lemon wedges tucked behind one ear.

The day swelled around us, bright and a little wild. I watched as Westley chatted with a group of old-timers near the barbecue pit, his voice low and steady, his smile easy. He belonged here in a way I envied, rooted as the citrus trees that lined the roads.

A band struck up on the stage, fiddles and guitar blending in a ragged harmony. The crowd thickened as the parade began—floats decked out with tissue paper flowers, kids in red wagon "fire trucks," the high school majorettes twirling with abandon.

Near the courthouse, someone set off a string of firecrackers, and for a moment, the air shimmered with the sound—bright, crackling, a memory made real. I leaned back against Westley, letting the crowd push us together, feeling the slow, certain burn of anticipation in my bones.

We sampled everything: slices of lemon icebox pie, sweet tea poured from a chipped pitcher, a bite of fried catfish shared on a paper plate. Joani insisted I enter the "best festival laugh" contest ("You're a shoo-in, sugar—nobody can fake joy like you"), and River dared Westley to try the jalapeño eating challenge ("Don't do it, Beckett, you'll be breathing fire all night").

And everywhere—always—the press of Westley's hand at the small of my back, the glance exchanged over a rim of lemonade, the quiet, growing certainty that I was exactly where I belonged.

Near the edge of the square, beneath a magnolia tree strung with lanterns, we found a moment's hush amid the noise. I caught my breath, savoring the cool shade, the lazy drone of bees in the branches overhead.

Westley's eyes found mine, soft and a little amazed. "You alright?"

I nodded, happiness blooming in my chest. "More than alright. I just—don't want to forget any of this."

He smiled, the kind that you feel before you see. "You won't, but I'll remember it for both of us, just in case."

And for a moment, the world went quiet. The crowd, the music, the sunlight—everything else faded, leaving only the promise of now. Of here. Of us.

The afternoon settled into a sweet, sunlit daze—the kind of lazy, high summer hours that seemed to stretch forever, stitched together with music and the shrill joy of children chasing each other through clouds of dandelion fluff.

Joani was everywhere at once. One minute she was coaxing a shy toddler into the sack race ("You'll do fine, sweetheart, just pretend you're running from your chores!"), the next she was behind the lemonade stand, arguing that no, you absolutely could not use Splenda in the peach sweet tea. When she swept past us, clipboard in hand and a daisy tucked behind her ear, she caught River lurking by the pie contest sign-up sheet.

"River, if you so much as sniff those pies before the judges do, I'll tell your mama you still can't fold a fitted sheet."

River grinned, unfazed. "That woman doesn't fold anything. She just wads it up and prays."

Westley let out a low laugh beside me, and for a moment I saw him as the town saw him—easy, rooted, just a bit untouchable. But not to me, not anymore.

Westley stayed close through the crowds—not hovering, exactly, but always right at the edge of my vision. He carried my bag for a while, handed me napkins when my ice cream started to melt down my wrist, and nudged me gently out of the path of a little boy wielding a sparkler like a lightsaber. It wasn't flashy or flirty. Just steady. Easy. Good.

We wound our way toward the courthouse lawn, the press of people giving way to a knot of onlookers and the unmistakable clang of the festival's most ridiculous tradition: the bell-and-hammer game. Someone had wedged the whole contraption between the popcorn stand and a booth selling homemade pickles. The mallet was propped at an angle, its handle worn slick from decades of sweaty hands.

I took one look at it and shook my head. "Nope. Not happening."

Westley grinned, one brow raised. "You scared?"

"Yes," I said, without a hint of shame. "Deeply and honestly. I don't even have health insurance yet."

River was already rolling up his sleeves beside us. "I'll go first. Let you see how it's done, March."

Joani tossed her purse at Westley and flexed her arms. "Move aside, gentlemen."

River made a dramatic show of lining up his shot. He hefted the mallet, swung, and the bell rang—barely. He bowed with a flourish, unbothered by the weak applause.

Joani stepped up next, skirts hiked, determination in her jaw. She brought the hammer down with a force that startled everyone. The bell shot up the rail and wobbled near the top. A few kids clapped, a little awe in their faces. "My great-granddaddy was a blacksmith," she declared, smoothing her dress. "And yes, I still have the biceps to prove it."

I took the hammer when it was offered, and immediately regretted it. It was heavier than it looked; my palms went slick, and the teenage attendant eyed me with that familiar Citrus Grove skepticism. I tried to plant my feet, but my sundress was no match for physics—or festival wind. As I shifted my grip, the skirt hiked dangerously up my thigh. I heard a snort from behind me.

"Oh, don't worry, babe," Joani called out, voice carrying clear over the crowd. "I've seen you naked twice. If you flash the mayor, at least give him a show."

The crowd burst out laughing, and my cheeks went crimson. "If I end up on the front page, I'm blaming you," I shot back, half laughing, half mortified.

Westley stepped up behind me then, his presence quiet but solid, steadying me in a way that had nothing to do with the hammer. "Here," he murmured, so close I could feel his breath warm at the shell of my ear. "Let me help."

His hands closed over mine—warm, calloused, familiar. His chest brushed my back, grounding me with just the weight of his touch. For a moment, the crowd and chaos faded to a hum.

"We swing together," he said, low and steady. "One. Two. Three."

We brought the mallet down in a single, hard arc. The bell rang out, bright and clear. For a heartbeat, I just stared at it, blinking, breathless for reasons I couldn't name. Joani whooped and River whistled. "That's what I'm talking about!" Joani crowed. "Strength and style!"

I turned to look up at Westley, heart pounding from more than just the effort. He didn't say anything, just stepped back and adjusted his shirt like nothing had happened. But his hand lingered a half-second longer at my waist as he did, a silent *I've got you* in the press of his palm.

Then it was his turn. He hefted the mallet, squared his feet, and missed so spectacularly that even the attendant winced. The mallet *thunked* off the side of the base with a sad little puff of dust. Joani cackled, slapping her thigh. "Now I've seen it all! Get that man a lemonade and a fresh start."

Westley looked right at me and winked, and something in my chest squeezed tight with affection. I laughed, giddy from the rush of adrenaline and embarrassment and belonging. For the first time in a long time, I didn't care who was watching.

As the sun began to dip toward the horizon, the Ferris wheel rose above the crowd, its silver spokes catching the late light. Westley extended his hand. "You ready?"

I nodded, nerves fluttering in my belly. "Only if you promise not to rock the car."

He grinned, eyes gentle. "You've survived this much, haven't you?"

The Ferris wheel attendant—a kid barely out of high school, wearing a shirt that read "Ask Me About Funnel Cake"—waved us into a seat. The metal was warm against my thighs, the little car rocking just a bit as Westley slid in beside me. The safety bar clanked into place, and for a moment, all I could hear was my own breath and the low hum of the machinery.

We rose slowly above the festival, the world shrinking beneath us: booths, blankets, patchwork quilts, the burst of red and blue against the green of the square. I looked down and spotted Joani and River waving like lunatics.

Westley groaned, face turning just a shade pinker. I couldn't help it—I dissolved into laughter, the kind that unspools the last of your nerves. I leaned against him, shaking with mirth, and for a moment we were just two kids at a summer fair.

At the top, the Ferris wheel paused, our car swaying gently in the breeze. Below us, the whole town looked impossibly small, a pocketful of memory and promise. The wind played with the loose curls at the nape of my neck, cool against the lingering heat on my skin. Westley's hand found mine, fingers weaving through. He said nothing—just held on, anchor-steady.

For a moment, neither of us spoke. The hush between us was wide and shimmering, full of everything we'd said and everything we hadn't. I turned to look at him, the last rays of sun painting his profile gold.

"It's beautiful up here," I said, my voice softer than I meant it to be. "It almost doesn't feel real. Thanks for coming tonight."

"I'm glad I did," he replied.

Our eyes met. For a moment, something passed between us, not fireworks, not exactly. Something quieter. Deeper.

The Ferris wheel began to move again, and I exhaled slowly as it dipped us toward earth and the bright, blooming chaos of the night. As we reached the bottom, the lights from the booths shimmered in the twilight, the music swelling into something that felt like celebration and longing, all braided together.

As we stepped back into the glow of the festival, laughter and music swirling around us, I knew that whatever else might happen—tonight, I belonged. Here. With him. With all of them.

We ended the night on the edge of the park, the crowd thinning as the sun dipped below the horizon and a hush of anticipation settled over the field. Joani had scouted a spot just beyond the oak trees, not too close to the bandstand but with a clear view of the sky, and unfurled a trio of faded quilts with a flourish like she was laying out fine china.

"Luxury accommodations," she said, kicking off her wedges and plopping down in the middle. "Front row to the grand finale."

River joined with two ciders in hand and a suspicious-looking thermos. "Tell me someone packed snacks."

"Watermelon, cheese sticks, and Joani's famous bourbon peaches," I said, digging into the picnic basket.

"For courage," she announced, passing it around. River took a swig and coughed so hard he nearly dropped the jar.

"Lightweight," Joani crowed. "Next time, I'll add more peaches and less bourbon. Or not."

Westley handed me a peach slice, sticky and sweet. Our fingers brushed, and for a heartbeat the festival receded—the world narrowing to sun-warmed skin and the quiet certainty in his eyes.

We all laughed and sprawled out on the blankets like kids at summer camp. My dress still held the warmth of the day, and I sank into the soft give of the quilt as Westley stretched out beside me, arms behind his head, boots crossed at the ankle. The distance between us wasn't much- just a few inches of faded cotton- but it felt like its own kind of gravity.

The first firework went up with a crackle and a cheer from the crowd, blooming above us in cascading gold.

I leaned back on my elbows, watching the sky blossom with color. Somewhere to my left, Joani whooped and grabbed River's hand without looking. He didn't flinch or tease, just curled his fingers around hers and kept his eyes on the sky.

It was nothing. It was everything. A quiet kind of intimacy; the kind that didn't need a name to matter.

I watched them out of the corner of my eye, wondering if they were something, or nothing, or something that didn't fit neatly into either box. Or maybe this was just how people loved here. Not with declarations and drama, but with *presence.* With a hand held during fireworks. With a blanket shared on the grass. With a slow rebuild of a house that had seen better days.

Beside me, Westley let out a low whistle as a volley of blue and silver exploded overhead. I turned to look at him and in that moment, I didn't see the gruff handyman or the haunted grandson or the guy who fixed things without asking. I saw him; laid out under the stars, his face lit with quiet joy, his heart so close I could almost hear it through the stillness. His laugh from earlier still echoed in my chest.

And it felt like home.

After the last volley of fireworks, we lingered on the quilt long enough for the world to start dissolving back into ordinary time—faces blurred by the dark, laughter muted under the hush that comes after too much joy. Somewhere behind us, vendors began packing up, and Joani threatened to "bodycheck anyone who tries to steal my quilt." River sprawled out with his arms folded behind his head, humming "American Pie" as if the night might never end.

But it did end. Festivals always do.

The first fat raindrops landed on my outstretched palm, warm and insistent. Florida's storm had finally caught up to us—no polite warning, just a sudden opening of the heavens. Joani yelped, grabbing her heels and bourbon peaches in one swoop. "If y'all aren't under shelter in thirty seconds, you're on your own!" she called, already dragging River toward the nearest oak. I shoved pie tins and stray lemonade cups into the picnic basket, adrenaline buzzing in my chest, and Westley was suddenly beside me, steady as ever, his hand on my elbow as we made a mad dash for the truck.

The windshield wipers beat in rhythm as we crept along the winding road back to the house, tires hissing over wet pavement. Lightning stitched bright, jagged scars across the sky, followed seconds later by the low rumble of thunder that seemed to roll up from the ground itself. The streetlights blurred behind streaks of water, casting everything in a gold-soaked haze. Puddles gathered in dips along the shoulder, and palmettos swayed like dancers in the wind, their silhouettes half-erased in the deluge.

The air between us held the same simmer it had back at the festival, like something had been said without being spoken, and we were both holding our breath to keep from startling it away. The truck cabin felt too small for the weight of it, the anticipation thick enough to press against my ribs.

When we finally pulled into the long gravel drive, the rain was still coming down in sheets. The citrus trees beyond the fence swayed and hissed, their silvered leaves catching flashes of lightning and the carriage house barely glowed through the haze of headlights cut across gravel, its windows fogged with condensation, as if it too was holding its breath.

Westley cut the engine. Neither of us moved.

"Ready?" he asked, voice low, turning to look at me.

I met his gaze and smiled. "Together."

We ran for it, splashing through puddles and ducking low branches, shoes slipping in the mud. My dress clung to my legs, soaked within seconds—heavy and warm, plastered to my skin in a way only a Florida summer rain could manage. I fumbled the key, rain running down my face, and laughed breathlessly when it finally turned and the door gave.

We tumbled inside, slamming the door behind us like the storm might follow.

It took a moment for us to catch our breath.

My dress clung to my skin like a second heartbeat. Westley's shirt had gone nearly transparent, stretched taut across the thick lines of his chest and shoulders. Water dripped from his hair, tracing a slow path down his temple and jaw before falling to the wooden floor in quiet taps.

I pushed a wet curl from my cheek. The air inside the house was warm, or maybe I was just aware of him; of us.

We stood in silence, the only sounds the thunder outside and the too-loud pulse in my ears.

"I never know what you're thinking," I said finally, voice barely above a whisper. "I thought… I don't know. There's been so many time, I thought maybe—"

"You thought I was going to kiss you."

I nodded, staring at the floor.

Westley's chest rose slowly. He stepped closer, slow, deliberate, letting the space shrink on my terms. His hand lifted—slow and sure. His fingers threaded through the damp hair near my temple, tucking it gently behind my ear. His palm lingered, cupping my cheek, warm and calloused, thumb brushing the edge of my jaw like he was memorizing the shape of me.

I closed my eyes and leaned into it. The steadiness of him. The strength. The safety I didn't know I'd been missing until it was right in front of me.

When I opened my eyes again, his were waiting. So close. So steady. So certain.

He leaned in, not fast—like gravity, slow and inescapable. Our foreheads touched first, and I felt the warm, rhythmic exhale from his chest.

I felt the hitch of his breath, sharp and low. My hands found his chest, resting there, the cotton of his shirt soaked and soft beneath my fingers.

He pulled back just enough to meet my eyes. "I meant what I said," he told me. "Whatever you want. Just tell me."

My fingers slid up from his chest, curling lightly at the base of his neck. "I want…" The words caught in my throat. So, he closed the distance for me.

His lips met mine gently at first—tentative, soft, almost reverent—like he was still asking. I answered with a breath against his mouth, leaning in, pressing closer, and then something in him cracked. The kiss deepened, not frantic but *full*. His hand at my waist pulled me flush against him, anchoring me like he could keep the storm out just by holding me tight enough. His other hand slid to the small of my back, fingers splayed, strong and claiming.

I melted. Into him. Into this. It wasn't fireworks like the Fourth of July; it was the kind of fire that starts low and deep, builds slowly, catches everything you thought was safe and steady and burns it into something new. It was real. For a moment, I let myself believe we could stay suspended in this heat and hush forever. But the world kept turning; the storm pressing at the windows, time urging us forward.

When he finally pulled back, just enough to rest his forehead against mine again, our breath mingled in the warm space between.

"Damn," he whispered.

"Yeah," I breathed, my fingers still tangled at the nape of his neck.

I could feel him pressed hard against me. I could feel *everything*. And it sent a flush up my spine, my ribs, my neck. He wanted me. I didn't have to wonder. I'd never wanted anything so much and so simply: not a promise, not a future, just this—him, here, now, wanting me too.

"I don't want to stop," I whispered, the words thick with truth. "But I don't want to ruin this."

Westley nodded, jaw tight, breath uneven. "If I stay…"

"I know."

He kissed my forehead—slow, steady, anchored.

"I should go."

"You could wait out the rain," I offered weakly, though even I heard the hope in it.

He looked out the window. The rain was still coming down in curtains. "We'd be waiting a long time."

We both knew what that meant.

He stepped back, slow and aching, like every inch was a goodbye. His hand slid from mine last of all, his thumb brushing my palm like a promise. Then he opened the door and stepped into the storm. I stood there for a long time after, my lips tingling, my chest rising too fast, too full. I pressed my fingers to the place where our kiss still lived. Tried to hold the moment in place, to etch it into my skin.

Outside, the rain kept falling.

Chapter Sixteen

The days after the festival stretched out, slow and golden and thick as honey. The house was quiet again, the echo of laughter still clinging to the corners, as if the boards themselves remembered how it felt to be full. I didn't wake with a sense of loneliness, only a soft ache where Westley's presence had been—a fullness that lingered even as the hours emptied themselves into routine.

I kept to our rhythms. I watered the porch plants, checked on Moo-donna at the fence, and baked bread in the warm, sunlit kitchen. The scent of yeast and citrus drifted through the house. My hands, used to reaching for Westley's steady help, now found their own confidence in the quiet. Every so often, I'd pass a window and spot the shadow of a man at work—a memory, not a ghost—and let myself smile.

Westley hadn't come by since the festival. He hadn't texted either. I told myself it was what I wanted: space to let my heart settle, to see if the feeling that burned between us was more than just a holiday spark. In truth, I missed him with a sweetness that surprised me—not a hollow yearning, but a kind of satisfaction, like the slow ache of fingers after putting your heart on paper. I missed him, and it felt… good, in a way. Evidence that something real had happened, and that it would last even in his absence.

On the fourth morning, I got up early, made strong coffee, and threw myself into work.

In the span of three days, I had patched drywall in the pantry, regrouted the tile in the downstairs powder room, installed new hardware on the parlor doors, sanded and stained the banister with a podcast playing in my ears, and even taught myself how to rewire a sconce without electrocuting myself. There was sawdust in my lungs and paint under my fingernails, but the house was beautiful. It wasn't finished or perfect, but it was mine.

I was in the kitchen, elbow-deep in flour, when the crunch of tires on gravel startled me. I wiped my hands on a dish towel and peered out the window, heart stuttering. Not Westley's truck, but a white Jeep stuffed with luggage and a familiar blonde head bobbing in the driver's seat.

Goldie.

She flung open the door before I could even reach it, arms wide, perfumed with Sephora and sunscreen. "You didn't think you could come down here and hog all this sunshine to yourself, did you?" she crowed, hugging me so tight my ribs squeaked. "Move over, cowgirl. I brought half the panhandle with me."

I laughed, breathless with relief and something like gratitude. "You could have warned me!"

"And ruin the surprise? Never. Besides, I wanted to see the look on your face. You look…" She stepped back, eyes scanning the tidy kitchen, the sunlit parlor beyond. "You look happy, Mina."

I shrugged, not trusting myself to answer.

She took it all in—her gaze lingering on the stack of mail by the door, the wildflowers on the sill, the faded quilt draped over the couch. "This is really your place now, huh?"

"It's getting there," I said, fighting the urge to apologize for the unfinished corners, the still-too-quiet air.

Goldie beamed, dropping her bags by the stairs. "Show me everything."

We spent the morning wandering the house, her laughter rolling through the halls like sunlight. She poked her head into closets, ran her hands over freshly sanded wood, declared the clawfoot tub "an absolute non-negotiable if I ever move in." I showed her my room in the carriage house, the little reading nook I'd carved out for myself, the old cedar chest I'd found at a yard sale and filled with extra linens. She listened, truly listened, her arm slung around my shoulders as if to say, *I see you.*

We sat on the floor together for a while, drinking lemonade and eating peanut butter crackers from a tin I'd forgotten I had. She told me about her experimentation with raves and body glitter and I told her about Moo-donna, and Joani, and how River might actually be three Florida raccoons in a trench coat.

Eventually, the conversation slowed, then stilled. She looked at me, something real settling behind her sunglasses. "Do you ever think we got stuck?"

I blinked. "Stuck how?"

"Me being the golden one. You being the strong one. Me needing. You giving." She paused. "You protected me for so long that I think I forgot you needed it too."

I looked down at my lap, fingers knotting the hem of my shirt. "I didn't know how to ask."

Goldie reached out and took my hand. "I should've seen it anyway."

We didn't say much after that. We didn't need to.

By midmorning, the air was already thick with heat. We grabbed wide-brimmed hats and made our way down the back path to the barn, where Moo-donna blinked at us like a sleepy goddess. I flipped off her halter and handed Goldie the stainless-steel bucket.

"Ever milk a cow?" I asked, arching one brow.

"Only in my nightmares," she muttered.

I showed her my hands—steady, sure—and guided her beneath Moo-donna's flank. The first squeeze was clumsy; warm milk splattered into the pail. Goldie laughed— soft but unstoppable—and I joined her, the sound echoing under the rafters. Before long, we fell into rhythm: squeeze, release, squeeze—each soft plop into the bucket a tiny victory.

When we were done, Goldie carried the milk to the kitchen; It smelled of hay and something sweet.

The world outside was ripe and humming. Cicadas whirred in the trees. The grove glittered; every orange still on the branch bursting with promise. Goldie and I wandered beneath the arching boughs, our arms brushing, juice sticky on our wrists from where we bit straight into the fruit, warm from the sun. We rounded up a cluster of fallen oranges—heavy, bruised, over-ripe with sugar. The grove had borne its finest just to let it fall. I wondered if I was the fruit, or the tree. If I was ready to let myself ripen—ready to fall, or to be caught. The grove was quiet except for the bees droning through the blossoms. We filled the wicker basket until the fruit tumbled over the sides.

"This place is magic," Goldie said, licking her lips, juice running down her chin. "You always did know how to find the good things."

I smiled, brushing pulp from my mouth. "Sometimes I need reminding."

Goldie reached over, thumb swiping a smear of juice from my cheek. "That's what sisters are for."

We laughed until our stomachs hurt, collapsed in the grass beneath the orange trees, and let the sunlight wash over us. For a long, slow moment, I didn't miss Westley at all. Or maybe I did, but the ache felt less like longing and more like... fullness. The kind of fullness you only get when you let yourself be loved, and then let yourself rest in that love, even when you're alone.

"I found the juice dream," Goldie said, hefting the load.

"Or a trap," I teased.

Her grin was wide. "Let's find out."

---

We drove east to the coast in her Jeep, which smelled like coconut lotion and stale glitter. She sang the whole way, off-key and loud, bare feet up on the dash, while I tried to remember how to relax. We drove an hour and change, singing loudly to old pop songs with the windows down and the wind tangling our hair. Somewhere near the outskirts of the sleepy beach town, a faded billboard loomed above the road: ENDLESS SUMMER STARTS HERE.

We both snorted. The sky behind it was graying with distant rainclouds.

"Guess nobody told them about July in Florida," I said.

Goldie glanced at me sideways. "Or about fall."

When we finally reached the coast, the beach was nearly empty; a stretch of white sand and blue-gray sea framed by dunes and sea oats waving gently in the breeze. No boardwalk, no tourist traps. Just sky, salt, and something soft I hadn't felt in a long time.

It was the kind of quiet Gulf shore that tourists overlooked, but locals kept sacred. We laid out a couple of old beach towels from her trunk and peeled off layers until the sun could kiss our skin properly. Goldie looked like she belonged there, tan and luminous. Meanwhile, I tugged at the edges of my swimsuit and tried not to feel like a broken seashell beside her.

"I can't believe you haven't been to the beach since you moved here," Goldie rolled onto her side, propping her head on one hand. "That's a crime."

"I've been busy."

"You've been hiding," she corrected gently.

I sliced the fruit and squeezed it hard, juice spilling over my fingers, running down my arms in golden rivers. We drank it straight from tumblers, laughing as the sticky sweetness stung our tongues. Goldie wiped a drop from my chin like it was some kind of spell.

I leaned into her, tasting salt and sweetness on her breath as she pressed her forehead to mine. We sat for a while like that, the hush of waves and children's laughter wrapping around us like salt-laced ribbon.

We talked about everything. And nothing. About the boy who broke Goldie's heart in college. About the teacher who once told me I'd never be brave enough to write anything worth reading. About our mother's peach cobbler and the way Dad used to hum when he washed the car. We talked about who we were. Who we are. Who we're trying to become. It wasn't dramatic. It wasn't perfect, but it was real.

"You know," she said finally, voice soft, "I always knew you were holding the world together. For Mom. For me. Even when I was too busy being the golden child to see the cracks."

I blinked against the sun. "You *didn't* see it," I said. "You were off at camp or homecoming or sleeping in while I paid the electric bill."

"I know," she said. "But I did see those things, Mina. I did know. You wanted to protect me, to fix everything, but it broke you." I looked at her then, and something in her expression—open, regretful, maybe even reverent—hit me square in the chest.

"It's okay to let go," she said. "You don't have to feel responsible for how we turned out anymore."

My throat tightened. "Then what do I do with all that weight I've been carrying?"

She reached over and took my hand. "You put it down. Then you go swim in the damn ocean."

We laughed, a little too hard, like we were teenagers again sneaking into places we didn't belong. And when we ran into the water together, breathless and squealing at the chill, it felt like shedding something invisible.

It felt like maybe summer *was* endless, if only for one afternoon.

Tired from sun-blistered feet and golden juice, we returned to the carriage house just as the sky bruised into twilight. There was just the one bed, so we squeezed in together, Goldie cocooned against my side.

I turned off the small lamp, the blue moon glow painting her freckles like constellations. She yawned, heavy-eyed but grinning.

"Thank you," I whispered. "For coming."

Goldie's hair tickled my cheek, her arm heavy across my waist. "Thank you for having me. This place… it needed more than walls. It needed us."

We fell asleep locked together in one soft nest, the hum of rain tapping on tin above us—water bringing quiet, water bringing promise. In that moment, I knew the house would heal, and so would I.

———————————

Goldie had stayed two more days. She leaned against the kitchen counter, sipping her coffee like she'd been here a hundred times already. I watched her take in the kitchen—the sun-warmed tile, the jars of herbs lined neatly by the window—and for the first time in years, I didn't feel the need to explain myself. She didn't tease me for the quiet or the stacks of poetry books, didn't ask if I was lonely here. Instead, she smiled like she understood it all without words, the way only a sister could. We'd spent our childhood making nests in the unlikeliest places—under quilts, behind locked doors, anywhere the shouting couldn't reach. Maybe this was just another nest, only this time, I'd built it big enough for her to breathe in, too.

She watched me work on the house with a mixture of awe and exasperation, occasionally offering a manicured hand to hold a ladder steady or fetch a new roll of painter's tape, always with a dramatic sigh and a "don't tell anyone I chipped a nail for you." Her presence grounded me. Her laughter filled the carriage house, her music echoed down the hallways, and her unfiltered commentary- about everything from citrus-scented hand soap to the "impossibly jacked" mailman- reminded me that life didn't have to feel so heavy all the time.

On her last evening, she hugged me tight and kissed both my cheeks before slipping behind the wheel of her Jeep, off to a concert in the city with glitter on her collarbone and a denim jacket sliding down one sun-kissed shoulder. "Love you, Mina. Try not to renovate yourself into a hermit."

Then she was gone, trailing pop music and perfume down the gravel drive.

But the ache her absence left wasn't sharp or hollow; it was full—like the sweet soreness after laughter, like the heaviness in your arms when you've carried something precious. I settled into the house's quiet again, not as emptiness, but as space made sacred by joy. The walls echoed with all that had been shared, the bedsheets still smelled faintly of her coconut lotion, and everywhere I went, I carried the evidence that I was no longer holding this place—or myself—together alone.

A week passed. Seven days since Westley kissed me like I was the last good thing in the world. Seven days since the rain poured around him like a blessing or a goodbye. Seven days without a word. Not that I was counting.

But I was. I counted the mornings he didn't show up. The afternoons I worked alone, sanding the parlor floors until my arms shook. The nights I fell asleep staring at the ceiling, heart split between gratitude and longing. I'd told him I didn't want to ruin things. Maybe that was the wrong phrase. Maybe it sounded like I didn't want him. But I did.

God, I did.

I promised myself if he ever came back, I'd make it clear. No more half-open doors or letters unsent.

One morning, as the sun spilled pale gold between the rows of citrus trees, I slipped out barefoot, the porch light flickering off behind me. The air tasted sweet and alive—dew clung to the leaves like tiny jewels, and the hush felt sacred. I left my phone and tools behind; today, I was just a visitor in this grove I'd claimed.

I stepped onto the soft grass, each blade whispering beneath my feet. Above me, oranges hung heavy, their skins glowing like lanterns. I reached up and cupped one in my hand—its weight a promise. I breathed in blossom and sun, feeling a thrill of new ownership in my chest.

A few paces on, I paused at a fallen tangle of fruit. Bruised, cracked, rotting at the edges. I knelt and let my fingers brush the sweetest, most perfect orange still clinging to a broken stem. I pressed my palm to a gnarled trunk, rough as truth. It thrummed beneath my fingers—ancient and patient.

Carrying the perfect orange against my apron, I wandered deeper, sunbeams dancing across cypress and branch. Pollen swirled like tiny fireflies, and somewhere a lone cicada called out. I settled beneath the largest tree and leaned against its broad trunk. My back curved to its shape, and for a moment I felt held, known.

When I stepped back toward the carriage house, I carried not just fruit, but a quiet resolve. I belonged here. I would guard this grove—and this self—through every season.

And I was ready for whatever came next.

Chapter Seventeen

The house was quiet in a way that felt earned, not empty. That morning, sunlight slipped in through the newly washed parlor windows, angling across the polished floors and painting bands of gold on the wall where I'd just finished a final, stubborn coat of paint. The air was soft and heavy with the scent of citrus wood polish and old pine; the kind of hush that only comes after hard work—real, honest work—has been done.

I had finally let myself move slow, like the rest of the town, and it felt as natural as sunrise. I made coffee in the French press, poured a cup, and carried it to the parlor, my footsteps whispering over the boards I'd sanded by hand, the same boards he once helped me patch and stain until their grain glowed.

The room was transformed. Where there had been dust and disorder, there was now warmth—floor-to-ceiling bookshelves flanking the bay window, each one brimming with my battered paperbacks, poetry collections, and a few old hardcovers from Ellie's library. I'd spent the last hour sliding my favorite volumes into place, pausing every so often to run a finger along the spines. Here was *Pride and Prejudice*, already soft at the edges; here was the slim green Keats that felt like a secret talisman. A shell dish from Joani sat atop the shelf, collecting stray hairpins and buttons. Even my grandmother's embroidery hoop had found a home, propped in the sunlight where its threads shone like wildflowers.

The velvet sofa—deep green, impossibly soft, found at a thrift store and revived with weeks of care—anchored the room. There were throw pillows that didn't match, exactly, but made the space feel layered, lived in. On the coffee table, a bowl of oranges glistened in the light, promising breakfast or a snack, or maybe just a burst of color in all that sunlit green.

I took my coffee to the sofa and let myself sit, tucking bare feet beneath me. I traced the line of the molding with my eyes, feeling the weight of all I'd done—not just with my hands, but with my hope. Every surface, every brushstroke, every shelf filled was proof: I'd made something lasting here. I could belong. I could finish things.

The parlor seemed to pulse with a new kind of light—sunbeams glancing off the fresh varnish, tracing lines up the whitewashed shelves and spilling in puddles at the baseboards. If I closed my eyes, I could still smell hints of turpentine and lemon oil, a memory of work and effort made sweet by success. The air felt charged, somehow, as if all the words I'd ever read in these books had gathered together, filling the room with stories. It was a room that invited me to linger. Here, time slowed to a hush. Here, I could almost believe I was safe.

I set my mug down and wiped a thumb over a stray fleck of paint on my wrist. The morning stretched out, honey-thick and slow. Outside, the porch plants were thriving, lush and green from the week's rain; Moo-donna's bell rang in the distance, low and contented. The citrus grove shimmered, leaves whispering in a breeze that smelled faintly of sun and promise.

It would have been easy to let the longing creep back in—to ache for Westley, to wonder if I'd said too much or not enough, to replay every moment since the night of the festival. But today I let the feeling sit, soft and warm in my chest. Longing didn't have to be empty, I was learning. It could be full—a slow, golden ache that reminded me I was alive, that I could miss someone and still be whole.

I had been so afraid that missing someone would hollow me out, but this ache was golden—quiet and humming, as if love was a root growing deeper, not a wound left open. I realized longing could be its own kind of harvest: proof of the seeds we'd sown, the tenderness that had taken hold. I wasn't waiting by the door, desperate. I was living, breathing, carrying the shape of him alongside the new shape of myself. There was a kind of gratitude in it. To have something—or someone—to long for at all felt, finally, like hope.

I moved through the house, letting my fingers brush the tops of doorframes and windowsills, touching each finished task with a private pride. It struck me, as I wandered, how much of myself I'd left in these walls. My fingerprints hid in the grain of the wood, my breath in the air that smelled faintly of citrus and varnish. Even the floorboards seemed to hum with recognition beneath my bare feet, as though they had been waiting for this kind of quiet all along. I paused by the parlor window, watching the afternoon light gild the glass,

and for a moment I imagined the house exhaling with me—
our rhythms matched, two survivors learning how to belong
to each other. I fluffed the pillows on the sofa, straightened
the mirror in the hallway. In the kitchen, the bread I'd baked
that morning cooled on a rack, crust split and golden. I let
myself taste a slice, still warm, slathered with honey and the
tiniest bit of salt.

Each room held a memory. Here, the parlor where
laughter echoed off half-bare walls, Westley's voice low and
gentle as he handed me sandpaper or advice. There, the
hallway, still marked by a scuff from a night of moving
furniture, Goldie's laughter bouncing between the walls. I
pressed my palm to the frame, feeling the cool wood,
remembering a time when the house felt impossibly big and
empty, all shadow and unknown corners. Now, every surface
bore some trace of effort, of love—my fingerprints, my
dreams, stitched into every board. I was part of this place
now.

There was peace in this solitude—a different kind of
belonging. I'd built a life that didn't require anyone else to
feel real. But sometimes, when the light hit just right, I wished
for someone to see it. Not to fix it, not to rescue me, but to
witness it. To say, *I see what you've made. I see you.*

By late afternoon, the house was nearly singing with
readiness. The parlor gleamed. The air hummed with the
clean scent of citrus and the hush of possibility. I'd lit a
candle on the mantle, just for the softness of it, and the
shadows had begun to grow long across the floor.

That was when I heard it—the knock. Three slow raps. Steady. Familiar. My heart skipped, then galloped, all that golden peace gone bright and electric in an instant. I wiped my hands on my skirt and crossed the room, every sense tuned to the hush that fell as the candle flickered.

I paused at the door, fingers on the cool brass handle. For a moment, I just breathed. I remembered every time I'd waited for someone who never showed, every time I'd opened the door and found only emptiness. I thought of how easy it had become, in this house, to trust that someone might come back.

I turned the handle.

Westley stood on the other side, backlit by the last light of evening, shoulders slumped, eyes rimmed in red. He looked like hell. He looked like hope. He didn't speak right away. He just held my gaze, letting the question hang between us like a ribbon. "Can I come in?" he asked.

I nodded, stepping aside, feeling the swell of invitation in my chest—an open door, an open heart. As he crossed the threshold, I felt the space shift, the hush growing warmer, fuller, as if the house itself had been waiting for this moment all along. The sunset painted him in bronze and rose; his hair was damp at the temples, his shirt still creased from the day. He looked at me like a man who had come home from a long journey, and for a moment neither of us moved.

"Hi," I managed, voice thin but steady.

He lifted his hand, hesitated, then let it fall. "Hi, Mina." His eyes searched mine, dark and intent, as if looking for something he'd left behind. His boots made a low scuff on the newly swept floor. I closed the door softly behind him, and for a moment, the hush between us was all there was.

He looked around the room, and I watched him take it in—the lemon-polished shelves, the books tucked in every corner, the old velvet sofa lit soft by the lamp's honey glow. He saw the space, but he was really seeing me, all the work and waiting made visible. "You did all this?" he said, finally, voice rough.

I nodded, the pride warming my cheeks. "It's almost done. Feels more like a home every day."

He gave a slow, approving smile, but it faded at the edges. His jaw worked, like he was fighting back words he didn't trust to come out right. "I'm sorry I haven't been around. I wanted to. I just… needed to be sure I wasn't going to make things harder. For you. For me."

I shook my head, not trusting my own voice yet. The silence wasn't awkward; it was thick with everything unsaid, a shared ache turned almost sweet.

He moved closer, slow as the tide, hands in his pockets. I could smell the citrus on his skin, a hint of soap, a trace of sawdust and sun. All the scents of this place, braided together and made new. He stopped just a breath away. "I missed you," he said, voice low.

There was no shame in it. No need for pretense. He missed me. I missed him. The truth of it hung between us like ripe fruit, heavy and sweet. I reached for him before I thought twice. My hand found his, warm and rough and trembling just slightly. He let out a shaky breath, like he'd been holding it for days. "I was afraid," I admitted. "That I said the wrong thing. That you'd hear 'don't ruin this' and think I didn't want you. But I did. I do."

He closed his eyes for a moment, gathering himself. When he opened them again, I saw nothing but devotion. "I heard you," he said, voice thick. "But I needed to know it wasn't just the rain or the night. That it was real. That it was you."

My fingers traced the back of his hand, the line of his knuckles. "It's always been you."

He moved then, just a step, but it felt seismic. His arms went around me, slow and careful, as if holding something precious. I melted into him, breathing in the safety and hunger and promise of his embrace. He pressed his forehead to mine. "Tell me to stop, and I will," he whispered.

I shook my head, nose brushing his. "Don't stop."

His lips found mine—not hesitant, not rushed, just sure. A kiss that wasn't about desperation or fireworks but about arrival, the deep exhale after a long longing. I felt it everywhere: in my fingertips, in the soft arches of my feet, in the slow curling of my heart around his name.

His hands stayed gentle, moving from my waist to my back, from my back to my jaw, mapping me as if re-learning a familiar song. My own hands were greedy, sliding up the strong lines of his arms, tangling in the cotton at his shoulders. He deepened the kiss, and I opened for him—heart, mouth, soul—welcoming the press and the promise.

When we parted, his eyes searched mine. "I want to be here. I want to take this slow. I want to remember every part of this."

I nodded, laughter trembling in my chest, half a sob. "We've both been running so long. I don't want to run anymore."

He kissed me again, slower, surer, hands cupping my face like a blessing. The room around us faded, and there was nothing but the hush of our breathing, the hush of rain on the eaves, the hush of finally being seen.

We moved to the sofa without breaking, bodies twined and trembling. His hands slipped beneath the hem of my shirt, fingers warm on my ribs, just resting there. He pressed a kiss to my temple, my cheek, the corner of my mouth. "You feel like home," he murmured.

I wrapped my arms around his neck and pulled him closer, closer, until I could feel the wild hammer of his heart against my own. The ache in my chest went from longing to fullness to something almost holy. Slowly, reverently, he brushed his thumbs along the delicate skin just below my ribs, his palms mapping the rise and fall of each breath.

Then, with a softness that left me breathless, he lowered his head and pressed his lips to the hollow at the base of my throat—just above my heart, right where my shirt dipped and the last of the sun's warmth lingered on my skin. His mouth lingered there, open and gentle, his breath warm against my chest. It wasn't possessive; it wasn't hurried. It was a kind of worship.

I felt something loosen in me, something I'd kept bound up for years. My head tipped back, exposing more of myself, my pulse wild beneath his mouth. I let him feel it— the drum of want and wonder, the rhythm of trust. It felt as if I was offering him my heart, bare and beating, and that he understood the weight of it. We held each other there, letting the desire crest and settle, neither of us needing to rush. It was enough—more than enough—to be touched and held, to be chosen and cherished, to have longing answered at last.

When he looked up at me, his eyes were dark and bright all at once. He brushed my hair back from my forehead, fingers gentle. "You're safe here," he said again, "with me." But now I understood it wasn't just a promise. It was an invitation—to let myself be loved, to give as much as I wanted to take.

I leaned in, pressing my lips to the corner of his mouth, tasting salt and sun and every wish I'd ever whispered into the dark and as we sat tangled together, the storm finally passing, I realized: desire was not the opposite of patience, and hunger could be holy. I was wanted. I was home.

When the world quieted and the storm outside faded to a low, contented hush, we stayed curled together on the velvet sofa, tangled but calm, the soft afterglow of something longed-for finally found. I was half-draped over Westley, his arm a steady weight around my waist, his thumb tracing slow, absent-minded circles along my hip. The golden lamp glow painted the shelves, and every book on them felt like a homecoming.

Neither of us seemed eager to break the spell. Outside, the rain slowed to a whisper against the windowpanes. I thought, for a moment, that maybe time really *could* pause—if only in our memories. Maybe that's what makes a moment last forever: the way you return to it, tuck it away in your heart and revisit it when you need to be reminded that joy is as real as the grass beneath your feet. I pressed my cheek to Westley's shoulder, breathing him in, letting the hush settle over us like a blessing. For just a heartbeat more, I let myself believe we could live inside this golden hush forever.

It was the hush between us that drew me most. Not the silence of absence, but the quiet that grows from being truly known. I reached for a familiar book on the shelf behind me—my slim, battered copy of J. H. Reynolds' *The Garden of Florence And Other Poems*, its cover soft from years of reading and the page edges worn smooth from being thumbed and loved and lived in. I opened it with one hand, careful not to disturb the weight of Westley's head against my shoulder. "Do you want me to read to you?" I whispered, my voice low as candlelight.

He smiled, eyes closed, and nodded. "I always do."

So I began, my voice quiet, each line like a thread pulled through the dusk:

*Sweet poets of gentle antique line,*
*That made the hue of beauty all eterne*
*And gave earth's melodies a silver turn,—*
*Where did you steal your art so right divine?—*

I read slowly, letting the words move through me, feeling him listening. Not just the polite nodding and humming so many men performed, but an active, patient presence. I could feel his breath change with the rhythm of the poem, the way his hand paused against my skin, the way he leaned in just a little closer with every verse.

I stopped after the second stanza, unsure why. Maybe I wanted to see if he'd notice, if he'd care. Maybe I just wanted to hear my favorite lines in someone else's voice, to see if he could.

Without opening his eyes, Westley picked up where I left off, his tone softer than I'd ever heard it—full of devotion.

*…The golden clusters of enamouring hair*
*Glow'd in poetic pictures sweetly well;—*
*Why should not tresses dusk, that are so fair,*

*On the live brow, have an eternal spell*

*In poesy?—dark eyes are dearer far*

*Than orbs that mock the hyacinthine-bell.*

He finished the poem, letting the final line linger like a kiss. When he looked at me, his gaze was clear and unguarded. "It's your favorite, isn't it?" he said, almost shy.

I blinked, startled. "How many times have I read it?"

A small smile. "Just once, a long time ago. But something in your voice changed. I could hear it—like you'd handed me something precious. I knew it mattered, so I listened. I remembered."

The air felt thick with wonder. All I could do was stare at him, heart fluttering, and reach for his hand. "Most people never notice things like that."

"I notice everything about you," he replied, soft and steady. "Especially the things you never say out loud."

I let the book rest on my lap, feeling the shape of his words settle inside me. For a long moment, neither of us moved. The hush in the room felt sacred, the kind of quiet you get only when two people are utterly at peace—no need to impress, no need to fill the air. "I love that you listen," I whispered. "Not just to my words. To me."

He kissed the top of my head. "Always."

The room dimmed around us, the only light the golden lamp, the only music the soft shifting of our bodies on the sofa. I tucked myself against his chest, his heartbeat a lullaby. He pulled a throw blanket over us both, and the velvet of the couch, the weight of his arm, the warmth of our tangled legs—all of it felt like sanctuary.

We talked a little, about nothing—about Joani's terrible lemon bars, about how Moo-donna always managed to escape the pasture, about the scent of rain on orange blossoms and the way the floors creaked differently now. Our words slowed, faded, became half-sentences and then just contented breaths.

Sleep crept in quietly, and I let it. For the first time in years, I didn't feel the need to guard my dreams. I let myself be held. I let myself rest.

Outside, the rain finally stopped, leaving only the soft hush of night and the heartbeat of two people finding shelter in each other. And in that parlor—books lining the shelves, lamplight curling across the floor, Westley's arms safe around me—I finally understood what it meant to be truly heard. To be loved, quietly and completely, without ever needing to ask.

The last thing I felt before sleep was the rise and fall of his chest beneath my cheek.

Chapter Eighteen

The parlor was still heavy with the memory of night—a gentle weight, not an ache. I woke with my cheek pressed to Westley's chest, his breath a slow tide beneath my ear, arms curled around me as if though he were holding onto the last few moments before waking from a good dream. Light seeped through the curtains, pale gold fanning out over the polished floors, filling the room with a kind of quiet warmth.

I untangled myself, careful not to wake him. The quiet was thick, almost luxurious. In the hush, I heard the distant call of a sandhill crane, the drone of cicadas already rising with the sun. Every inch of the house seemed to exhale, as if it, too, was waking from a long dream.

I crept down the hall, passing the cooled kitchen, the newly bright entryway. I slipped out the back door, the wood cool and worn beneath my feet, and crossed the gravel path toward the carriage house. There was dew on the grass, the scent of earth and growing things, and something sweeter still—gardenias blooming wild along the fence line.

I was halfway up the carriage house steps when I saw it:
A single gardenia laid across the porch rail, petals already bruised, dewdrops clinging to the soft white edges. A familiar notecard positioned beside it, one I didn't need to read. The flower was unmistakable—a gesture meant to be tender, but only dredging up something old and unsettled.

Luca.

The scent was heavy—familiar in a way I didn't want.
For a moment, I was back in that shadowed restaurant,
Luca's laughter glinting across the table like cheap glass:
bright, brittle, and sure to cut if you held it too long. Then the
unraveling, the way even his gifts became warnings. I pressed
my thumb to the notecard's edge but didn't turn it over. He
always signed his name with a flourish, as if the right
signature could rewrite endings.

He seemed to find a way to haunt the corners of my
new life, leaving small offerings that felt more like warnings,
reminders that unfinished business doesn't end just because
you turn your back on it. For a second, I felt the familiar
prick of dread—the tightness in my chest, the urge to shrink
or hide. But I didn't.

Instead, I let the feeling pass through me. I held the
gardenia in my palm, rolling the stem between my fingers,
letting the fragrance rise—sweet, almost cloying, a little too
much for the morning air. I looked back toward the house,
where the parlor window would be sending slanted sunlight
across the old green sofa, where Westley still slept,
untroubled, steady.

Not today, I told myself. Not anymore.

I pressed the flower between my hands, petals soft as
a secret, then tucked it gently into the compost bucket by the
carriage house door—letting it go, letting it rot, letting the
earth have the last word.

Inside, I found comfort in small rituals: I measured coffee, poured water in a slow, practiced spiral, letting the grounds bloom, the air filling with something rich and grounded. I put the kettle on for tea—Earl Grey and a pinch of dried lavender—letting the steam curl up in ribbons, fragrant and soft. I moved quietly, trying to disturb nothing, not even the hush I'd claimed for myself.

Carrying two warm mugs, I stepped outside. The light was brighter now, spilling over the grass and catching in the wild tangle of orange trees. I paused, feeling the sun on my face, letting the gardenia's ghost dissolve in the fresh air. The world was bigger than one bad memory. Brighter, too.

When I reached the main house, I paused at the threshold, coffee and tea warming my palms, and looked back at the path I'd just walked. The porch was empty; no trace of the flower remained. I breathed deep—the scent of citrus, the promise of bread rising in the kitchen, the pulse of new life everywhere.

Westley was stirring on the couch as I slipped inside, his eyes just opening, slow to focus. For a moment, he seemed almost younger, softer—no walls, no weariness, just the sweet bewilderment of waking in a place you want to stay.

"Hey," I whispered, setting the mugs down, letting the morning settle between us like a blanket.

He reached for his coffee, eyes closing in quiet gratitude as the warmth seeped into his hands. I sat beside

him, letting my knee brush his thigh, letting the hush
remain—not needing to fill it, just letting it be.

There was stillness, and there was peace. Outside, the
gardenias bloomed. Inside, I let myself belong. Westley
sipped his coffee in slow, savoring gulps, stretching out his
long legs beneath the coffee table, looking more at ease than
I'd ever seen him. The parlor glowed gold and green around
us, dust motes spinning lazy pirouettes in the sunbeams. We
didn't speak at first; we didn't have to. The quiet between us
felt earned, the hush of two people no longer circling each
other.

After a while, he set his empty mug aside and reached
for my hand, rough fingers tracing idle patterns across my
palm. There was something reverent about the way he
touched me now—not urgent, but with a kind of *everyday
devotion*. Like he'd never tire of the small rituals: hand to hand,
breath to breath, morning to morning.

"Sleep okay?" I asked, my voice still soft from all the
hush.

He nodded, thumb circling my knuckles. "You always
sleep better when you know you're safe. This house… you.
It's the first time I've really rested in years."

A flush crept up my neck. I wanted to say I felt the
same, but instead I just squeezed his hand and pressed a kiss
to his shoulder—a small, anchoring thing. Sometimes love
didn't need to be declared. Sometimes it just needed to be
lived.

He stood first, stretching, then offered me a hand up. "You ready to tackle that wallpaper?"

I groaned, but took his hand anyway. "If we must."

The dining room was cool and shaded, morning light painting patterns on the faded wallpaper. We'd cleared out most of the debris weeks ago, but it was only now—with Westley beside me, sleeves rolled, laugh lines deepening at the corners of his eyes—that the work felt like something we could claim as ours.

We fell into a rhythm: Westley pried loose a stubborn length of baseboard; the scent of old pine rising as nails groaned free. There was something sacred in the sound of it—the groan of old wood, the scrape of our tools, the way our laughter stitched itself between the cracks of this tired house. Dust hung in the sunlight like tiny ghosts, but even they seemed to settle at ease with us. Every time our hands brushed in passing—a putty knife traded, a rag offered—I felt a quiet promise in it.

This was how love was built, I realized. Not only in the grand confessions or the kiss-stained silences, but in the small, steady acts of two people making something last. I knelt with a putty knife, coaxing the wallpaper from the plaster in long, satisfying curls.

Billie Holiday crooned low from the old radio, her voice a velvet ribbon winding through the dust and daylight. Westley hummed along, off-key but certain, and I found

myself smiling as he wiped sweat from his brow and grinned
back.

At one point, I reached to brush a smear of white
paint from his jaw, my thumb lingering. He caught my wrist,
eyes searching mine. Instead of letting go, he pressed a kiss to
my palm, warm and soft, then held it there against his cheek.
The moment stretched, humming with something unspoken.

We worked in companionable silence, the kind that
only comes when you've chosen someone—not out of need,
but out of want. The hours slipped by. Sun moved across the
floor, shadows shifting, settling, then sliding away again.

By noon, we'd cleared half the room; the air fragrant
with glue and dust, laughter echoing off bare plaster. Westley
settled onto the floor, back against the wall, legs stretched
out. I dropped beside him, knees bumping, and let my head
rest on his shoulder. The world felt simple—sawdust and
sunlight, the lull of summer heat, his hand idly tracing circles
on my thigh.

"I like this," I murmured. "Not just the fixing, but
the… after. The together."

He smiled, turning so his lips brushed my hair. "I've
never wanted to build anything with anyone before. Not
really. But with you… it feels different. It feels real."

I tipped my face up to his, catching the earnest glint
in his eyes—the longing, the gratitude, the certainty. For a
moment, I let myself be seen, let myself believe that maybe I

was worthy of all this newness. I touched his cheek, let my thumb graze the stubble there, and felt the echo of his heartbeat in my own chest.

He leaned in, lips finding the soft place just above my jaw, right where my pulse beat wild and hopeful. I closed my eyes, feeling the warmth of him, the steadiness, the way he always asked with his touch—*is this okay? am I welcome here?*

I answered with a quiet yes, pressing closer. His arms wrapped around me, anchoring me. We didn't rush. We just breathed together, hearts settling into the same slow rhythm.

For the first time, I understood what it meant to *build* something with someone—to create a life not out of halves made whole, but from two people standing side by side, each bringing their own weight, their own worth, to the foundation. Westley took pride in his hands, his steadiness, his work; I took pride in the warmth I could weave into these rooms, the way I could turn a house into a haven. We met in the middle—not to rescue or be rescued, not to fill some emptiness, but to make something greater than either of us could alone.

It wasn't about being claimed or claiming, but about choosing—again and again—to show up, to shoulder our share, to give and receive with equal measure. He never treated my homemaking as less than his labor; I never saw his strength as overshadowing my care. We were partners, both needed, both necessary.

In that sunlit hush, kneeling beside him on the scarred floor, I felt the quiet power of what we were building: not a fairy tale, not a prize to be won, but a home that bore both our fingerprints. A place sturdy enough to last through any storm, not because one of us held it up alone, but because we held it together.

When we finally stood, dizzy from the nearness, hands still tangled, the room looked different. Brighter. Ours.

For a long moment, we just stood there—tools scattered around us, the scent of lemon oil and old glue clinging to the air. My fingers ached from scraping, his shirt was streaked with dust, but neither of us wanted to break the spell. I let my hand rest against his, palm to palm, our work-worn lines meeting in the middle. The light shifted on the faded wallpaper, turning every flaw to gold.

He glanced down at our joined hands, then back up, his expression open and almost awed. I saw the same wonder I felt: not just at the room, but at how easily we fit together in it, how ordinary the extraordinary had become. How our labor and longing had woven themselves into something solid, something beautiful, right here in this battered house.

Westley's voice was quiet, thick with the emotion he never tried to hide from me. "You know, I used to think I was the only one who could fix things." His thumb traced the back of my hand, slow and careful. "But you… you make it feel like I don't have to do it all alone. Like maybe I was never meant to."

I smiled, brushing my thumb along his knuckles. "Maybe fixing things isn't the point," I said. "Maybe it's just… making them yours."

He took a breath, steady and slow, as if he were weighing each word. Then he squeezed my hand and led me to the bay window, sunlight painting us in gold. He let go only long enough to brush a stray curl from my cheek, the gesture so gentle it made my chest ache.

The world outside shimmered with heat, the orange grove swaying in the breeze. For once, I didn't feel like an outsider peering in. I was here—barefoot, dust-streaked, entirely present.

He spoke first, voice low and sure. "Mina, I don't want to just fix this house, or fix you, or be fixed by you. I want to build something with you. Something that lasts."

I felt the weight and lightness of it all at once—the history behind us, the ache of what we'd survived, and the hope of what might still be possible. I watched his jaw work, the furrow in his brow, the vulnerability there.

I stepped closer, closing the last bit of distance. My hands found his shoulders, thumbs pressing into the soft cotton of his shirt, grounding myself in the steady strength I found there.

He looked at me then as if he could see all the secret places I'd tried to keep hidden. His hands came up, slow and tentative, until his palms cupped my jaw, thumbs brushing beneath my ears.

I let my eyes flutter shut, surrendering to the moment. The hush of the room pressed close, the only sound the distant hum of bees in the garden. He waited, giving me space. I opened my eyes, searching his face for fear or doubt and finding only hope. His smile broke slow and sweet, like sunrise after a long storm. He pressed his forehead to mine, his breath warm on my cheek.

"Be mine," he whispered, voice rough. "Please. I can't go another day without you being mine. It would be cruel."

I didn't answer right away. I wanted to linger here, memorize the way he looked at me like I was both sunrise and shelter. I traced the shape of his jaw, the stubble catching at my fingertips, and felt my heart crack wide open.

"Okay," I said, voice trembling, but sure. "I want to choose you. Every day, if you'll let me. Not because I have to, but because I want to. Because what we make together… it's better than anything I could build alone."

He let out a shaky breath—a sound half-laugh, half-sob—and pulled me into him, wrapping his arms around my waist.

We didn't rush the kiss. It was gentle, certain, the kind of kiss that lingers at the corners of your memory long after it's over. His lips found mine, soft and sure, and I answered with everything I'd kept bottled up inside—all the longing, all the hope, all the relief of being chosen, and choosing in return.

When we finally parted, I saw the shimmer in his eyes, the quiet awe, the gratitude. We held each other there, forehead to forehead, the room gone golden around us. He laughed, pressing a kiss to my temple. "You make it easy to believe in second chances," he said.

I brushed my nose against his. "That's what homes are for."

We drifted to the old velvet sofa, still tangled up in each other. I tucked my feet beneath me, settling into the soft green cushions, and Westley stretched out beside me, his arm finding its way around my shoulders. The lamp on the side table cast a honeyed glow, the afternoon hush settling over us like a benediction.

He reached for my hand again, twining our fingers together. "I love this," he said quietly. "Not just us. The work. The building. The ordinary, everyday things."

I smiled, resting my head on his shoulder. "Me too. I think I always wanted someone to share it with, but I didn't know how to ask."

He squeezed my hand, his thumb tracing lazy circles over my skin. "You don't have to ask. Not with me."

The room was still, but it wasn't empty. It was full— of light, of memory, of everything we'd made together. We sat in that fullness for a long time, letting the weight of it settle deep in our bones. At some point, I reached for the book of poetry I'd left on the coffee table. The cover was battered, the pages soft and familiar beneath my fingers. "Read to me?" Westley's voice was softer now, almost a plea.

I opened to the page I knew by heart and began, my voice low and steady, each line another page in the story we were writing. He closed his eyes, listening—not just to the words, but to me, to the hush of the room, to the song of our summer—and  as the last morning light burned into something brighter, I knew with a quiet certainty: I hadn't just found a partner. I'd found my match. Someone to build with, to rest with, to begin again.

The house breathed around us, new and old all at once, and I let myself believe—for just a moment—that we could stay here forever, side by side, building something true.

------------------------

The drive into town felt different with Westley's hand on the wheel and the July sun pouring through the windshield. My legs were bare, feet kicked up onto the dash, the old truck humming beneath us as the world ripened on either side of the road. I fanned myself with the Sundrop's paper menu from last week, already wilting in the heat.

Westley reached across the seat, his palm sliding up my thigh, thumb drawing slow, lazy circles over my sun-warmed skin. It was a gesture so casual, so familiar already, but my heart kicked up anyway. The citrus groves blurred by, all green and gold, the scent of summer thick in the air. He rolled the window down and the wind tangled my hair, wild as laughter. Every so often, our knees bumped, and I let my hand settle on his, fingers tracing the line of his knuckles, memorizing the way our lives fit together.

He squeezed my thigh gently at a stoplight, shooting me a sidelong look that was all affection and promise. I felt lit up from the inside—a different kind of warmth than the sun, deeper, steadier. There was a song on the radio, something old and crooning, and Westley started humming along under his breath, tapping the beat against my skin.

We didn't need to say much. The road unwound beneath us, the windows open, his hand never straying far. It was a new kind of quiet—not the hush of waiting or the ache of absence, but the contentment that comes from knowing you are seen, chosen, and wanted, right here, right now.

By the time we turned down Main Street, my cheeks hurt from smiling and my skin was tingling with the leftover imprint of his touch. I wanted to bottle the feeling, keep it tucked in my pocket for the hard days. I glanced over at him—hair mussed by the wind, sunglasses sliding down his nose, looking for all the world like a man who'd just stepped into a life he never thought he'd get to keep.

"Don't look at me like that," he said, voice low, half-laughing.

"Like what?"

"Like I'm your whole world."

I grinned, unashamed. "You are, a little."

He shook his head, smiling, the lines at the corners of his eyes deepening. "You're trouble."

The truck rattled to a stop in front of The Sundrop, dust settling in the late afternoon sun. Westley hopped out, came around to open my door, and when I stepped down, his hand lingered a half-second longer on my waist than it might have before. No one watching would have noticed—but I felt it in my bones.

Inside, the bar was cool and busy, laughter rolling through the air. Joani was behind the bar, stacking glasses. River leaned against the counter, twirling a straw in his drink.

When we walked in together, hand in hand, River groaned theatrically and slapped a crumpled twenty into Joani's waiting palm.

"Told you," she said, grinning like a fox in a hen house.

Westley rolled his eyes, but the corner of his mouth betrayed a smile. I slid onto the barstool next to him, close enough our knees brushed beneath the counter. No one commented; there was nothing overt about it, just an easy togetherness, like a song settling into its refrain.

Joani slid a lemonade across to me, basil leaves floating on top. "You're glowing, sugar," she said, but it was more observation than tease.

I ducked my head, feeling Westley's hand brush the small of my back, grounding me. "It's the Florida humidity," I managed.

River leaned in, eyebrows raised. "The A/C's been working for once. Can't blame the weather for that look."

Westley grinned, half-shrugging. "She's always glowed. Y'all just never noticed."

Joani raised an eyebrow at that, her gaze flicking between us. "Maybe we notice more than you think."

River, already halfway through his sandwich, leaned on one elbow and gave us both a long look. "So what did it? The sink? The storm? The Fourth of July kiss heard 'round the county?"

I rolled my eyes. "We've been working on the house."

"And each other," Joani added with a wicked grin, delivering two heaping sandwiches on sourdough, thick with bacon and tomato.

Westley cleared his throat. "We're taking things slow."

River snorted. "Right. Just like I take whiskey neat—slow and restrained."

Joani slapped the counter with a laugh. "Leave them alone, Riv. Look at them. They're all gooey and ridiculous."

"I'm not gooey," Westley muttered into his sandwich.

A basket of kettle chips appeared in front of us, and Westley swiped one, popping it in his mouth like it was his right. I rolled my eyes, nudging him with my shoulder, and he nudged me right back, the sort of gentle ribbing that spoke of shared history and new tenderness.

Conversation swirled around us—River's complaints about the heat, Joani's story about a couple who'd danced barefoot on the bar the night before, plans for the coming week. I found myself listening with one ear, the other half of me tuned to the warmth of Westley's thigh pressed against mine, the little looks we exchanged—soft, startled sometimes, like we still couldn't believe our luck.

At one point, Joani leaned in, dropping her voice so only I could hear. "You know, it's a rare thing when love makes folks more themselves, not less. Don't lose that, honey."

Her words landed somewhere deep. I squeezed her hand, grateful.

Westley returned from talking with River at the bar, brushing his arm against mine as he sat. The energy between us felt quiet but alive—no grand declarations, just the way his smile curved softer when he looked at me, the way my laughter found its ease in the space he made.

We finished our drinks and Westley insisted on paying. Joani tried to argue, but he slid a card across the counter with a look that said *don't push me*. When we stepped out into the late golden sun, it felt like stepping into the rest of our lives—not different to anyone else, but everything had shifted for us.

Once in the cab, the quiet fell over us again, but it wasn't empty. He rested his hand on my knee, thumb tracing idle circles, his gaze fixed on the road but his smile soft as dusk.

I leaned back, feeling the heat of the day still radiating off my skin, letting my hand drift over his.

"We're different now," I said quietly.

He squeezed my knee, glancing over with a look that said he knew exactly what I meant. "Yeah. But I like it."

And in that ordinary truck, on that ordinary drive home, it felt like we had begun something that belonged to us alone—visible to anyone who cared to look, but real in all the ways that mattered most.

Outside the window, the sky was wide and cloudless, summer spilling ahead of us like a road with no end. I let my head fall back against the seat and thought of all the mornings still to come—the porch light burning late, the smell of bread in the oven, the echo of Westley's laughter down the hall. I didn't know what the next season would bring. But I was ready to find out.

I reached for his hand, and he laced our fingers together, steady as sunlight.

Chapter Nineteen

The morning broke heavy and low, the sky a bruised, shifting slate pressed down on the grove. The sun hid behind dense clouds, its gold snuffed out to a thin, blue-grey wash. It was the kind of light that made the colors of summer go muddy; leaves dulled to olive, the bark of the old oaks streaked with silver, even the orange blossoms paling to a ghostly white. Everything looked dimmed, underwater, like the world was quietly drowning.

Even the air tasted different. Instead of sweetness, there was the faint, metallic tang of ozone and the wight of something sour and unfinished, like a summer fruit gone just past ripe. The usual hum of bees was stilled; even the chicken kept to the barn, restless and fussing over nothing, their feathers fluffed up in the muggy air. Somewhere in the field, Moo-donna's lowing was plaintive, sharp and uncertain. It sounded less like a greeting and more like a warning, as if she, too, felt the press of the sky.

The house held a kind of silence like the hush before a downpour, the kind of silence that warns you to listen closely. My coffee tasted bitter, no matter how much cream I stirred in. I tried to busy myself with small, familiar things. I checked on the jars of honey cooling in the pantry, folded a basket of linens I'd washed yesterday, watered the porch plants even as the sky threatened rain. But the weight in my chest wouldn't lift.

The kitchen felt cavernous, too quiet. I found myself glancing over my shoulder, unsettled by the click and whir of the old fridge, the scrape of tree branches against the tin roof. The radio on the counter played a voice slow and syrupy, but instead of filling the space, it seemed to seep into the walls and linger in the corners, too low and mournful to lift the mood.

I filled a basket with towels and took them out to the porch, telling myself I'd hang them before the rain came. But outside, the light was wrong—grey and shifting, with the wind tugging at the hem of my skirt. The towels hung limp, colorless, as if they too were holding their breath. The air pressed in around me, dense and unmoving. I wiped sweat from my brow and squinted at the horizon, where the sky rippled with shades of blue and violet, thunderheads building, swallowing the sun.

That was when I saw it. On the top step, where I'd almost set my bare foot—another gardenia, limp and brown at the edges, petals wrinkled and dark as old paper. The stem was snapped, oozing sap onto the wood. There was no note this time, just the bloom itself, dropped or left behind, an offering gone to rot. The perfume rose as I crouched beside it—overripe, cloying, with an undertone of mold. I felt my lip curl. It was nothing like the bouquets at the beginning. There was no beauty left to pretend at tenderness, just this: a flower past saving, collapsing in on itself, the ghost of what it once was.

Halfway through sweeping the carriage house steps, I saw it—another gardenia, limp and brown at the edges, petals shriveled as if they'd been pressed beneath a boot. There was no note this time, only the wilting bloom resting against the rail, its scent gone sour, more rot than perfume. I didn't have to wonder: Luca. Always finding ways to slip through cracks, to remind me that unfinished things can fester if left alone.

I crouched, gathering the wilted flower in my hand. Its petals left a dark stain on my palm, sticky with decay. I thought of the first bouquet—lush, showy, almost beautiful. Now, all that was left was this: a warning, a memory gone wrong.

A shudder went through me. I picked it up with two fingers, careful not to let the sticky petals brush my skin, and for a moment just held it there, letting the rot seep into the moment. I could feel a prickle of dread, an old echo deep in my chest—the knowledge that some things don't simply end, they linger. They haunt. Luca. Always finding a way to slip through the cracks.

Joani texted—*You good out there?*—and I replied without thinking, *All's well, just tired*, the lie quick and easy. My thumb hovered over the keys. I almost said more, almost told her about the flower, the feeling. But I let it go. I wasn't sure if the denial was for her sake or my own.

A gust of wind rattled the porch screen, carrying the scent of sour earth and wet bark. The orange trees beyond the yard swayed and whispered, their green dulled to pewter in the storm light. Like the one before, I tossed the wilted gardenia into the compost bucket with a flick of my wrist, watched it tumble into the peelings and shells, already half-dissolving, claimed by the earth.

For a moment, I lingered there, fingers tight around the edge of the bucket. It was such a small thing, watching rot return to soil—but I felt it like a lesson I'd been waiting my whole life to learn. Maybe this was what healing looked like, quiet and unglamorous: not erasing what had been spoiled, but letting it sink down, break apart, and feed something better. I pressed my palm to the porch rail, grounding myself in the solid grain of it. Beneath the storm-heavy air and the hollow of my ribs, I swore I could almost feel the house agreeing with me—its old bones steady, its silence not empty, but listening.

Inside, I moved through the house like a ghost in my own skin. The clock ticked too loudly. My steps felt muffled, every sound warped by the storm's threat. The light coming through the windows was sickly and my own reflection in the glass startled me—a pale shape, eyes ringed with shadow.

I made the bed, straightened the kitchen, refolded the towels I'd just hung, but each task left me more unmoored. The air was so thick I could feel it pressing against my lungs, a kind of humidity that made breathing an effort. Even the house felt different; rooms darker, corners deeper, doors creaking and sighing as if the walls themselves remembered something I did not.

Every so often I caught myself listening, straining for a voice that wasn't there, a footstep on the path, a laugh cut short. I thought about calling Westley, but the urge made me angry, suddenly—resentful that I still felt small sometimes, that I wanted rescue when I'd come so far on my own. Instead, I shut the windows, cranked up the radio, and tried to lose myself in the rhythm of work. The storm was coming, but I told myself I was ready. I'd survived worse. Hadn't I?

By mid-morning, thunder was rolling in earnest, echoing over the groves and rattling the old glass. The animals huddled in the barn, even the birds silent. My heart tripped in my chest with every distant crash. I pressed my palm to the window, feeling the cool glass, watching as the sky turned from blue to bruised violet, clouds boiling overhead. All the warmth had gone out of the world, leaving only this—suspense, uncertainty, the knowledge that something was moving closer, unseen.

I told myself it was only a storm, but I knew better. Some storms begin long before the rain. Some start in the pit of your own stomach and don't break until the sky does.

All day, a restlessness haunted me. Shadows seemed longer. The light itself felt uneasy, sliding through the clouds in odd, slanted ways. Every chore I finished left another undone, every attempt at peace interrupted by a flicker at the edge of my vision—a memory, maybe, or just the sense that something was coming. And so I waited, house sealed and silent, heart beating too loud in the hush.

The light never changed. Clouds pressed low over the grove, swallowing the hours until everything bled together: morning, noon, and the long, bruised stretch toward night.

The rain still hadn't started, but I could feel it gathering—thickening the air, weighing down every living thing. I moved from room to room, windows closed, lights on, as if I could ward off the dark by force of will.

I kept myself busy because the alternative—sitting still—felt impossible. I kneaded bread dough until my arms ached, the sticky flour clinging to my wrists, the air heavy with yeast and worry. I set it to rise and washed my hands in water that never quite warmed. I checked locks, tightened the bolt on the side door, swept the kitchen floor again though it was already spotless.

Outside, the wind rattled the magnolia leaves, their broad faces slick with dew, and the chickens made uneasy noises in the barn. It was the kind of day that made you believe in omens. When I stepped onto the porch for air, the world felt thick and colorless—cicadas silent, even the distant road gone quiet. My hair clung damp to my neck. My skin prickled.

I tried to remind myself of all the ways I'd made this place mine. I opened the linen closet and breathed in the scent of lavender sachets, felt the cool cotton on my fingertips, tried to root myself in the comfort I'd built here. But even the familiar was off kilter; the sheets felt damp, the air sour. I made tea I didn't want and stood by the window with the mug warming my palms, watching the trees writhe in the wind. The citrus grove—usually a tangle of green and gold—had turned sullen, all hard shadows and shifting leaves. The barn doors banged in the gusts. Farther out, the grove's edge blurred into the oncoming dusk, trees bending and shuddering, the grass pressed flat by the air's invisible hand.

I set my tea down untouched and moved through the rooms again, closing curtains, checking the doors. I turned on the radio and then turned it off—the static too sharp, the music too sad. Each time I tried to settle, I found myself rising again, unable to keep still.

The sky had deepened to a shade of blue-black; lightning flickered soundlessly at the horizon, and every so often thunder rolled across the groves, making the windows tremble. I kept thinking about that gardenia, how it had stained my palm, how the rot had clung to my skin even after I'd scrubbed it away. I imagined the scent still lingering in the rooms, curling around corners, haunting the air.

A memory surfaced—my mother closing all the blinds, moving methodically from window to window, her lips pressed tight, refusing to say what she feared. I'd always wondered if I'd inherited that anxiety, the way it built and built until you were sure something would break, even if nothing ever did.

The shadows grew. I moved through the house lighting lamps, candles—anything to keep the dark at bay. I told myself it was just the storm, that I was being silly, but I still paused at every sound, every gust against the glass. When the clock in the kitchen struck six, I jumped, heart hammering, hand pressed to my chest as if to steady the beat.

I made a simple dinner and ate half of it standing at the counter, staring into the gloom outside, appetite gone. I left the dishes in the sink, hands trembling. The wind rose and fell in long, eerie sighs. Branches clawed at the windows. Every noise felt amplified, warped, as if the house itself was straining to listen. I wished I'd asked Westley to come by. I wished I didn't need anyone.

I checked my phone again—no new messages. No headlights winding up the drive, no boots at the door. Just me, and the hush, and the mounting pressure that said something was coming.

I tried to read but couldn't focus on the words. I wanted to be strong, to prove I'd outgrown the old fears, but as the last light died, and the wind pressed up against the house with a strange, insistent hand, I felt that old, familiar thrum beneath my ribs. My heart beat loud—too loud. The storm was here, but something else was coming with it.

I sat by the window and waited, counting the seconds between flashes of lightning, measuring my own breath. The world had narrowed to shadows and sound, and the unspoken certainty that the worst things don't always arrive with thunder—they slip in, silent, when you're most tired, most alone.

And so, I waited, lamps burning, heart tight, knowing the night was far from over.

When the knock came, I didn't move at first. I held my breath and listened again. My heart hammered against my ribs—loud, insistent, like a bell tolling through my body. Each beat felt impossibly heavy, reverberating through my throat, drowning out every other sound.

*The dead bell, the dead bell. Somebody's done for.*

The phrase drifted up from nowhere, chilling in its finality. I wasn't sure if it belonged to a poem or a nightmare, only that it belonged to endings, to the sound a life makes when it's about to change. I pressed my palm to my chest, as if I could quiet the bell, steady the trembling. But the echo wouldn't fade.

A shadow moved outside. I saw it through the glass: a shape, tall, too familiar. For a heartbeat I hoped it was Westley, but the hope died quickly. Luca. I could feel it before I saw his face—a chill that settled into my bones.

He knocked again. Harder this time. I wanted to run, but my feet wouldn't move. My childhood returned in a rush—every moment I'd learned to freeze, to shrink, to hope that if I just made myself small enough, invisible enough, the bad thing would pass me by.

I edged toward the door, more out of old habit than courage, and peered through the glass. The porch light caught Luca's face, washed pale and unfamiliar. His smile was tight, a practiced thing—a smile that might have once seemed charming, now stretched thin and strange under the yellow bulb. His eyes scanned the doorframe, searching for a weakness.

I hesitated, instinct screaming at me to lock the door and turn away, but the old fear of being rude, of inviting trouble by acknowledging it, kept me rooted.

I opened it.

"What are you doing here?"

He tried for lightness, but it faltered, slipped into something sour. "Couldn't sleep. Figured you wouldn't be either—not after the way we left things. You haven't answered my texts. No thank you for the flowers." He leaned closer, his voice dropping as if we shared a secret. "That hurt, Mina."

His presence filled the entry like a cold draft. I gripped the edge of the door, suddenly aware of the dampness gathering at the back of my neck. "I asked you to stop, Luca. We're done. I want to move on."

He looked past me, eyes searching the dim hall as though expecting to find evidence of someone else. His voice shifted, too smooth. "It doesn't have to end like this. I'm willing to forgive—whatever this is. We can start over, if you'll just talk to me."

I shook my head, stepping back. "Luca, you're starting to scare me. I'd like you to leave."

He stepped forward—just one step, but it brought him into the doorframe, and I backed up without meaning to. He took that as permission. Suddenly he was inside.

His face twisted—hurt, then something colder. "Why are you making this so hard?" he said, voice thick with disbelief. "You're acting hysterical. Do you know that? This whole thing—you're blowing it way out of proportion."

The air behind him felt charged, the night rolling in on a breeze that raised goosebumps along my arms. My voice came out smaller than I intended, but I stood my ground. "I don't want to talk. I want you to go."

"There it is," he muttered. "The real you. Playing innocent. But I know what you are. You led me on. And now you want to cry victim—"

He reached for me then, and before I could stop myself, I let him catch my wrist. His grip was strong, not quite painful, but the heat of it sent a shudder through me—a memory, old as childhood, of being trapped, of voices so loud it filled my ears and hands that didn't let go.

I tried to pull away, panic rising in my throat, but he only held on tighter, eyes wide with expectation, as if waiting for me to fall back into the role he'd cast for me—a role I no longer wanted, never really had.

The room shrank to the span of his arm, the shape of my fear. I tasted metal on my tongue, sweat cooling in cold patches at the base of my neck. For a moment, I remembered—not a scene, not a word, but a sensation; a child again, the press of fear, the certainty that no one would come, a flicker of wild, impossible hope: maybe this time, someone would.

But then the screen door crashed open behind him, the sound splitting the night like thunder. Westley stepped into the frame, shoulders squared, a weight in his gaze—assessing, protective, furious, and steady all at once.  Luca whirled, startled. "This is private—"

"No, it's not," Westley said, his voice deep, controlled. "You're done here." He didn't say my name, not at first, but I heard it in the way his gaze fixed on my wrist, the tremor in my body, the silent plea in my eyes. "Mina," he said gently. "Come here."

I moved like I was underwater, heart thudding, skin still prickled and damp. The spell breaking the second I passed Luca, my shoulder brushing his—my skin crawled at the contact. Westley reached for me, but didn't pull, just waited, open and steady, the way you might wait for a frightened child to decide if she's safe. I stepped into his arms and exhaled, the breath wracking out of me in a sob I hadn't meant to release. I let myself lean into the steadiness of him, the safety.

Behind us, Luca scoffed, his mask slipping into a sneer. "Of course."

Westley jaw tightened. "Leave. Now."

Luca lingered, pride wounded, but he left. He had to. Someone like him always does when they realize they've lost their grip. The door slammed shut behind him, punctuation on everything that had come before. I flinched at the sound, but it was over. He was gone.

I stood trembling and Westley caught me before I could collapse. His arms wrapped around me, solid and unyielding. He didn't speak; just held me, safe. The sweat on my skin cooled in the warmth of his chest. I pressed my face to his shirt and breathed, heart slowing, the storm outside at last giving way to the quiet between us. After a moment, he lifted me effortlessly off the floor.

"Let's get you upstairs," he murmured. I rested my head against his chest, breathing in the steady beat of his heart as he carried me up the stairs to my bedroom in the loft. The way he held me was like he was trying to ground both of us. His heartbeat slow and steady against my cheek, his voice low in my ear, murmuring something I couldn't quite hold onto. A lullaby I never got as a child. For the first time, I let myself believe I could be soother—could be kept. It didn't erase the ache, but it softened the sharpest edges, enough to let the sleep come.

I must have drifted off in the tangle of his warmth, then turned restless. I startled awake more times than I could count, heart pounding, throat raw, breath shallow, the whisper of my name in his voice calling me back. "Mina," soft, urgent. "It's just a dream."

His fingers rubbed slow circles on my skin, pulling me back from the edge. Sometimes he kissed the top of my head—a small gesture that carried more tenderness than words ever could. He stayed awake when I couldn't, a silent sentinel against the dark.

I couldn't speak. Couldn't even open my eyes. I only knew the tightness in my chest, and the sensation of something slipping through my fingers. Maybe control. Maybe the mask I'd worn since childhood. Maybe both.

In those quiet hours, I realized how different he was from Luca. Where Luca's presence had been storm and heat, Westley was calm, steady—roots deep in the earth. I let myself lean into that steadiness, even when my mind fought to pull me away. And slowly, very slowly, the nightmares faded, until finally, dawn slipped through the window, pale and hopeful.

The sun was already pouring in when I woke, blinking against the soft light and the surprising weight of Westley's flannel shirt draped over me like a blanket. For a moment, I lay perfectly still, letting the morning filter in—the distant call of birds, the slow churn of the ceiling fan, the ache behind my eyes where tears had dried. The scent of laundry soap and something steadier clung to me, a hush in my chest where last night's fear had been.

Westley sat in the armchair in the corner, one foot tucked under the other, elbows on his knees. He watched me quietly, as if I might startle, hands folded together to keep from reaching for me too soon. He didn't speak right away. Just passed me a glass of water, his fingers careful, and waited as I sat up, still a little fuzzy, the heaviness of the night lingering at the edge of my awareness.

"I got rid of everything," he said finally, his voice gentle but careful. "The flowers. The notes." He glanced at his hands, then back at me. "Not because of pride or anything like that. I just… I didn't want you to wake up and see it."

"Oh," I whispered, curling my knees to my chest, the glass cool in my palms. "Thank you."

He nodded, his gaze never wavering. "You were crying in your sleep." My throat caught, tears prickling again before I could swallow them down. "I didn't know what to do," he admitted quietly. "I can fix a cabinet door or a busted sink or a wasp nest under the porch. But not that. I didn't know how to fix that."

I blinked hard, trying to steady my breathing. Then I looked at him fully, at the worry etched into the lines around his eyes, the patience in his silence, and something in me finally—finally—unclenched. "You stayed," I said, voice barely above a whisper.

His eyes met mine, steady as always. "Of course I did."

## Chapter Twenty

The days after the storm passed in a hush, the house and
grove still holding their breath. For the first time in weeks, I
woke with sunlight in my hair and the promise of a new
season on the air, not the taste of fear. Yet even in the gentler
quiet, I carried a watchfulness with me—like some part of my
body was still waiting for the next shadow, the next sound
out of place.

It was a Tuesday, ordinary and bright. I padded
barefoot through the kitchen, feeling the cool tile soothe the
ache in my arches. The window above the sink was open,
letting in a thin line of breeze that carried the scent of citrus
blossom and cut grass. Somewhere out in the grove, I heard
the distant crow of a rooster—confident, insistent, as if the
world might start again if he simply declared it enough times.

I filled the kettle, the familiar click and whoosh of gas
settling my nerves in ways I couldn't quite name. The
comfort of small rituals: tea bags lined up on the counter,
sugar spoon glinting in the bowl, a single cracked mug waiting
for my hands. I ran a thumb over the faded pattern—blue
cornflowers, chipped at the rim—and felt the odd, anchoring
pride of having survived another day.

The house itself seemed to have softened. Where
once there was only the tense hum of what might break, now
there was a warmth—shadows grown gentler, corners filling
with the low, golden hush of morning. I found Westley in the

front hall of the main house, kneeling at the baseboard with a pry bar, sleeves rolled, the muscles in his forearms jumping with each careful movement.

He didn't look up at first, lost in the rhythm of sanding and scraping, as if coaxing the house back to life inch by stubborn inch. I watched him for a long moment, letting the sight of him work its way under my skin—his steadiness, the patience in his hands, the way he worked quietly but never alone. Not anymore.

I cleared my throat, voice tentative. "You missed a spot."

He glanced back over his shoulder, grinning. "You offering to supervise or help?"

I knelt beside him, jeans catching at the worn floorboards. "I'll let you decide."

We fell into the kind of partnership that needed no instruction. I handed him the sandpaper when his fingers cramped, brushed away the dust before he needed to ask, and found the right size nail in the tray without being told. For a while we worked in silence, the good kind—full, companionable, as honest as touch.

A shaft of sunlight caught in the curls at his temple, and I reached to brush a stray lock back, my thumb grazing the soft place just above his ear. He closed his eyes at the touch, a small sound escaping him, half-laugh, half-sigh. I felt the warmth of his trust settle deep in my chest.

We didn't talk about Luca. We didn't need to. There was no more rot in the corners, no unwelcome blooms to cast a shadow. I thought of the gardenia, the last one, and how I'd dropped it into the compost and watched it disappear. Maybe that was what this was—the quiet undoing of something that had once held me in its grip. Not an erasure, but a burial.

I brushed my fingers over the floorboards Westley had sanded smooth and imagined the house breathing easier because of it, as though it, too, understood what it meant to be remade. The air smelled of sawdust and citrus, and I didn't flinch from the stillness. I stood there, palms flat against the wall, and let the hush settle in my chest like a promise: nothing was rotting here anymore. Not even me. The only thing between us was the work, and the pleasure of it—the ordinary, sacred joy of making something whole with your own hands.

I lost track of time, measuring the hours not by the clock but by the progress we made: a baseboard smoothed, a crack filled, a patch of paint left to dry. The sun shifted higher, warming the boards beneath my knees. A fly buzzed at the window, the only interruption in the slow, golden drift of the morning.

At some point, Westley paused and looked at me, his eyes clear, open, full of something I didn't have to name. "You sleep at all last night?"

I shrugged, tracing a swirl of wood grain with my thumb. "Some. Enough."

269

His hand found my knee, squeezing gently. "If you want to talk—about anything. You know I'm here, right?"

I nodded, the words sticking behind my teeth. "I know." I meant it. For once, the truth of it didn't make me flinch.

We worked until the dust motes floated thick in the slant of light, until my arms ached with honest use and my breath came easier. Westley put away his tools, and I followed him out to the porch, blinking in the sudden brightness.

He settled beside me on the steps, stretching his legs out, hands folded behind his head. I tucked my knees to my chest, letting the late-morning sun warm my skin. For a while, we just watched the yard together—the bees tracing lazy lines through the clover, a stray cat prowling along the fence, the orange trees shimmering in the heat.

There was peace in the stillness, a new kind of hush. I let myself lean into it, shoulder bumping his. He didn't move away, just turned his head and smiled, the kind of smile that said I see you, whole and unhidden.

Inside, the kitchen clock chimed the hour, and I felt the rhythm of my life start to stitch itself back together. I thought about all the places I'd tried to run from—houses and cities and old hurts—and how none of them had ever felt like this: not perfect, not painless, but possible.

Westley nudged me with his knee. "Hungry?"

I nodded, the simple need feeling good, uncomplicated. We went back inside, moving easily around each other as we fixed breakfast: eggs cracked into a skillet, bread slid into the toaster, the small comfort of food shared between two people with paint under their nails and hope in their bellies.

I watched him for a moment, the way he buttered his toast, the way he poured his coffee and set the mug down exactly where I'd always left it, as if he'd been doing this all his life. I felt the old loneliness lift, just a little, replaced by something lighter—like opening a window after a long rain.

The house felt fuller, my own skin less strange. I sipped my tea, savoring the taste, the heat, the quiet, and thought: This is what coming home feels like.

The afternoon sun climbed higher, scattering coins of light across the kitchen floor. I'd just finished washing the breakfast plates when I heard the screen door slap and Joani's voice drifting in before her—bold, unhurried, full of that unbothered confidence I'd always envied.

"You got anything stronger than coffee, sugar?" she called, toeing off her sandals and letting them clatter on the tile. A breeze trailed behind her, citrus-bright, carrying the promise of mischief and company.

I grinned despite myself. "It's barely noon."

She waved a hand, sliding into a seat at the table. "Honey, I'm not here to drink. Just came to check on my favorite troublemaker." Her gaze swept over me, assessing, sharp as a paring knife but just as useful.

I poured us both iced tea and set the glasses between us, the sweat beading on the sides. For a moment we sat in companionable silence, the kind I was only just learning to value—the silence of women who know what it means to wait out storms, who've patched more than their share of holes in leaky roofs and stubborn hearts.

Joani sipped her tea, then set the glass aside with a soft clink. "You doing all right?"

It wasn't small talk. There was nothing casual about the way she watched me, elbows planted, chin resting in her palm. She waited—not for performance, but for honesty. I hesitated, tracing a ring of condensation on the counter. "Getting there," I admitted. "Some days are easier than others."

She nodded, her eyes warm. "That's the thing nobody tells you about starting over—it's not one decision. It's a thousand tiny ones. Every day you wake up and choose to keep going. Even on the days you'd rather crawl back under the covers and let the world spin on without you."

I swallowed, letting her words settle, grounding me in the comfort of her matter-of-fact wisdom.

Joani leaned forward, voice dropping. "You know what I see, Mina? I see someone who stopped waiting for a knight or a miracle and started building her own rescue. I see a girl who came here broken but didn't stay that way. You're not who you were when you walked through that door."

My throat tightened, a mixture of pride and old grief welling up. "Some days I still feel like a mess."

She smiled, soft but unyielding. "You're supposed to. Life isn't about being tidy, sweetheart. It's about learning to love the mess you are and making a place where you can rest without shame."

Her hand covered mine, warm and sure. "Don't you forget—no one gets through this world unscarred. But scars are proof you healed, not that you failed."

We sat with that for a while, the light shifting across the floor, time stretching in that easy way it does with true friends. Joani told a story about a summer she'd spent chasing dreams in a city that never cared to keep her, about the heartbreak that sent her running back to Citrus Grove, about the ways you make peace with the world by making peace with yourself.

Her words were a balm, and a challenge—gentle, yes, but also a reminder that there was no shortcut through becoming. No magic cure for loneliness, no single victory that made you whole. Only days and days of choosing, and the steady hands of those who loved you through the process.

Eventually she rose, smoothing her skirt, glasses glinting as she peered down at me. "Come by The Sundrop tonight. There's talk of a little gathering. It's time you let folks celebrate you for a change."

I shook my head, embarrassed, but she only winked. "Let yourself belong, Mina. Sometimes that's the bravest thing you can do."

She left with the same easy grace she'd arrived, her laughter trailing through the kitchen like the scent of orange blossoms in spring—sweet, fleeting, but impossible to forget.

After she was gone, I poured myself another glass of tea and sat with the silence, letting her words echo in the spaces I'd once filled with doubt. I looked around the house—at the way the light had found its way into every corner, at the faint scuffs on the floorboards and the clean lines of the windowsills Westley had repaired. For the first time, I let myself imagine staying, truly staying. Not as a visitor, or a guest in someone else's story, but as a woman who had made a life she could claim as her own.

And in that moment, with the sun dappling the table and the taste of mint and lemon on my tongue, I felt the first real flutter of belonging take root. Not just to the house, or the town, or even to Westley—but to myself.

***

The late afternoon settled over the grove like a prayer. Shadows stretched long and cool beneath the trees, cicadas humming their slow benediction. I was rinsing paint from my hands, halfway listening to the clatter of Westley working in the entryway, when the first car eased down the drive—then another, and another, a line of vehicles trailing dust and sunlight in their wake.

At first, I thought it might be a mistake—a neighbor come to borrow sugar, a delivery truck turning around. But then the doors swung open, and people began to spill out: arms full, voices rising in greeting, laughter bubbling up so unexpectedly that it nearly knocked the breath from my chest.

It felt like the opening notes of a hymn. One by one, they made their way up the gravel path—Joani in the lead, a vision of retro grace in her cherry red lipstick and sun-bright dress, wielding a massive mason jar in one hand and a casserole dish in the other, her stride both queenly and familiar.

Behind her came River, grinning wide, a battered cooler slung from one arm and a box of old records balanced on his shoulder. There was Mrs. Castillo, from the bakery, bearing a tray of sticky buns still warm from her oven. Mr. Lane with a crate of tools, two kids in tow. Families I barely knew, faces I'd seen only from a distance at the market, even the old men who gathered in the corner of The Sundrop to play dominoes and argue about the weather.

The line wound its way up the drive, a slow and joyous procession, every hand full—paint cans, spare wood, garden gloves, pies, and folding chairs. The hum of their voices rose like a chorus, and for a moment I just stood at the door, unable to move, heart thudding with the wild certainty that I was witnessing a kind of miracle.

Westley came to stand beside me, saw the stunned look on my face, and burst out laughing—a real, helpless sound. He threw up his hands in mock surrender, looking back at the crowd. "Don't look at me! I didn't do this. I swear!"

Joani, already halfway up the steps, called over her shoulder, "That's right! This is all me. No one does anything alone in Citrus Grove, especially not on my watch." She beamed at me, the kind of smile that gathers people in like arms.

It was almost too much—the generosity, the effortless way they just arrived, expecting nothing, asking nothing, simply there to give. The air was thick with the scent of fresh bread, sawdust, cut grass, and the faint tang of sun-warmed orange peel. I felt tears prick my eyes, and Joani noticed. She handed me the mason jar—her own homemade "sacrament," sweet tea laced with bourbon and mint, cold and strong enough to make you believe in the goodness of people.

"Drink, honey," she said, her tone gentle for once. "It's tradition."

We moved as one into the heart of the house. Tools were laid out on the porch, casseroles lined the kitchen counter, records spun on the old player Westley had set up near the window. There was laughter, instructions barked good-naturedly, children running through the hallways like they belonged there. Every room filled up with voices, stories, the easy shuffle of feet and the sound of wood being planed, glass polished, curtains pinned and rehung.

Someone started hauling debris from the back porch, and soon a bonfire bloomed in the yard—at first for the scraps and cast-offs, then, as dusk fell and the work slowed, for warmth and gathering. String lights were draped from the porch to the old oaks, a canopy of gold beneath the indigo sky.

When the sun dipped, everyone circled the fire— some in lawn chairs, others sprawled on blankets, red solo cups and mason jars passing from hand to hand. Joani poured her "communion" for all who would take it, telling stories that made the kids blush and the adults roar with laughter. River produced a battered guitar and plucked out old country songs, voices rising in ragged harmony, the kind that only comes at the end of a day spent building something together.

I sat cross-legged at the edge of the circle, feet bare in the cool grass, bonfire light flickering up my shins. I watched the faces around me, each one aglow—paint-streaked, sweat- damp, tired, and impossibly alive. They passed food, clapped hands, argued over the best way to hang a cabinet door. I realized, with a kind of awe, that I had never felt so included, so wholly present, in any place before. Not because I'd earned it, not because I'd done anything to deserve it, but because I'd shown up, and that, in Citrus Grove, was enough.

For a little while, the house behind us glowed with the light of a hundred small kindnesses, every corner a little brighter for the work of so many hands. The bonfire snapped and sang, sparks rising to join the stars. And the song—sweet, off-key, full of joy—stretched from one edge of the grove to the other, like a blanket of night, tucking us all safely in.

When the last embers of the bonfire collapsed into ash and the laughter faded to a soft undercurrent, the yard emptied out by degrees. Voices drifted to cars, screen doors thumped, and porch lights winked out across the grove. The house was full but no longer loud—just the hush that lingers after something holy, the slow return of breath and quiet.

I slipped onto the porch steps, knees drawn to my chest, the wood still warm beneath me. The night was velvet-dark, cicadas a steady thrum in the distance, fireflies rising from the grass in silent bursts. My hands were rough from cleaning, my hair smelling of woodsmoke and orange blossom; I felt the exhaustion of joy rather than loneliness. The ache in my muscles was proof of a day spent among people who showed up because they could—because that was the only reason anyone needed.

Westley joined me without a word, settling beside me with a long sigh. He stretched his legs out, boots scuffed, palms splayed on the step between us. His shirt was damp at the collar, a smear of white paint still on his forearm. I watched him, watched the easy way he tilted his head back to look at the sky, the slow curve of a smile at the corners of his mouth.

We didn't speak for a long while. The night felt too wide for words. Everything important had already been said in a hundred small gestures: a pie left on the counter, a chair sanded smooth, a curtain straightened and knotted to let in more light. Love, I thought, didn't always announce itself. Sometimes it just filled the space you left empty.

After a time, Westley reached over and took my hand, his fingers threading through mine, warm and sure. His thumb traced the back of my hand in slow circles, grounding me, reminding me this was real.

I leaned my head on his shoulder, watching the fireflies blink across the yard, feeling the steadiness of his breath. "Did you ever think you'd have this?" I whispered, more to the night than to him. "A place that felt like yours?"

He didn't answer right away. Just squeezed my hand, his voice quiet but certain when it came. "Not until you. Not like this."

I felt the tears slip down my cheek—soft, grateful, more release than sorrow. "I keep waiting for it to disappear. For the world to remind me I don't belong."

Westley turned, his gaze so gentle it hurt. "Mina. You belong because you're here. Because you stayed." He brushed a stray tear from my cheek with the back of his finger. "They love you because you let them."

I laughed, a watery sound, leaning into the warmth of him. "I'm learning. I don't know if I'll ever get used to it."

"Don't try," he murmured, voice thick with affection. "Just let it be good."

We sat that way until the cicadas faded and the stars wheeled overhead. The house glowed behind us, gold spilling from the kitchen windows, the music from the record player faint as memory. Everything felt possible, for once—not because I'd done anything to deserve it, but because I was willing to be here, to be held, to be seen.

Westley's arm slid around my waist, gentle but sure, anchoring me in the newness of belonging. His voice was a low rumble in my ear. "You ready?"

I tipped my face up to him, searching his eyes for any trace of doubt, and found only patience, hunger, and something that looked a lot like awe.

"Let's go," I whispered, and felt the whole night shift—stars tilting overhead, the world making room for what would come next.

Chapter Twenty-One

Outside, the heat hit us like a silk curtain—heavy but forgiving. We walked the garden path slowly, the gravel crunching beneath our feet. The overgrown lavender brushed my bare legs. A hibiscus bloom caught on the curve of his boot. When we reached the carriage house, I opened the door without hesitation, but I could feel him at my back, not crowding, just... there. His presence laced through the air like a thunderstorm waiting to break.

Inside, it smelled like tea leaves and lemon oil and something clean; us, the space we'd made. I turned and Westley shut the door behind us. He hadn't said a word, but I could feel it; the gravity between us shifting, the tension he'd swallowed all morning, the control he was barely holding. His chest rose and fell in deep, steady breaths. His eyes didn't stray. They locked on mine and stayed there and I knew.

"Come here," I said, softly.

Westley closed the space between us in two steps. His hands found my hips, big and warm and steady, like he was anchoring himself in me.

*His hands, his hands, his hands.*

I reached for him, palms smoothing over his chest, the stretch of cotton thin over the muscle beneath. He smelled like cedar and salt and something faintly citrus. Like the woods and the sea and every piece of him I was already starting to memorize. His shirt hung open just enough to catch the light on his broad chest, the thick muscles taut beneath skin kissed by years of hard work and quiet restraint. When his voice dropped to that low, rough growl, it vibrated through my ribs, deep and unyielding.

"You sure about this?"

The tremble in my breath was the only answer he needed.

His hands moved like they owned the space; one cupping my jaw, thumb tracing the hollow beneath my cheekbone, the other sliding down my back, pulling me flush against him.

*His hands, his hands, his hands.*

The solid weight of his body pressed into mine was impossible to resist; every line, every curve, commanding and protective. His jaw twitched then he bent his head, brushing his lips over mine—not a question this time, but a promise. The kiss deepened fast. His arms wrapped around me, strong and sure, like he couldn't get close enough. He kissed like he meant it, like he felt it in his bones. I broke away only long enough to whisper, "Bedroom."

He reached down and gripped the backs of my thighs, lifting me in one swift motion. I gasped as my legs wrapped instinctively around his waist, arms around his neck. His mouth found mine again, deeper this time, and I felt the growl rise from somewhere low in his throat.

"You don't have to hold back," I breathed against his lips. "I trust you."

He pressed his forehead to mine, closing his eyes, before climbing the stairs, one slow step at a time, like we had nowhere to be but here; like the whole day had been leading to this. I could feel every part of him; his strength, his heat, the way his grip flexed just slightly on my thighs, as if anchoring himself with me, the way his breath faltered when I kissed his neck, the deep hum in his chest when I whispered his name.

He set me down at the edge of the bed with aching care, but when I tugged him toward me by the collar of his shirt, all that carefulness cracked. He groaned into the next kiss, deeper now, hungry. His hands slid under my shirt, palms splayed across the small of my back, up my spine, until I felt fabric lift and his fingers brush the bare skin beneath. When he pulled the fabric up and over my head, I shivered at the cold night air mingling with the warmth of his hands exploring me like worship.

*His hands, his hands, his hands.*

He sat back just far enough to look at me; like he needed a second to absorb the sight. His lips parted slightly. His hands didn't move. "God, you're beautiful," he growled, teeth grazing my jaw as his lips burned a path down my neck. "I've been holding back for too long. You make me lose myself, Mina. I can't be careful with you anymore" His voice shook through me. The words hit somewhere deep in my chest, knocking the breath out of me.

"I've been trying to be good," he said, kneeling in front of me. His hands slid slowly up my thighs, warm and deliberate. "Take it slow. Make sure I don't scare you off. But you…" His mouth found the soft place below my ribs. I gasped. His hands curled around my hips.

*His hands, his hands, his hands.*

"You undo me," he said.

"You don't have to be good," I whispered, dragging my hands over the thick lines of his back, the curve of muscle that flexed beneath my fingers. "Not with me."

His arms wrapped around me, one hand threading into my hair, the other dragging me tight to his chest. He kissed like he worked; purposeful, focused, steady; like a man who knew what he wanted and wasn't afraid to show it. The sheer weight of him made me dizzy. Solid muscle pressed against me, his size enveloping, unyielding. I felt small in the best way—not diminished but held—caged in something safe and wild all at once.

"You're gonna be the death of me," he growled, voice deeper now—rougher, more raw.

I arched toward him, aching for the feel of his skin against mine. "I hope I'm worth it."

He leaned in close, mouth brushing my ear. "Christ, Mina, you don't even know." Then he kissed me again, slower now, but no less hungry. It was the kind of kiss that claimed. That whispered promises beneath every brush of lips and tongue. He moved over me like he'd dreamed of this for longer than he could admit; like he meant to make it last. His hands roamed, exploring without hesitation, and every touch left me gasping.

*His hands, his hands, his hands.*

Then his fingers found the waistband of my jeans. When he slid them down, the low, guttural groan he gave sent a shiver straight through my core. He settled between my thighs, and I felt him; the weight and size of him pressing hard against me, undeniable. My breath caught, sharp and sudden, and then he pulled back, just enough to meet my eyes. His thumb brushed the edge of my bottom lip, like he couldn't stop touching me. "You can take me," he said, low and rough and so sure it made my knees weak. "I'll go slow. Every inch, every second...yours."

It felt almost holy, the way he filled the quiet between us. There was no rush, no pretense, only this slow, devastating certainty that every inch of him was offered, not taken. I had never been worshiped, not like this—not by hands that steadied rather than claimed, not by a body that didn't just want but stayed. He kissed me like he was memorizing every breath, every sound, until I stopped thinking of the years I'd spent running and started believing I'd finally arrived.

*The ache of him unbearably sweet—*

*like trying to hold on to thunder.*

*My body stretched around him, breath stuttering as he eased forward—*

*devastating care; every inch was a new kind of surrender.*

*Clutching at his shoulders, nails digging in—*

*the overwhelming rightness, not of pain, but of him.*

*And God, his hands, his hands.*

*His mouth found mine again, swallowing the whimper—*

*"I know, baby. I know."*

*He groaned as he pressed deeper and*

*I didn't know where I ended and he began.*

*There was only heat and pressure, his strength braced above me,*

*arms trembling slightly,*

*eyes never leaving mine.*

*Deep, focused—*

*each thrust a confession,*

*each drag of his hips a vow.*

*Like he was giving me something more than his body—*

*something unspoken. Something whole.*

*I want you, whispered against his lips.*

*A wicked, knowing smile. "You've got me, all of me."*

*And I did.*

*Every inch, every breath, every beat of that wild, patient heart.*

*I took him in and let go of everything else;*

*the noise, the fear, the years of being too much or not enough.*

*Because with him, here, now… I was perfectly enough.*

I didn't know how long we stayed wrapped in each other—limbs tangled, breathless and shaking, hearts still thudding out matching rhythms—but eventually, I stirred. "I need a shower," I whispered against his chest, my voice rasped and raw. "I'm not sure I can walk, but I need it."

Westley chuckled, low and soft in my ear. "You go ahead," he murmured, brushing a kiss to my temple. "I'll be right behind you."

I slipped from the bed, skin still flushed, legs unsteady, and headed down the stairs on trembling feet. The night air met me again, warm and full of the scent of lemon balm and spent desire. The house was quiet, still humming from what we'd just done. I could feel it in the floorboards.

In the tiny bathroom, I turned on the water and let it heat until steam clouded the mirror, then stepped into the small, tiled shower. It was barely big enough for one, but I didn't care. The spray hit my skin, and I sighed, letting the water run down my spine, rinsing the last remnants of restraint from me.

I closed my eyes.

Then the door creaked open.

A beat of silence and then Westley's voice, warm and low and already sending shivers across my damp skin. "I tried to stay upstairs," he said. "I really did. But knowing you were down here… wet and naked and glowing like that… I couldn't stay away." He stepped in behind me, and I felt him all over again. His presence filled the space, made the steam thicker, the air heavier. My breath caught as his hands found my waist.

"Still want that shower?" he murmured, mouth brushing the shell of my ear.

"I did," I said, but it came out more like a gasp.

He reached past me for the loofah, poured a generous stream of soap into it, and began to move it over my shoulders, slow and careful. Suds slid down my back as he swept the soft mesh across my skin, his other hand following behind, smoothing over the trail of lather with his palm.

*God, his hands.*

"I like seeing you like this," he said against my neck. "All flushed and clean and mine." The word *mine* settled in my chest like a stone dropped in water—spreading ripples through every part of me. I leaned back against him, and he groaned low, his soapy hands sliding down the curve of my waist. He filled the shower behind me completely, solid and strong, his chest flush to my back, thighs bracketing mine. There was nowhere to go, nowhere to escape the slow, deliberate glide of his hands over my ribs, my belly, the inside of my thighs.

*His hands, his hands, his hands.*

"You're taking your time," I breathed.

"I told you," he said, fingers dipping lower, sliding between slick skin. "I'm gonna give you every second."


*Hands against cool tile*

*Heat circling, pressing, teasing*

*Breath fogging glass as he worked me open*

*Coaxing sounds out of me I didn't know I could make.*

*Whimpering, moaning, arching*

*"That's it, baby. Let me hear you."*

*Fingers slipping inside with exquisite, patient precision*

*Perfect, deep, pressure*

*He moved like he knew my body already;*

*like he'd mapped it out from memory.*

*"I can feel you shaking," teeth grazing my shoulder.*

*"You gonna come for me, just like this?"*

*Whimpering, eyes closing*

*Body taut and trembling.*

*"I've got you," he promised. "Always."*

*He pulled his hand away, and I made a soft sound of protest*

*But only for a second*

*Because the next moment, I felt him again, hard and thick*

*"Tell me you want this."*

*"I want it," I breathed. "God, I want you."*

*"Then take me."*

*One hand braced beside mine on the wall, the other on my hip.*

*"Let me ruin you for anyone else."*

*Pushing forward, slow, relentless*

*Knuckles white against the wall tile*

*Filling me all over again—more, somehow*

*The new angle, the slick heat, the confining space—*

*everything heightened, everything deeper.*

*"Oh my god—" I sobbed.*

*He pulled back and drove forward again—*

*a slow, devastating rhythm*

*that stole the air from my lungs.*

*His hips moved with a controlled power*

*that shuddered the whole shower.*

*"Look at you," he groaned. "bent over for me. So tight you feel like sin."*

*Hips meeting his on every thrust*

*Chasing the pressure, the edge, the high only he could bring me to.*

*Reaching forward, fingers finding me again, circling in time with each stroke.*

*I shattered.*


For a long moment, the only sound was the water and our ragged breathing. He wrapped his arms around me from behind, pulling me upright against his chest, his lips pressing soft, reverent kisses to the curve of my neck. "Glad I didn't stay upstairs?" he asked, his voice a satisfied rumble against my ear.

I laughed—dizzy, blissed out, completely wrecked. "I'm never showering alone again."

The rain had stopped. The windows of the carriage house steamed slightly from the heat we'd created, and every lamp had been dimmed to a golden hush. I was wrapped in one of Westley's old college T-shirts, the hem falling to the tops of my thighs, skin still damp from the shower. He was stretched out beside me in nothing but boxers, his hair a tousled mess from my fingers, one arm curled beneath his head.

The bed creaked as I shifted closer, tucking into his side, my leg thrown over his. His hand instinctively came to rest on my hip, fingers tracing over the curve of it like he couldn't stop touching me. "I should be asleep," I murmured into the space between us. "But I don't want to miss any of this."

His lips curved into a smile. "Then don't."

From the nightstand, I reached for the battered poetry book we kept tucked there—the same one we'd opened a dozen times now—its pages soft from thumbed corners, the spine threatening to split. Westley pulled me close and held the book open between us, letting his voice drift low and warm through the quiet.

He read, this time, flipping to a page I had dog-eared weeks ago, one he knew I loved.

*But we loved with a love that was more than love—*

His voice trailed off, and the silence after the words felt like a held breath. I turned to him, brushing my lips along his jaw, letting my hand rest over his chest where his heartbeat lived steady and strong beneath my palm. "That was one of the first poems I ever memorized," I said softly.

Westley looked at me like I was the only thing he'd ever memorize. Then, after a beat, he reached over and set the book down. Turned toward me fully, his face half-shadowed in the amber light, the other half lit like a promise. "Can I do something for you?" he asked, voice low, a hush against my collarbone.

I blinked, warmth already flooding my chest. "You already have."

His lips brushed a path along my throat, then lower. "No," he murmured. "Not yet."

He kissed a line down the center of my stomach, slow and sure. The sheets rustled as he slid down, hands warm and certain on my thighs, spreading them with reverent care. I gasped at the first brush of his mouth, my head falling back against the pillows.

And then he began.

*He read my body like he'd written it,*

*like every reaction was a line of scripture.*

*There's nothing to compare*

*I was nowhere;*

*I was everywhere*

*My hands curled into sheets*

*But I was gripping the stars*

*His mouth moved in slow, devastating patterns*

*He didn't stop when I started to beg.*

*He didn't stop when I came apart.*

*He held me through every wave,*

*until I was half-sobbing, half-laughing, limbs limp and shaking.*

*I didn't even realize I'd said it until he paused—*

*just for a breath—*

*the most unbearably smug, satisfied look on his face*

*like he'd been waiting to hear it.*

"You don't have to take it back," he said, voice thick—everything about Westley was thick. "I already know."

I was blushing so hard I thought I might combust. "I think you just made me black out."

He grinned, eyes flicking over me like I was a miracle he'd never stop marveling at. Then he leaned up, kissed me softly, with so much tenderness it almost undid me more than everything that came before. "Round two in the morning?"

I bit my lip, still catching my breath. "If we make it to morning."

He smiled again—slower this time—then he pulled me on top of him, guiding my legs around his hips, wrapping me in the safety of his arms and the heat of his body. And as I curled against his chest, he whispered one last thing in the dark: "I'm never going to stop making you feel like that."

Chapter Twenty-Two

The morning arrived on tiptoe, gentle and weightless as a prayer. I woke in a bed made up with clean sheets and a heart that felt less like a stone and more like an offering. The house—no, the inn—felt transformed, both fragile and enduring, as if the very walls were holding their breath for what the day would bring.

I moved quietly through the rooms, sunlight slanting across floors scrubbed smooth by a hundred small labors. Every surface gleamed with the care of many hands: Westley's, Joani's, River's, and—though it still astonished me—mine. I let my fingers drift along the baseboards as I passed, as if my touch could bless the work we'd done. The wood was cool in some places, sun-warmed in others, carrying the memory of seasons I hadn't been here to see.

In the parlor, I paused to straighten the framed photograph of the grove in bloom—a picture I'd found in the attic, edges curled, colors faded like an old dream. I thought of Ellie seeing it again and wondered if memory would rush toward her or come in slow, halting steps. There was something holy about preparing a space for someone you love, not in the way of performance, but as if setting the stage for a prayer to be answered. Even the air felt changed, richer somehow. There were no more bruises on the doorframes, no broken windows or angry stains, only the scent of lemon oil and bread rising in the oven, a promise of welcome. The kitchen clock ticked a steady pulse as I wiped down the counters, setting out a vase of cut gardenias—white, fresh, redeemed from memory.

Today was the day Ellie would see what we'd made. My heart fluttered with nervous hope. It felt sacred, this work; a house built from ruin, made whole again for the woman whose story had become part of mine. I wondered if she would recognize the rooms, if the light falling through the bay window would call her back to herself, if she'd see her legacy woven into the soft hush of morning.

I straightened the stack of linen napkins on the dining table, fingers lingering on the embroidered edges—Joani's handiwork, a testament to patience and care. Outside, the garden shimmered in early sunlight, dew pooling in the cups of caladium leaves, and the wild grapevines climbing the porch railings seemed to tremble with anticipation. Even the chickens seemed quieter than usual, as if sensing the occasion. Moo-donna bellowed once from the field, low and content; in her voice was her own kind of approval.

I opened the windows to air out the last of the paint fumes, letting the breeze stir the curtains. It carried the scent of orange blossoms, just past their prime, and a hint of rain far off to the west. I breathed it in, steadying myself, remembering all the days I'd felt like an outsider looking in. Today, this house belonged to all of us. To Ellie, most of all.

I checked the clock again, nerves coiling tight beneath my ribs. The hands crawled toward ten. I moved room to room, dusting where there was no dust, smoothing already-perfect pillows, picking up stray feathers from the parlor rug.

The anxiety didn't feel like the old kind—paralyzing and raw—but a fluttering sort, edged with hope. I wanted everything to be perfect for Ellie, not because I needed her approval, but because I wanted her to see herself here, to recognize the home she'd built—through love, through endurance, through absence and return.

Downstairs, I lit a candle in the entryway, the scent of beeswax mingling with citrus and bread. I paused, letting the glow settle into the quiet, letting myself feel the gravity of the day. This wasn't just a tour; it was a homecoming, a blessing for all we'd repaired and all that would endure beyond us.

At the sound of a car in the drive, my hands trembled, and I pressed them to my apron, grounding myself in the feel of cotton and callus and certainty. I was ready, or as ready as I'd ever be—for this moment, for Ellie, for what it meant to open a door and say, *welcome home.*

River's old truck pulled into the gravel drive just before ten, its slow approach announcing the weight of the day. The breeze picked up, rustling the oaks and scattering pale sunlight across the porch. I stood at the door beside Westley, our hands just touching, the kind of contact that says more than comfort or habit—just presence, in the face of something sacred.

The truck idled a long heartbeat, as if even the engine understood ceremony. Westley's thumb brushed my knuckle once—an unthinking circle—then stilled. Somewhere in the yard, a hen announced herself to no one in particular and then fell quiet. The house took that quiet in and made more of it. I had the sudden, tender thought that places know when they're about to be forgiven, and they hush the air so the moment won't miss itself.

When the car door opened, Ellie Beckett stepped out with a steadiness that surprised me. Her dress was the soft color of cream and peaches, worn and clean, her white hair pulled back in a careful bun. She moved slowly, no rush in her gait, but her eyes—her eyes were clear. The cloudiness that had haunted her for months was gone. She looked at the house as if she recognized it for the first time in years.

She paused at the foot of the porch steps, one hand on River's arm for balance. "Would you look at that," she whispered, voice bright as morning dew. Up close, I could see the fine tremor in her fingers and the steadiness in her gaze, unlikely companions. She lifted her hand and let it hover over the rail—blessing without words. The boards creaked lightly as she climbed, not in complaint but in greeting. It struck me that memory wears more than one face: sometimes clear as a name, sometimes only the feel of grain beneath a palm, the tilt of light across a familiar threshold. Ellie's mouth parted, a soundless oh, as she stepped onto the porch—as if the house had reached back.

Westley released my hand and stepped forward, as if drawn by something deeper than memory. "Hi, Grandma."

Ellie blinked up at him, gaze roaming his face with the same reverence she gave the house. "There you are," she said, a soft, astonished smile on her lips. "Westley, my heart. You came back."

He nearly choked on his words. "Yeah. I'm here. I'm
so sorry—about the house, about leaving it like I did,
about—"

She touched two fingers to his lips, the gesture so
gentle it ached. "None of that matters now. You came home.
And I remember."

River gave me a little nod and stepped back down the
walk, his keys jingling in his hand—a quiet exit, giving us
space. I crossed the porch to join them, feeling the hush
thicken, not heavy but holy.

Ellie's fingers brushed the rail, then the frame of the
screen door. "The light's different," she murmured, voice
thin as thread. "Not worse. Just… kinder. Like it knows it's
been missed."

She crossed the threshold slowly, one palm pressed to
the wall just inside, finding the faded sliver of wallpaper we'd
left untouched behind the coat hooks—a deliberate remnant.
"That's where I used to mark Westley's height," she said, a
secret laugh in her throat. "He never thought I'd remember."

He swallowed, eyes shining. "I didn't know if you
would."

"I don't always. But I do right now." I watched her
thumb skim the edge where old pattern met new paint—sun-
bleached roses dissolving into cream. We could have sanded
it clean, made it seamless. We chose not to. In the parlor she
paused again, laying two fingers on the dent in the sill where a

window sash had once fallen hard. "Storm of '84," she murmured, almost to herself, "and I swore we'd move the piano away from the draft. Never did." She smiled, not apologizing to anyone, not even the past.

The house seemed to lean toward her as she moved, her palm grazing the banister, tracing the curve of the old sideboard, pressing to the glass of the parlor window. She wasn't just walking through rooms; she was unlocking something buried, each touch drawing stories back up through the grain of the wood.

"I had so many tea parties in this room," she said, pausing by the velvet settee. "I'd set the table for no one but myself, and still there'd be ten cups. I liked the sound of laughter, even if it was pretend."

Westley knelt at her side, one hand steady on her knee. "Do you want to see the kitchen? Mina redid it. You wouldn't believe the tile."

Ellie smiled at me, eyes twinkling. "Oh, I would. She has good hands."

Warmth bloomed in my cheeks, but I didn't look away.

The kitchen made her smile wider. She ran her hands over the drawer pulls, opened the cabinet doors, lingered at the stove like she was reacquainting herself with old friends. In the dining room, her gaze lifted to the chandelier. "The chandelier," she breathed. "That's your grandfather's work."

Westley's jaw tipped toward the ceiling. "Took three evenings and a spool of patience," he added. "New wiring, old crystals boiled in vinegar and sun." Ellie stepped beneath it, letting the prisms pepper her dress with trembling light. "He loved a job he could do with his hands," she said. "Said a thing doesn't need to be loud to be beautiful." She tugged the pull-chain gently; the room bloomed. For a moment, all three of us stood inside that light like it was a story we'd agreed to tell together.

Ellie's eyes brimmed, but she only smiled. "He would've loved this. And he would've loved her," she added, nodding at me.

I blinked hard, swallowing the tightness in my throat.

We settled in the sunroom, soft light filling the corners, and I brought in iced tea—lemons bobbing in the glasses, condensation beading on the table. Ellie talked: about jars of apricot preserves, about the summer she let every neighborhood girl swim in the creek in their slips, about reading poems aloud to her husband on rainy days. Her words drifted through the room like a blessing.

When her voice thinned, I set a small saucer of orange slices near her elbow, a habit I'd picked up from Joani. Ellie pressed a segment to her lips, eyes crinkling. "We used to do this during canning," she said. "One for the jar, one for the cook." Westley laughed, low and broken in the sweetest way. The sun made lace of the curtains and patterned her hands. Each time she paused, I resisted the urge to nudge, to guide. I let the silences be their own kind of path—wide enough for stories to find their way back without getting lost. "I forget so many things," she said, fingers curled around her glass. "But some memories come back when I need them most. Some bloom again if the soil's been tended."

She turned her hand over Westley's. "You tended this place. And me."

He shook his head, voice hoarse. "I didn't do enough."

"You did what mattered. That's all any of us can do."

A hush fell. The sun moved down the wall, painting gold over everything. I realized I was holding my breath.

We finished the tour as dusk slipped in, the porch awash in honey light. Westley brought out a blanket and tucked it over our laps on the old swing. He handed me a mug of chamomile. For a long time, we just sat, letting the quiet wrap around us—cicadas buzzing, the scent of grass and coming rain, the slow, deep exhale of a house that had found its people again.

The porch quieted around us, the last light catching on the window glass and turning everything soft at the edges. Westley shifted beside me, the blanket pooled around our knees, his fingers curled over mine. Ellie sat between us now, her eyes searching the twilight with a calm that felt newly hard-won.

For a while, none of us spoke. It was enough to simply be—to listen to the hush that lingered, the cicadas buzzing low, the gentle creak of the porch swing as it swayed beneath us. The day's heat had faded, replaced by a cool, damp breath from the orchard.

Ellie broke the silence first, her gaze fixed on the house's shadow stretching across the yard. "When I was a girl, my mother used to say that homes remember who tended them. Every cupboard, every floorboard, every garden row. They hold it all, long after we're gone."

I nodded, throat tight, and Westley reached over, squeezing my hand. I swallowed. It was time. "There's something I want to show you both," I said quietly. "It isn't finished—not really, not in the way things ever are. But I think it's time."

Westley's brow furrowed, but he didn't question. He simply rose, offering a hand to Ellie, steadying her as she got to her feet. I led them back inside, the lamplight glowing gold in the entry. My heart thrummed so loud I wondered if they could hear it—a bell, a beginning.

I stopped at the newly polished sideboard in the foyer, the wood still warm from the afternoon sun. On top sat a hand-painted sign, its letters soft and imperfect, the edges still a little rough. I remembered the night I painted it in secret— the board steadied across two saw-horses in the driveway. Moths kept flinging themselves at the shop light like tiny, winged blessings. I debated the curve of the O, whether the blossom should lean left or right; in the end it leaned toward the door, like a bow. When the paint dried, I ran my thumb along the serif of the N and felt something settle in me—the way a word becomes itself when you say it aloud.

Ellie reached out, fingertips trembling, and traced the words as if coxing music from old piano keys—tracing the name into her memory by feel, by heart: THE ORANGE BLOSSOM INN. I watched her fingers linger over the letters, slow and reverent, as if she could anchor herself in them. And for a moment, I saw her not as the woman memory had unraveled, but as she must have been when the house was young—steady, certain, luminous with the kind of love that leaves an imprint on walls. My throat tightened. It wasn't just for Ellie, I realized. It was for all of them—the ones who had laughed here, wept here, built and lost and still dared to call this place home. Their ghosts didn't haunt these halls; they kept watch. And for the first time, I didn't feel like an intruder. I felt like I had been invited to stay.

Her breath hitched, and for a moment, I thought she might not understand. But then her face softened, her eyes shining in the lamplight. "It's yours," I said softly. "Not just for you, but for all of Citrus Grove. For everyone who needs a place to rest, to begin again. I wanted you to see it while you could remember."

Westley watched his grandmother, his eyes wide and vulnerable in a way I'd never seen before. Ellie's gaze flicked between the two of us, the smallest, knowing smile curving her lips. "My husband would have loved that," she whispered. "And so do I." She looked at me then, and for a moment I felt the full weight of what I'd made—what we'd made. "You brought it back to life," she said, her voice a little shaky. "You gave us back our stories."

Westley stepped forward, sliding his arm around my waist, grounding me with his presence. I felt the heat of him at my back, solid and certain, as if to say: You did this. You, with your stubborn heart and gentle hands.

Ellie turned her face to me, and in her expression I saw something I hadn't expected—relief. Not just for what had been restored, but for what could still be carried forward.

"I don't know how to thank you," she said softly.

"You don't have to," I replied. "This is yours. It always was."

"No, Mina," she held my hand between hers like she was passing me something small and delicate, something sacred, "It's yours."

We lingered there, generations, lives, stories bound by memory and hope, as the house settled around us with the quiet sigh of old walls remembering new names.

In that hush, I realized I was no longer afraid—not of losing, not of letting go. This was what I'd wanted all along: to build something that would last, not just for me, but for all the ones who came before and after. To say, here is a place you are wanted, a place you belong.

Outside, the first crickets began to sing, their chorus swelling into the dusk. I pressed my palm to the cool wood of the sideboard, feeling the thrum of the house—the pulse of legacy and love—and knew, with absolute certainty, that we had done something right.

The sun slipped lower, stretching honeyed light across the porch and painting long shadows over the grass. Ellie sat for a while in the old rocker by the steps, her hands folded in her lap, her gaze drifting out over the grove as if she could see every summer of her life superimposed on the trees. When River came to walk her to the car, she pressed his arm with a gratitude that needed no words.

Westley and I watched them go, standing side by side in the hush that always follows a leaving. The wind had settled, and the world outside felt rinsed and new—a different kind of quiet than the storm-silence from weeks before. This was the quiet of something whole, finally at peace.

We stayed on the porch until the gravel stopped ticking under the tires and the gate sighed shut. A bat unstitched the sky above the grove; somewhere near the fence line, a frog tried out his evening voice. The kind of sounds you miss when your life is too loud. I could feel the day draining from my shoulders the way rain drains from eaves—slow, clean, inevitable. Westley didn't speak. He didn't have to. His palm found the small of my back, warm and steady, and the house—our house—answered with the soft tick of cooling wood.

I leaned into him, tucking myself under his arm. He rested his chin on my head, and for a long time, we didn't speak. There was nothing urgent left to say. The air between us felt soft, like the space in a well-loved quilt—patched, mended, stronger for every place it had been worn thin.

From the yard, the last golden light glinted on the sign above the door, the name shining clear and true. The house looked different in the dusk—not just fixed, but claimed, and at the same time claiming me too. The porch swing creaked as I settled into it, pulling my knees up, letting Westley push off with one slow foot so we rocked, slow as the breath that carried the day to its close.

"I didn't think she'd remember," I said softly, watching fireflies bloom in the shadows. "Not really. Not like that."

He squeezed my hand. "Maybe some things wait for the right day to come home."

We watched as River's truck turned out of the drive, taillights flickering between the trees. The whole world felt slowed, suspended, as if the house itself was listening for the last of Ellie's stories to linger in the rooms.

"She called me her heart," he said quietly. "I thought I'd lost her. All that time I spent away, I thought I'd lost everything that mattered—the house, her. But it was never about the walls. It was the stories."

"You gave them a way to come back," I whispered.

He tucked a strand of hair behind my ear, his fingers lingering at my cheek. "You did that yourself. All I did was show up."

A small smile tugged at my lips. "Sometimes that's the hardest thing."

We sat until the first stars blinked awake. I reached for his hand and held it tight, and when he turned to me, I kissed him—slow, certain, like sealing a promise in twilight. The light thinned, turning from gold to blue. In the yard, a pair of owls called back and forth, their voices low and secretive. Crickets began to sing. The first stars appeared, pale as chalk against the velvet sky.

We sat until the darkness thickened around us, letting the swing sway, listening to the house creak and settle. Inside, the old clock chimed the hour, gentle as a lullaby. The house felt blessed, somehow—safe, for once, from all that had haunted it.

"I think this is what I always wanted," I said at last, my voice no more than a sigh. "Not just a place, but a story that could hold everyone I love. That could keep growing, even after I'm gone."

Westley turned to me, his brow furrowed, gentle. "You built it. It's yours. It's all of ours now."

I let my head rest on his shoulder, the scent of cut grass and old wood drifting on the air. I closed my eyes and listened to the easy rhythm of his breath, the soft crackle of cicadas, the distant laughter from the last of the neighbors making their way home.

Somewhere inside, I could still hear Ellie's voice—brighter, surer than it had been in years—echoing through the rooms, blessing every corner with memory. I let myself believe that her stories would live here, tucked between the floorboards and woven into the light. That the house would keep them, even when memory failed.

We sat in the swing until the night was full, stars pressed thick above us, the whole world gathered in a hush as sweet as prayer.

And for once, I didn't feel like I was waiting for anything at all.

Chapter Twenty-Three

The mornings had started coming cooler—gentler, almost cautious, like the world was testing its memory for autumn. The sun still rose bright and gold over the grove, but the light came in at an angle that made everything look softer, more honest. I woke to birdsong that was a little less frantic, as if the sparrows had finally decided there was no need to rush. The air through the window was sweet, tinged with the first, clean edge of fall.

I lay in bed for a long while most mornings, the quilt heavy over my legs, watching the changing shapes of light slip across the ceiling. Sometimes Westley's arm would find me, loose and warm, his breathing deep and even. His shirts hung beside mine now on the hook by the door—a little more crowded, a little more lived-in. One drawer in the old dresser held his things; a handful of loose change, a faded photograph of his grandmother, a tin of balm that smelled like pine.

I didn't mind the evidence of him here. I welcomed it. Every time I folded one of his shirts into the basket, or found a sock peeking out from beneath the bed, it felt like some small affirmation: you are not alone, not anymore.

Most days began slow. I'd pad barefoot across the cool boards to open the curtains in the bay window, watching as the pale sheer fabric caught the sun and turned the room into a watercolor. Outside, dew silvered the grass. Bees visited the last of the zinnias; a blue jay splashed in the birdbath with a joy so reckless it made me laugh.

The kitchen was my next stop, the old tile cold under my feet. I'd start the kettle, measure coffee, press my palm to the windowsill and breathe deep. Lemon oil, flour, the faintest memory of yeast from yesterday's bread. This was how home announced itself—quiet, persistent, always returning. Some mornings I played old records while I wiped down the counters or watered the herbs by the sink.

The house felt different now. Not just mine, not just Westley's, but a thing being built and rebuilt, alive with our careful tending. The air held the memory of laughter and hard work, of arguments resolved, of the hush that followed storms. There were still shadows sometimes—corners where the old fears liked to gather—but they felt smaller, easier to name and face.

I spent hours some days arranging books, dusting shelves, tucking sprigs of rosemary into glass jars on the windowsills. It was not about perfection. It was about the small ritual of noticing: the way the light fell, the soft creak of the stairs, the way the house sighed and settled when the wind picked up. I'd catch Westley watching me sometimes, a half-smile at the corner of his mouth, as if he could see the changes happening in me the same way I noticed the world outside turning.

Sometimes, in the quiet after breakfast, I'd walk the length of the hallway and touch the walls. The paper was still faded in places, the floor still worn, but I could feel the echo of every choice we'd made. Every patch and polish, every nail driven home. The house was not perfect, but it was alive. Like us, it was still learning how to stay.

As August ripened, the world around us seemed to slow its frantic pace. Even the stray cat, usually wild and restless, took up permanent residence in the barn, spending long stretches of afternoons curled in a patch of sun at the threshold.

There was peace in these rituals. Not a flashy, storybook kind, but a peace that settled into the bones and stayed there. A peace that came from belonging, from choosing again and again to show up—to love this place, these people, this life.

And so the mornings slipped past, a little cooler each day, the world quieting and waiting for whatever came next.

By late morning the air was warm again, but not with the heavy, unyielding heat of high summer—more the easy gold of a season letting go. I moved through the house with the windows cracked just wide enough to invite in the soft chorus of neighbors' voices drifting from porch to porch. Someone was mowing down the lane; I could smell cut grass, and somewhere a radio played an old country song so faint it felt like memory more than sound.

The mailboxes for the whole lane sat clustered at the bend where the gravel drive met the road. I reached mine just as Mrs. Greene pulled up in her battered Ford, checking her mail, her hair tucked under a wide-brimmed sunhat.

"Morning, Mina!" she called, sorting letters into a straw basket. "You survived the summer, I see."

"Just barely," I called back, smiling.

She grinned, the lines at her eyes crinkling. "Wait 'til the chili cook-off. Then you'll know you're a local."

The mailbox held a handful of envelopes and a small brown paper sack. Inside I found a note from Mrs. Horton down the road—"For you and your mister—fig preserves, just like my grandmother made"—and a jar warm from the sun, the fruit inside glinting gold. I pressed it to my cheek, savoring the sweetness of the gesture, before carrying everything back up the walk.

Inside, I placed the preserves on the counter, the note tucked under a magnet. I made tea and sat by the kitchen window, watching a blue dragonfly chase its reflection in the glass. The town was quiet, August's hush settling over the grove, but it was the kind of quiet that felt full, not empty. It was the lull of something finished well, the pause before a new chapter.

After lunch, I propped my phone on the windowsill and tapped Goldie's name. The screen filled with her face, golden-haired and bright-eyed, chin in hand, all mischief and love.

"Look at domestic goddess Barbie over here," she teased, eyes scanning the kitchen behind me. "You're glowing. You baking sourdough next?"

I grinned and held up my hands, dusted with flour from the morning's batch of biscuits. "Don't tempt me. I might."

Goldie's eyes softened. "You really did it, didn't you? This whole… life. It's not temporary anymore."

I looked around—the sunlight on the table, the zinnias in a chipped vase, Westley's jacket slung over the back of a chair. The evidence of a life I hadn't just inherited, but chosen and tended, piece by piece.

"No," I said, quietly. "It's not."

She went still for a moment, her face shadowed with distance and pride. "I'm thinking of coming down for Labor Day. Bringing swimsuits and screwdrivers—the drink, not the tool. Let the Citrus Grove boys try and keep up."

I laughed, picturing the two of us as teenagers, daring each other to leap from the dock at midnight, bright with want and unspent dreams. "Deal."

She glanced away, then back. "I'm proud of you, Mina." Her voice was soft as a lullaby.

The call ended, but her words lingered, sweet and heavy, sinking down to settle somewhere new inside me.

I washed dishes at the sink, the warm water running over my hands, and watched the shadows of clouds slip across the lawn. I remembered arriving here, trembling with uncertainty, measuring my worth in the silence of empty rooms. Now, I moved through the days without apology—leaving footprints, not worrying about the marks I left.

Later, River stopped by, leaning into the kitchen doorway with a carton of eggs from his hens. He caught sight of the jar of preserves on the counter and grinned. "You getting spoiled already, Mina?"

I shrugged, a little shy but mostly pleased. "I think this means I'm in."

He grinned wider. "Told you."

When he left, I lingered at the threshold, looking out across the grove, the afternoon sun slanting through the trees, every leaf edged in light. The world felt known. It felt possible.

In the distance, I could hear laughter—a child's high, skipping joy. The sound drifted on the breeze and wrapped around me, light and easy as hope. For the first time in a long time, I understood what it meant to belong, not because I'd earned it or demanded it, but because I'd stayed. Because I'd let myself be seen, let myself need and be needed in return.

The days moved on—slow, golden, gentle—each small kindness rooting me deeper into this life, this town, this unfinished, imperfect home.

The last week of September settled in slow and golden, the kind of days that felt half-awake, half-dreamed.

Nights lingered longer, and dawn arrived with mist pooling over the grove, wrapping the trees in ribbons of pale blue and lavender. Even the chickens moved quieter, pecking in the dew-damp grass with a sleepy reverence, as if they too could sense the season shifting. On the porch, the air felt cooler— just enough for me to pull Westley's flannel around my shoulders and tuck my bare feet under his thigh.

We spent those evenings side by side on the swing, not always talking. Sometimes Westley read aloud from the newspaper or a tattered gardening book, his voice a familiar background hum. Other times we just listened to the sound of the world winding down: cicadas giving way to crickets, a dog barking far off, the quiet thump of a screen door closing two houses down. I would close my eyes and breathe in the scent of rain-soaked earth and sun-warmed citrus, memorizing the way it all felt—so full and simple and real.

One night, the sky cracked open in a late summer storm. The rain drummed hard against the roof, silver sheets sliding down the windows, thunder rumbling close as a heartbeat. We stood at the kitchen window, watching the grove blur and fade, and Westley pressed a mug of tea into my hands. I cupped it close, feeling the warmth in my palms and the steady presence at my back.

"We made it, didn't we?" I said quietly, almost surprised by the truth of it.

Westley's hand came to rest at the nape of my neck. "You did," he said. "You made a life here."

A memory flickered: my first day in Citrus Grove, the sharp, clean smell of sawdust, the loneliness edged with hope. I remembered wanting to run, wanting to stay, wanting something I couldn't even name. Now, with the rain singing against the glass and the house full of soft lamplight, it was hard to imagine ever belonging anywhere else.

After the storm, the world outside glistened—each leaf burnished with water, the orange trees heavy and shining. We stepped out into the night barefoot, the earth cool and forgiving under our toes. Westley led me by the hand to the edge of the grove, where the trees arched overhead and the grass lay flattened by rain. Above us, the stars had come out in clusters, trembling in the clean-washed sky.

We stood there a long time, neither of us needing to fill the silence. My fingers tangled with his, strong and warm, and I leaned into the steady beat of his breath.

"I never thought I'd be grateful for a broken thing," I said, tracing circles over his knuckles. "But this house—this place—it's everything I needed."

Westley didn't speak right away. He just pressed his palm against mine, his thumb steady, grounding. I thought of the cracked floorboards we'd sanded smooth, of the walls scrubbed clean of their stains, of every nail we'd driven home with our own hands. Maybe that was the thing about broken things—they remembered what it felt like to be mended. Maybe I did, too. The grove shifted in the breeze, a thousand leaves whispering at once, and I realized it wasn't only the house that had been remade. I had. Piece by piece, until I almost couldn't see the seams anymore. He smiled, slow and quiet, his thumb sweeping over my hand. "It was waiting for you."

A breeze rustled through the grove, carrying the faintest whisper of autumn—something brisk and wild at the edge of the warm air. It curled between us, raising goosebumps on my arms and making me pull closer to his side. I tipped my face up, feeling the hush, the potential, the sweet ache of a door about to open.

Westley pressed a kiss to my hair. "Summer's almost gone," he said.

I nodded, feeling a pang—not regret, but something gentler, the ache of loving what you know you can't keep forever. "I'm ready," I answered. "I think I finally am."

We walked back toward the house, grass slick beneath our feet, arms around each other's waists. The porch light glowed ahead of us, bright and welcoming, a beacon against the night. Inside, the air smelled of lemon oil and fresh bread, and every lamp was turned low. Our home—ours in every sense.

Later, I sat at the kitchen table, journal open, pen moving slowly across the page. I wrote about the heat and the storm, about Westley's hands and the feel of the earth after rain. I wrote about belonging, about the soft ache of change. The words came easier now—less searching, more knowing. The story of my life, no longer something I was running from, but something I was running toward.

As the clock ticked past midnight, I went out one last time to the porch. The night had settled deep and still, the air tinged with that mysterious edge—the knowledge that tomorrow the wind might shift, that the world would turn, and everything would begin again.

Westley came to stand beside me, silent and solid as ever. I took his hand, and we watched the horizon, waiting for the first hint of dawn.

In the quiet, I realized: I was ready for the next season. I was ready for what would come after summer—for the slow burning gold of autumn, for the comfort of roots sunk deep, for whatever stories the wind might bring.

Epilogue

The house felt so much fuller. Full of morning light and the
music of windows flung open. Full of the hush of old
floorboards that no longer groaned with loneliness, but with
life—quiet, unhurried, and whole.

I wandered barefoot through the grove, grass cool
and spongy under my feet, a basket hanging from my arm,
half-filled with oranges, the skin still slick with dew. The trees
had thickened with summer's labor, their leaves a deeper
green, the branches heavy with fruit not quite ready to fall.

Above me, the sky held that honeyed blue that
belongs only to late August. The world was changing, and for
once, I wasn't afraid. Each breath was easier; each step sure. I
let my hands trail over the rough bark, touching what had
outlasted storm and drought, what had bent and not broken.

There was sweetness here, threaded through
everything. In the scent of orange blossom clinging to my
dress. In the distant laughter from the porch, where Westley
was oiling the old swing, humming off-key. In the memory of
Ellie's voice, bright and clear, naming the house with her
hands.

I thought of the first day I stood on this ground—
uncertain, longing, convinced I was only passing through.
The ache of beginnings, the terror of being seen. And now,
the ache was softer, shaped by belonging. I had made a life

here that fit around me like sunlight fits a window, like roots fit the earth.

I knelt at the edge of the grove, running my fingers through the grass. The earth gave beneath my touch—rich, dark, and patient. The world spun quietly, inviting me forward. The future no longer looked like a shadow but a field waiting to be sown.

For a while, I just listened. The rustle of leaves, the low hum of bees, the distant hush of the river. The same sounds as that first morning, only now they felt like mine. I closed my eyes and let the moment hold me.

Somewhere, a cardinal sang from the tangled hedge, sharp and scarlet against the green. I smiled, tucking another egg in my basket. The house stood behind me—smaller, yes, but bright with memory and promise. A place built not of fairy tales, but of labor and forgiveness and the daily choosing of love. I had found myself in its rooms, had lost and reclaimed and become.

Tomorrow, the season would turn. The light would change, the trees would let go. But today—today, I belonged.

I tilted my face toward the sky, watching the sunlight spill through the branches like it had been poured there just for me. Once, I would have been afraid of this quiet— convinced it was only the calm before another storm. But now, I knew better. The hush wasn't a warning. It was an answer. Every breeze through the grove, every creak of the porch boards, every heartbeat against Westley's chest had been teaching me this: belonging isn't loud. It doesn't demand. It simply waits, steady and sure, until you're ready to walk into it. And today, at last, I was.

I stood and walked back toward the porch, the basket heavy with fruit, my heart lighter than it had ever been. Behind me, the grove shimmered in the golden hour, and ahead, the house waited—open-doored, full of everything I'd ever hoped for, and all the rooms still left to fill.

And as I crossed the threshold, bare feet and sun-warmed shoulders, I knew this was only the beginning.

www.ingramcontent.com/pod-product-compliance
Lightning Source LLC
Chambersburg PA
CBHW051304130726
47987CB00004B/1650